XAN &

ZAK ZYZ

Cover Art: Design by Adam Priester
adampriester.com

Editing: Margot Atwell

Cover and Interior Design: Zak Zyz

Wanna get in touch? Drop us a line at info@gutpunchpress.com.

Gutpunch Press
Brooklyn, New York
www.gutpunchpress.com

Xan & Ink

C'est le Diable qui tient les fils qui nous remuent!
Aux objets répugnants nous trouvons des appas;
Chaque jour vers l'Enfer nous descendons d'un pas,
Sans horreur, à travers des ténèbres qui puent.

Charles Baudelaire - *Fleurs du mal*

The white tower of Joymont had seven bronze bells, imported all the way from the foundries of Aran. It took a team of oxen and twenty men a week to raise them into the high tower and mount each on its beam. The work was pure murder, a labor like none of the men had ever done, but when it was all through, how fine the tower looked! A fluted shaft of white stone capped in a cone of gleaming copper, seven levels, seven bells engraved with glorious scenes from the epics. Atop it all they raised the flag of Joymont, a seven-pointed green star rising over white-capped mountains on a field of indigo.

For years the laborers had worked on this keep, hauling stones and timber, swinging hammers until their bones rang, and now they looked out across the tall ramparts they'd built, the thick walls and the fine white bell tower, and beamed with pride. Here was something for the ages!

Even the King seemed moved. A few workmen thought they saw a tear gleam in the corner of his eye as he gazed up at the grand tower. His own flag flew above the tower he'd designed, crowning a keep that would repel slavers and bandits. More than that, he'd built Joymont from nothing, he hadn't simply inherited it by accident of birth. He was a conqueror, he'd seen a kingdom where others had seen naught but wilderness.

Joymont's cronies were flopping over themselves, each trying to find their own angle to praise. How stately it looked, how clever the design! What a fine choice he'd made selecting the scenes!

Wasn't it just perfect to have the Calamity of Rapaxoris beneath the Beheading of the Limitless Light? And if you were going to choose a battle of Grimbalgon to depict, what better than the final one? Didn't the figure of Harlan remind you of a certain King in his youth? On and on they went until his stomach nearly turned.

When at last it was time to sound the bells, each rang more pure than the last, resonant tones that you could hear from any corner of the keep, and far out into the fields. Every man, woman, and child in Joymont was looking up at those bells as they rang, one, two, three, four, five, six...

Seven.

They rang the seventh bell, and all winced. As sour as the others had been sweet, a bitter, jarring note that made teeth ache and bones lurch. At once they knew the bell had cracked, and their eyes were on King Joymont, their breath caught in their throats. The head stonemason took off his hat and wrung it, his mouth working like mad with little half-spoken excuses.

For a moment, Joymont's eyes twitched with fury, but he swallowed it. He could feel the weight of the years to come balanced on this moment. It had to be salvaged at all costs.

"We'll save that one for the hangings!" Joymont roared at last, winking at the head mason. There was a titter of nervous laughter. Relief rippled through the crowd, and the stonemason looked as if he'd been pardoned at the gallows. He was as pale as the white stone he worked.

"Still the traitor bell! Let the rest ring!" Joymont shouted, and they rang the other six bells until everyone's ears ached.

As the years went on, there were few hangings worthy of ringing a cursed bell. The seventh bell grew quite dusty and forgotten at the top of the tower while the others sang out for weddings and feasts, holidays, and all other occasions for joy.

Today they rang the seventh bell.

"BANISHED!" screeched the old woman, raising her spindly fist above the furious crowd.

Gregary slowed and turned to the woman as a flung crabapple pinged off his helmet. All around him the mob hooted and screamed, a tangled roar of voices. Above the din the bitter traitor's bell rang, buzzing like an angry beetle.

"BANISHED!" she cried again as he stared her down. Another apple struck him in the shoulder but he did not flinch. He wore armor beneath his padded cloak.

"I know you. You're Sarid. We drove the wolves off your land. They were eating your sheep." He spoke slowly, as if he'd forgotten the throng around them. As if he couldn't quite believe it was happening, that the widow Sarid stood before him, one hand full of dung, the other curled into a fist.

"BANISHED!" she screamed, flinging the dung at him. He turned his head away from it, just as a rock sailed toward him and struck his helmet with a tremendous clang. Everything flashed white and his ears rang hard.

"Move, idiot!" hissed Sandros at his side. Gregary's brother was in a cloak so stuffed with straw that he was twice his normal size, slick from head to toe with the slime of rotten vegetables. Sandros grabbed him by the arm and jerked him forward through the jeering crowd. The pair nearly slipped in the mud—the sky had turned to stone and a mist of rain had been falling all day, beading everything it touched. It was the most miserable day.

There were fifteen others with them, marching toward the western gate to Red Ravine. Drunks and wake fiends, paupers and beggars, thieves, and outlaws. Outlaws Gregary and Sandros had captured in the first place, enough of them that there would surely be a reckoning past the gate. If they even made it to the gate. It seemed half of Joymont had come out to join the mob, and all their stones were meant for the brothers.

"How's it feel, you fucking shants?" A large man with a thick black beard stood before them, blocking their way. Gregary drew a sharp breath and regretted it immediately. He'd been hit with a lot of dung. Another face he recognized. Raenwheld the shepherd from Blackberry Bole.

They had a history with the man.

Three seasons ago, Raenwheld had fenced off the whole length of a stream that ran along the edge of his land, claiming it for his own and demanding a toll from any neighbor who wanted to water their herd. His neighbors had simply knocked down the fence, again and again. Any fool should have known to give up then, but Raenwheld was not just any fool.

The next time the fence was knocked over, his neighbors didn't simply break the slats, they stole an entire section, even digging up the posts and carrying them off. When Raenwheld found a twenty-foot length of his fence missing, he snapped. He rebuilt the fence, and then hid in a blackberry briar with his two sons.

Hours later, Minamore Trant appeared with his cows and kicked through the fence. Raenwheld and his boys gave no warning but the volley of arrows they loosed. They missed Trant, but killed one of his cows and lamed another. Trant escaped and soon the whole of Blackberry Bole was calling for Raenwheld's blood.

That night, his barn was set ablaze, and when he screamed fire and called for help, no one came. He and his sons worked long into the night with buckets, but they could not quench the fire by themselves. When morning came, the barn was a skeleton of blackened beams. Defiant, Raenwheld marched into the town square with his sons and swore an oath of vengeance on the cowardly arsonists and any who concealed them.

It was an ugly enough scene that King Joymont caught wind of it and sent Sandros and Gregary to deliver his judgment. The fence was to come down and Raenwheld was to pay five cows to Minamore Trant and five more to the crown for raising the King's ire. Most thought Raenwheld had gotten off lightly, it was a perilous thing to anger Joymont.

But Raenwheld hadn't seen it that way. He'd cursed the town, cursed Joymont, and sworn vengeance on the brothers, though they were little more than messengers. Last they'd heard of him, he'd been driven from his farm and into the northlands.

Now here he stood, with his sons at either side of him, all three of them holding cudgels. The guards sent to escort the procession to the gate made no move to intervene.

"Should I?" Sandros offered.

"Don't! I'll deal with—" Gregary began, but as he prepared to draw his sword, a huge man stepped past them. Where Raenwheld had half a head on Gregary, the big man who'd stepped between them had a whole one on Raenwheld.

"Get out of my way," the big man ordered, and though he walked among the brothers and the others turned loose from the dungeon, he was nearly clean. No one wanted to anger him. Most in the crowd had heard of the murder in Solem Square, the story had been told a hundred ways from a hundred mouths. The murderer glared down at the shepherd with wild blue eyes, his mouth hidden behind a huge red beard.

"Fuck off, Brakkar! Idiot priest, I've no quarrel with you. It's them I want!" Raenwheld hissed, stepping sideways to edge around him.

Brakkar's hand shot through the air and clapped against the side of Raenwheld's head with a tremendous crack. Raenwheld spiraled into the muck, out cold. Silence fell over the mob. Gone were the shouts, now they only gasped and gaped. The rabble looked at Raenwheld's sons for a response, but the boys dropped their cudgels and ran, leaving their father unconscious in the mud.

"Swine," the big man rumbled, clearly disappointed that they'd fled. The crowd murmured to each other in hushed tones. The traitor bell rang on and the rain grew tired of merely drizzling and began to pour.

There were no more crabapples flung, no more dung, no more shouts. No one wanted what Raenwheld got. The crowd before the brothers began to break apart, and by the time they reached the Horizon Gate, the spectators had nearly dispersed.

"Stopped a mob with a slap. Gods," Sandros said beneath his breath, nodding at the priest.

The procession of exiles swept forward and the brothers along with it, toward the Horizon Gate and out of Joymont. They crossed the bridge over Red Ravine and stood in the clump of former prisoners who were all looking at each other, streaked in slime and shit, wondering where to go from here. The last man in the line was pleading with the guards, they had to drive him across the drawbridge with their spears. Once the guards drove the last of the banished across, they began to winch the bridge up, and the broken bell tolled its last. The drawbridge slammed against the stone wall and they were locked on the other side of the ravine.

The brothers looked up at the heavy black oak of the drawn bridge, neither wanting to look at the other.

No one had ridden up to the procession to offer them a pardon. No guard had pulled them aside at the end to explain that the whole thing had been a test of loyalty.

They were banished.

"Take my back," Gregary said, breaking the moment. He drew his sword, and Sandros threw off the straw-stuffed helmet and took up position behind him. They were ready to go down fighting, back to back, and take as many attackers with them as they could. Gregary had his eyes on Brakkar, waiting for the big man to try something.

But there were no attackers. Most of the prisoners had been rotting in the dungeons for months, and the damp air and thin gruel had taken all the fight out of them. The brothers were armored, they had supplies. Gregary had his sword, and word had gotten around what Sandros could do... it was no secret why they'd been banished. The big priest raised an eyebrow at the maneuver, as if he couldn't quite believe they were serious. After a few sheepish moments, Gregary lowered his blade.

Men were slinking away, headed up the road. A few had joined into groups, but none of them seemed intent on fighting. Most were alone. At the drawbridge ledge, a slight man in a thin cloak streaked with eggs stood looking down into the ravine.

"I think he means to jump," Gregary whispered, looking back at the figure.

"That's his right. Probably a cleaner end than he'll find in the wilds. Gods, I can't believe they turn them out like this. Not a scrap of food, not so much as a pointed stick to defend themselves with. Do you think any of them are going to take that oath seriously?"

"I am going to talk to him." Gregary spoke as if he hadn't heard a word and sheathed his sword.

Sandros shook his head in disbelief. *The eternal knight. Banished and cast into the muck, and he looks at once to rush to the aid of some miserable wretch.*

"You," a voice rumbled behind Sandros, and he nearly leapt out of his skin. He spun to find Brakkar behind him. At his side hung the heavy ceremonial mace he had used to bang on his copper kettle in Solem Square as he thundered that he could purge the blood of the sick and demon-possessed. The priest was staring down at him, close enough that Sandros could smell the dungeon stink, see the filth in his flaming beard and eyebrows.

"They tell me you can call the flame. Do you worship Urth'Wyrth?"

It was a demand, and Sandros had no doubt if he answered wrong, the big man would try to kill him, just as he'd killed the Sun Cult hawker. For a moment, fear held his tongue, but he knew the right answer. He'd had to learn the doctrines of dozens of religions during his apprenticeship, though he didn't need the training for this answer. Few worshiped Tyrias the Sanguistar in Joymont, but nearly everyone had heard Brakkar bellowing about it.

"Urth'Wyrth is a demon. Only a fool would worship a volcano."

"YES!" the huge man shouted in agreement. "They pile skulls atop the devil, they feed a monster that will destroy them all! But the Red Giant shall cast down the firemountain, I have seen it! I have bathed my face in blood, I have seen the truth of it!"

Sandros could only nod, shying away from the huge man's zeal. The way his eyes lit when he spoke of it, the way his hands tightened with excitement… it was a perilous topic.

"GET AWAY FROM ME!" screamed a high voice. Sandros and Brakkar wheeled toward the ravine to see a flash of steel, and hear the squeal of metal on metal. The hooded man was attacking Gregary!

Gregary was backing away, trying to deflect the blade. The swings came in a wild frenzy, until at last the dagger snapped in half against his bracer. His cloak hung in shreds, and the wild one's hood fell back to reveal eyes flashing like a cornered beast.

It wasn't a man!

Sandros recognized her at once, the Ibexian. For weeks, things had been going missing in Millmauth, a little stream town at the far north of Joymont. Accusations flew until the townfolk were on the brink of murdering one another. Then a keen-eyed child spotted the dark-haired woman sneaking out of the woods to pilfer a haunch of venison from a smoking shed. The Millmauthers wasted no time forming a posse to track her down with dogs. It was a stroke of good fortune for the town: the Wyrth paid a good bounty for escaped slaves.

Yet it was no simple thing to capture her. She eluded them for days, and when at last they wore her out, they found her as fierce as a cornered badger. She killed two of the dogs they'd set on her and cut one of the men so badly he had lost the use of his hand. The farmers beat her for it, and tied her up in an ox stall. In the dead of the night, the stableman ran screaming out of the barn, half his nose bitten off.

He could have died of shame, for the whole hamlet knew how he'd gotten bitten. Instead, he died of rot; the wound festered and he went out in a bloody mess, thrashing mad with fever.

By the time the brothers arrived to collect the Ibexian, she was nearly dead too. The locals thought she was plagued and had given her neither food nor water for days. The brothers had to bring her back to Joymont in a cart, she was too weak to stand. King Joymont raged, not only because the Millmauth stableman had tried to rape her, but because they'd beaten and starved her so badly he could expect almost no ransom for her from her masters in Wyrth. He'd cast her into the dungeon until she could recover enough to be of value.

Now here she stood, looking half-ready to leap into the ravine to escape them.

"I mean you no harm," Gregory said with his hands up. Blood was streaming down his left bracer from a cut on the knob of his wrist, but he seemed not to notice.

"Go away from me. Leave me alone or I will jump." Her accent was strange. Sandros had never met an Ibexian before.

She had dark, suspicious eyes and the burnished skin of the river people. The Ibexian might have been pretty once before the farmers set their hands on her. She wasn't now. On either ear she had two triangular notches. The first told the world that she was a slave, the second that she could not be trusted. Small wonder she'd fought so hard.

The Wyrth didn't notch ears a third time. If she were brought back, they would notch her neck instead, and give her skull to Urth'Wyrth.

The four of them stood there for a moment, at an impasse. Gregory neither moved closer nor backed away.

"Where the hell did you get a knife?" Sandros asked at last, anything to get her to talk.

"Guard."

"A guard gave you a knife?"

"He might as well have. It was right there in front of me, he wasn't watching. Some knife. Garbage, like everything else in the north. I didn't expect armor or I'd have had you in the throat."

Their eyes widened at the arrogance in her voice, the prideful way she'd boasted of stealing the knife.

"The smiths are better in Wyrth. You can't get good steel out here in this backwoods village. Just a bunch of hicks and infidels," Brakkar offered.

"Joymont is hardly a village," Gregory said, turning to the giant.

"Call it what you want. It isn't a city. It stands only because it isn't worth the trouble to conquer," the priest shot back, raising his chin at the woman.

"The Wyrth have been attacking us for years!"

10

"Skirmishes to train greenlings and weed out weaklings only. The Legion would crush this little keep like an ant," Brakkar said, squeezing his thumb and forefinger together and rolling them.

"It wouldn't take them a season," the woman agreed. "This shitty little castle will stand only so long as there's sweeter fruit to the east. Yokel scum."

"Ha! She speaks truth. Fuck this pissant burg!" Brakkar's voice rose in a shout at the walls. From behind the arrow slits, bowmen squinted down at him.

Gregary was open-mouthed, his cheeks coloring with anger. In all his life, no one had ever slighted Joymont to his face.

"Come with me, little one. I can protect you from the Wyrth. The Bloodstar will guide us both," Brakkar offered, making his move.

"I'm not a savage. I don't worship stars," the woman rebuffed.

"Ha! Only because you don't know any better. The Red Giant is a true power. Follow me and learn the truth."

"No. Take your star and cram it up your ass," she said, her eyes narrowed.

Sandros lurched inside, he felt certain she was trying to goad them into killing her. He shook his head from side to side at the priest, who gave a quick nod of understanding.

"Fine, hop in the ravine! You will learn the truth either way!" Brakkar shouted, and then he swiveled and began to march off.

The woman turned and stared back down into the ravine. The rocks below were banded in layers of red and gold, and a long way down, the rapids roared. Sapirion Brook ran white and swift through Red Ravine, forming a natural moat along Joymont's western border. She drew a deep breath.

"Don't… you can come with us, if you want," Gregary offered.

Sandros glared at Gregary, shaking his head.

"We have some food and supplies," he offered, ignoring his brother. "I don't know if you remember us, but we brought you back from Millmauth in a cart. You were weak and had a bad fever. Sandros brewed a tea for you that broke it. He saved your life."

The woman looked as conflicted as a stray cat offered a fish. At last, she looked back at the gate and nodded.

"I remember," she said. "My name is Osolin."

"Gregary. This is Sandros. Hey, big man!"

Ahead of them, Brakkar turned around too quickly. He'd been walking away quite slowly.

"Brakkar of the Red Giant. Thank you for knocking those fools out of our way. Do you want to travel with us? We have some food."

The priest's face lit up as Sandros' darkened.

"Oh STARS, how much food do you think we have? Look at the size of him!" Sandros griped, unable to hold his tongue. The big man snorted.

"Ha! Listen to that skinflint. As if there were anything so valuable as the favor of the Red Giant. I am one of his chosen!" Brakkar announced, his voice loud. He was grinning. Sandros was certain he'd been hanging around, hoping for exactly this.

Sandros rubbed at the back of his head, but there was nothing to be done, they were already walking together, four lost souls trudging into the rain.

The rain never let up. They walked the whole way along the Snake Road that wound down the western edge of the Red Ravine Rise, through the Flinderwood where they expected an ambush from behind each tree they passed. They found the first body there, crumpled at the base of a pearlwood tree. Someone had brained him from behind with a stone and taken his cloak. The cloaks were nothing but sackcloth and twine, exactly like the one Osolin wore, nearly worthless, but the man had died for his.

They found another facedown in a stream near the wood's edge. This one still had his cloak. He'd been clubbed to death— why, they could not say. They paused to drag his body out of the stream so it wouldn't taint the water as it rotted, all four chiming in with outrage at the sort of scum who would leave a body in a water source. Here was something they could agree on. They were all travelers, each had suffered from bad water more than once. For a time they rested and used the stream to clean the last bits of filth from their gear.

They hadn't seen the sun all day.

Before they set off, Gregary broke a round of bread into four and handed out quarters. The priest wolfed his in three huge bites, then looked to Gregary for more like a hungry dog. Sandros ate his quickly, without interest.

Osolin worried hers, sheltering it from the rain under her cloak, taking the tiniest bite imaginable and chewing it so slowly her jaw barely moved. The hunger she must have known in her life! It was only a small piece of bread, but she made it last for well over an hour, and Sandros was certain she'd squirreled away better than half of it in her cloak.

They slogged through the long and grueling leagues, trudging through mud in squelching boots, scrambling over uneven ground as the Flinderwood petered out into the hills of Rapscallion. Still, Gregary drove them on, while the other three wondered at his hurry.

"How far do you intend to march? Soon it will be too dark to see," Osolin spoke at last, and Sandros and Brakkar exhaled with relief that they hadn't been the first to ask. Sandros was used to it, at least, but the big priest kept looking ahead at Gregary and shaking his head. His brother marched in armor, with a full pack, and still he'd worn the others down to nothing.

"We should be about a quarter-league off from the Math-iscene stead. Do you know them?" he asked, and Osolin and Brakkar shook their heads.

"Dairy folk, they come to Joymont every season to sell their cheese and try to marry off their daughters. Seven daughters, no sons."

"Who needs a son, have you seen the size of those Mathiscenes? Enormous women, absolutely enormous. Old Mathis tried to get me to go for his eldest, Sarabele. She could carry two of me under either arm and balance another on her head." Sandros tried for a laugh, waggling his bowed arms but he could get no more than a smirk from Brakkar. Osolin scowled at him.

"That's why we're marching so hard. To try and get there be-fore," Gregary said, giving Sandros a withering *younger brother* look.

"Before... oh. Oh stars!" Sandros groaned, realizing what Gregary meant and feeling a fool for not thinking of it first. He knew the stead was ahead but he hadn't considered... Joymont hadn't warned them. He'd turned his dungeon loose on the Snake Road without a thought for the Mathiscenes. For all of Gregary's haste, the men ahead of them had nothing to carry, nothing to lose.

Brakkar's face was sewn up in confusion, and at last he tilted his head for an explanation.

"We want to get there before the others, because northmen are filthy savages who can't keep their pants laced," Osolin explained, her eyes narrow with contempt. "Do you have a weapon for me?"

"Hopefully there won't be fighting. If there is, we can handle it," Gregary said, trying to be diplomatic.

"If that knife weren't trash, you would be dead. Give me something to fight with."

Gregary's eyebrows shot up.

"That wasn't even a fight. In a real fight—"

"Here. Take this," Sandros said, seeking to head off an argument. He shrouded his pack with his cloak as he rummaged so water couldn't get in and warp his flute. He produced a dagger with three silver rings worked into a black leather sheath. When he offered it to Osolin, her eyes lit up as if it were made of solid gold. For the first time all day, Sandros smiled.

"Don't you need it?" she asked, though she'd already tucked it away into her cloak.

"I prefer to use my words to settle disputes," said Sandros the Sanctimonious.

At his side, Brakkar snorted and hefted his mace.

"Words," spat the priest.

"Why did they let you keep that?" Sandros' eyes narrowed. "And the robe," he added, indicating Brakkar's garment, a blood-stained white robe trimmed in black.

"The gaoler returned them to me. That one is a righteous man, a former warrior who has seen for himself the true power of the Red Giant. He applauded me for silencing that blaspheming dog of the Sun Cult."

"Murdering him. In broad daylight, in the middle of Solem Square in front of women and children. A crazy old man who sold lucky pennies." Sandros's voice was heavy with scorn. He'd seen Brakkar's handiwork that day, the Sun Cult hawker's arms and legs twitching on the cobbles, breathing his last in great whooping gasps.

"All should witness the fate of heretics. Would that they shared a single skull so that I could crush them at one go!" Brakkar fixed Sandros with a zealous stare, and Sandros glared right back at him.

"Enough! We are all weary and hungry. The past is gone. We must forget what has come before." Gregary stepped between the pair, but they stared on through him.

"The past is gone!" Gregary repeated, raising his voice. "Now is now. There's work to be done ahead. We swore an oath! I shed my blood and swore I would find a way to save Joymont. You all swore the same. Are you going to keep it?"

"What value has an oath if it's coerced from you? Rot in a cell or swear an oath, what choice is that?" Osolin asked, and Sandros nodded in agreement.

"No. He is right," Brakkar said, pointing his mace at Gregary. "I bled and swore. Nothing can break the bond of blood. Cursed forever are the oathbreakers, hated in the sight of the stars."

"Then enough squabbling, enough talk. All of us carry the burden of our crimes. Let's get to the stead," Gregary said, and he lurched forward into the rain. They had to hurry after him to catch up.

The Mathiscene stead lay ahead of them, unlit, the hearth fire dead and the chimney cold. The house stood silent and still at the top of the hill. Then the last threads of day failed them, and the moon was gone. The skies swallowed the stars and the darkness was so thick they could not set one foot before the other without stumbling. At least the rain had stilled.

"Sandros."

"They'll know we're coming."

"I don't fear an ambush. I fear breaking an ankle tripping over a clod of shit."

"I can sneak up and scout. Probably get two or three of them," Osolin offered, drawing a line across her throat with her finger.

"No. If they've taken the Mathiscenes hostage, they may hear you and hurt them in a panic. Better they see us coming."

"They won't hear me," Osolin said with absolute certainty.

"Let him," Gregary ordered. Osolin frowned but said nothing.

Sandros began to chant, weaving together heavy words that twisted and hissed in the air. Brakkar and Osolin drew back, their shoulders seizing with discomfort, but Gregary had seen it all before. The air roiled and seethed, a spark blooming into a flame, bursting into a spinning ring of fire. Within the ring, a flaming eye winked open, a pit of black at its center darting left and right.

"He summons a demon!" Brakkar cried, hefting his mace.

17

Osolin had drawn the dagger silently and slipped around behind Sandros.

"Ha! That's what they'll think. It's merely an illusion wrought in flame," Sandros said, heedless of their discomfort. In the light, they could see he'd grown pale from the effort, his eyes squinting with concentration. He sent the burning eye high above them, so that it cast its light all around them. "Let's move, this is harder than it looks."

Gregary was already walking. Osolin and Brakkar gawked and then followed, blinking their eyes.

Beneath the flaming eye they climbed the hill to the Mathiscene dairy, straining their ears for the slightest sound of ambush. There was nothing but the trilling of insects and the crackling of flame. At the top of the hill, the stead stood, a handsome building of black oak beams and glossy birch slats. Downhill and downwind was the barn. All was still. No cows lowed, no dogs barked, and even the wind was mute. The four strained their eyes, peering into the dark, but there was nothing.

"Perhaps they took them…" Sandros offered, his eyebrows pointed with concentration.

"Why would they take them? And where?" Gregary wondered, and Sandros could only shrug.

"BANISHED MEN!" Gregary shouted. "SHOW YOUR-SELVES!"

No one answered. Gregary motioned toward the house, and Sandros brought the fire eye closer to loom before the door. The windows were calfskin, certainly the Mathiscenes couldn't afford glass, and they could see nothing moving behind them. They began to creep closer when the breeze turned and stopped them in their tracks.

Death on the wind.

They grimaced as the smell of rot washed over them. Brakkar snuffled the air, scenting it like a dog.

"I smell corpses. Rotted three days or more. They died before the banishment. What killed them?"

Gregary and Sandros shared an uneasy look.

"Let's check the barn, see if anyone's still alive in there," Gregary said, and Sandros nodded. The others squinted, the flaming eye overhead had begun to burn much brighter. Beads of sweat gleamed on the sides of Sandros' face despite the chill of the night air.

The barn was down the far side of the hill, and as they approached, the smell was far worse. With a gasp, they found the first bodies, clad in the sackcloth cloaks of the banished. They'd been ripped apart and hollowed out. Something had devoured their innards and left the rest of them scattered all over the yard. Their faces remained, pale eyeless masks.

The three fighters tightened their grips on their weapons and Sandros' eye of fire grew so bright it could have been noon. The barn door had been flung wide and at the threshold a man lay, still moving.

They drew closer and saw that he had been impaled, a long spike pierced his guts and pinned him to the ground. The man cried for help, but his strength was gone, and his words came out as a choked gurgle. The spine driven through him was a silvery chitin, trembling as he struggled. Above them, the eye was searing and whistling, they could feel the heat from it on their brows.

"It's them," Gregary said, his voice leaden.

Within the barn they could see more carnage, a slaughter-house of disemboweled cattle, an arm, ghostly pale with all the blood drained from it, and then something glinted in the light, a pair of iridescent violet eyes. The eyes glittered like jewels, a thousand gleaming pomegranate seeds.

"Burn it all!" Gregary hissed, and there was no hesitation from Sandros. The eye roared into the barn and exploded just as there was a crack like a bullwhip within the barn. A spine came singing at them from the darkness. The spine shot at Osolin, but she ducked with blinding speed. Brakkar was next in its path, he raised his sacred mace reflexively and the spine clanged against the barbed head and deflected into the night.

Inside the barn, bales of hay caught and suddenly the whole building was ablaze, flames pouring from the chinks, rising to the rafters. Within, there was a terrible angry chittering. Sets of violet eyes were winking open on the roof, blinking out of the hayloft window.

"RUN!" Gregary shouted. Another whip-crack, and a spine thudded into the ground where he'd been a moment earlier. Brakkar and Osolin wasted no time, but Sandros stood there, gesturing at the fire. He moved his hand and a wave of flame swept toward the hayloft, the eyes there vanishing behind a wall of white fire.

"Sandros!" Gregary turned back, rushing toward his brother. Reaching low, Sandros made a lifting motion and the flames followed his hand. A ball of flame lifted from the burning barn and flew in an arc to strike the stead, splashing out against the roof and setting the tarred shingles ablaze.

Gregary threw an arm around Sandros' waist and lifted him over his shoulder. Sandros reached out to the flaming house with both hands, as if could hang on to the blaze, and the flames grew brighter, licking toward his grasp.

When he worked the flame, Sandros grew stiff as steel, every muscle in his body tensed. Afterward, it would all slip out of him, and Gregary felt it now. The fire fled and left Sandros limp.

Gregary ran for thirty paces, and then Sandros began to squirm, wanting to be set down. He was too exhausted to speak. Gregary sloughed him off and then gripped him by the shoulders, scanning his face to be sure he was in control. Sandros was glassy-eyed but at last he nodded, and the two of them set off running down the hill after the others with wild shadows from the fire behind them.

"What the fuck was that?" Osolin demanded.

"Manticores," Sandros said, his eyes still a little far-off and wild. He kept glancing back up at the flames and shuddering. "That's what destroyed Black Brook. We tried to fight them at Barleymore but..." Sandros trailed off. His hands clenched and unclenched, and he could not stand still.

Osolin and Brakkar stared expectantly, but he turned away from them, his eyes glistening.

"Gods. They spread so fast. There's no way to fight them. Arrows bounce right off them. Those spines they fling, they'll go right through plate. I lost a whole company trying to purge them," Gregary shook his head.

"I heard the tales...but I didn't believe. Who can believe a thing like that without seeing it?" Osolin said.

"They'll all see it soon enough," Sandros said, turning back to them. "I've served Joymont since I was nine. I've fought wolf packs and criminals, battled the Wyrth. I trained under the Scourer. I spent years in that miserable tower! And then when they sent me to battle these monsters, when I did what had to be done...they threw me away."

Sandros' voice broke and he began to weep in front of all of them. Osolin and Brakkar stared at him as if they'd never seen a man weep. Gregary drew close and threw an arm over his shoulders. It struck Gregary how used to it all he'd become. He knew every step of the way, from the crooked words to the glaring light to the flood of emotion that sometimes accompanied his brother's sorcery.

"He sets the whole stead to the torch and then he bawls like a child," Osolin said, eyeing Sandros.

"Disgraceful," Brakkar snorted.

"It's been a hard day," Gregary offered, his glare at odds with the gentle tone of his voice.

Osolin raised an eyebrow, holding out the edge of her sackcloth cloak between thumb and forefinger, then tapped her notched ear with the other. She gestured back at the burning stead. Even down the hill, they could smell the bodies burning. *You could have it worse.*

Behind them there was a groan as the timbers finally gave. The barn collapsed in a roar, sending unnatural spirals of sparks and smoke into the night. Soon the house followed, and the stead was no more.

21

"Ashes."

The big man looked up at her as she said it. She had learned this was his *Brakkar no understand* face. She'd seen enough of it. The man had that Wyrth slowness, hints and abstractions were lost on him. You had to almost literally hit him over the head with something before he would grasp it.

"A whole stead of supplies, food, tools, weapons. Nothing remains but ashes."

Osolin's face was coated in soot. She'd combed every part of the stead that wasn't too hot to walk on and come up with nothing. Her frustration was evident, her dark eyes kept stabbing at Sandros, but he did not notice. Sandros was walking around, scuffing his feet in the wreckage. He would find a piece of ground where the ashes had sifted into a pattern and stare at it for a long time, as if he could still see the fire burning there. Brakkar had caught her watching him and raised his eyebrows, then indicated Sandros with a tilt of his chin, tapping the corner of his eye.

He's dangerous.

Of course he was. She'd never seen a fire burn so hot. The hearth had melted as if it were glass, and the air above it still seethed with heat. Fire didn't burn like this, didn't leave scorched spirals twisted around everything, didn't bake the ground into a crust that snapped underfoot like ice.

I am dangerous too, she thought, drumming her fingers along the ringed handle of Sandros' dagger. In an instant she could put an end to the magician and be gone. She was certain she could outrun the others.

Unless there was some sorcery in the dagger, and as she thought about it, that was just the kind of thing a magician would do. Give her a knife that was only an illusion and then laugh at her when she tried to stab him with it. She drew the blade from its sheath, pressed her little finger against it until she felt it break skin and inspected the line of red welling there.

Real. Sharp.

For a moment she imagined the dagger turning into a serpent the moment it tasted blood. Who knew what the magician was capable of?

Her thoughts were strange this morning after so many days spent in the cell. Everything felt different, raw and new. Never had she dreamed they would actually release her, she was certain it was just the beginning of their torture, to raise her hopes and then crush them to nothing. She'd truly meant to leap into the ravine yesterday until she realized the whole thing wasn't just a Set'Assul.

That was the Wyrth sport. Dangling something before a slave only to snatch it away and replace it with something terrible. They considered it an art, and went to great lengths to outdo one another. She'd seen a public Set'Assul in the arena once, before the second notch. When they still trusted her to go outside un-chained.

The Set'Assul was a Yarlee boy no older than eleven. They had him stand blindfolded on a platform near the entrance, for everyone to get an eyeful of before the spectacle. His back was unscarred, he'd never known the lash. With his milk-white skin, his ample flesh, he stood in stark contrast to the other slaves in the audience. They'd actually been feeding him. She remembered hating him for that, even though she knew it had simply been preparation for this day, no different than fattening a calf.

Within the amphitheater, the barker told the assembled crowd the boy's tale.

The outrunners of the Legion had captured his entire family as they sailed not half a day from Yarlsbeth in a nobleman's pleasure boat, crafted in the shape of a graceful swan. They could never have expected the Fearless Wyrth would sail so deep into their waters, could never have dreamed of what awaited them.

The barker was a tall spindly Terhaljatani man with waxed mustaches and a pointed goatee. He spoke with relish, lingering on every detail of the capture. He told the crowd how the boy had never been beaten, never been told the fate of his parents or siblings.

"He doesn't even know where he is! He's been kept caged like a bird, he thinks he is still in Yarlsbeth!" The barker announced each word with delight, his eyes glowing with foreknowledge. "We've told him that he will be reunited with his family!"

The crowd tittered and began to laugh at the barker's exaggerated movements and his open-mouthed grin.

"We've told him… that we're setting him free!"

Now the whole amphitheater roared with laughter so loud Osolin's ears rang. When it was stilled, they brought the boy in, still blindfolded, and walked him up to the gallows. Four robed figures entered the arena and assembled in a line beside the Set'Assul. Two were tall, two were the size of children. They drew off the boy's hood and he was startled by the hundreds of eager faces peering down at him. He looked around, frantic, and called out to the four hooded figures.

"Mother! Father! Sister, Brother!" the boy had cried in Yarlee, and laughs were stifled all over the audience. It was bad form to laugh too early in a Set'Assul. The four cloaked figures did not move, and a dwarf came in, leading a bird taller than he was on a golden chain. It was a swan.

That was what she remembered most clearly, the swan. Not the look on the boy's face as they had clapped him into the stocks, nor the moment the two tall robed figures threw off their robes

24

and hoods to reveal they were not his family, but scarred pit fighters, tattooed head to foot. The short ones were not his siblings, but dwarf clowns like the one who'd led in the swan.

The highlight of a Set'Assul is the moment when the slave realizes the whole thing is a set-up, and this was a vicious one. At once, the pit fighters and the dwarves set upon the swan, stomping it to death as the boy looked on in horror. The crowd was silent with awe, each of them drinking in the boy's anguish, mesmerized by the horrible revelation.

Even the vileness that followed could not approach that wretched moment, when the slender neck was bent and broken by a boot, the wings beating uselessly, feathers flying as the boy began to weep. How the crowd had roared! And what followed… she could not leave, could not even shut her eyes if she didn't want to be whipped. She had to watch the whole thing. There were many other slaves in the crowd—it was thought to be a wise investment to send a household slave to a Set'Assul every so often, to remind them how good they had it.

Standing among the ashes of the Mathiscene stead, Osolin shook her head, willing the memory to go away. Many times she'd wished she could simply forget it, but it was there to stay, burned into her with all the other scars from Urth'Wyrth.

Until two days ago, she had been certain she would be sold back to the Wyrth. No Set'Assul for her: a twice-escaped slave was too callous for their "art." Instead, they would chain her in a public square for the use of any passerby, and when she was too far gone for that sport, they would flay her alive and let the birds finish the job. She knew it, for she'd seen it happen time and time again. There was no third notch. Her skull would be crushed into the streets for the glory of Urth'Wyrth, like so many others.

But now she was free, and her thoughts were frenzied, bounding ahead, spinning with possibility. It had been so long she'd forgotten how to do anything but survive. She stared out at the world all around her, expanding forever in any direction, and had no idea where to go or what to do.

Gregary returned from washing at the well down the hill. He spoke a few short words to Sandros, snapping the magician from his reverie. With a nod, Sandros hoisted his own pack and headed down the hill.

Gregary came to her smiling and she was immediately on guard. *What the fuck did he have to smile about?*

A startling transformation had taken place. The thick padded cloak he'd worn was gone, as were the shapeless tabard and leggings he'd worn over his armor. Now he had a midnight blue cloak, embroidered with fine silver thread to make it look like wings draped from his shoulders. It was clasped with a silver insignia, a falcon in flight, the eyes glittering jewels. He'd polished his armor, and over it he wore a royal blue tabard, conspicuously without an emblem. Osolin stood in rags among the cinders and this one could have marched in a parade and none would bat an eye.

A change of clothes.

They'd packed a change of clothes so their finery wouldn't be spoiled by the mob. Even as they were banished, they were treated differently. They'd been given supplies, weapons, food. Her lip curled at the privilege of this noble-born shant, with his talk of oaths and the burdens of crimes. Spoonfed from birth without a clue how the rest lived and…

"It's a little big for you, perhaps you can uh… alter it somehow. I should have thought to offer it to you last night." Gregary held out the padded cloak. The four had spent the night shivering under a tree along the Snake Road, nudging each other awake for watch. They hadn't dared sleep near the stead.

She looked at him in disbelief. He was giving her his padded cloak. Her first instinct was to throw it back in his face, to spit on his charity. But the memory of the cold night held her tongue. The sackcloth cloak was almost worthless for keeping warm. The cloak was damp. He'd washed it for her.

"Thanks," she said, accepting it with her eyes down.

"It's nothing," Gregary said, and he left her there, humming as he walked away.

She shook her head at his back. He called it nothing, because it was nothing to him. He hadn't paid for the cloak, hadn't paid for anything. They collected taxes, and clapped people in prison, and sold them. They made nothing, earned nothing. Noble leeches.

Still, a cloak was a cloak. She threw it around her shoulders and found that it was a fine size. Gregary was no more than two inches taller than her.

How grand he thinks himself! She wondered if he could even read, or speak any language besides that backward Aranic drawl.

There was clarity in anger. She shut her eyes and felt herself drift free from the chains of this place, hunger, the stupid oath she'd sworn, the hooks of charity. In that sweet, stabbing isolation she could make a plan to get free. Lay low, catch them sleeping, slit their throats, take the supplies, make for the west. It would be a trick to get all three without rousing any of them. If she could get them drunk or poison them somehow...

"Oh, here."

Sandros had come up behind her, and she jolted from her scheme. Could he read her mind and tell what she was planning? He spoke an arcane word and she felt the air around her grow warm. In a panic, she clenched her eyes shut and balled her fists, trying to somehow resist the sorcery. A long moment passed, and she did not feel herself burst into flame. She dared to open her eyes and saw wisps of steam drifting up from her cloak.

"A handy cantrip. Nothing worse than a damp cloak," Sandros said, carefully ignoring her overreaction. Her eyes were wide as she watched the damp patches on the cloak shrink until it was dry.

"He's a bit of a clod, but he means well. This isn't the first time he's literally given someone the clothes off his back," Sandros said, nodding toward Gregary. "He's always charging ahead, playing the hero, and Sandros the Steward is left to clean up after."

Sandros rubbed the back of his head. Osolin nodded, trying to sort out what was genuine sibling pique, and what was a calculated offering to gain her trust.

Sandros had washed and changed. He wore a crimson cloak clasped at the neck with a golden medallion inset with rubies in the shape of a flame. Did he really intend to wear gold on the road, where anyone could see him?

"Who will clean up after Sandros?" Osolin asked, gesturing to the devastation around them.

"Wind. Rain. Time. In a few years it will be just another hill. If you're alive to see that, you can thank me. Twice."

How hot his voice had become! How he glared!

It gave her pause. This was no rube, bashfully offering her a cloak. The way he looked at her, not trusting her but at the same time dismissing the threat… perhaps she ought to simply steal what she could and vanish when the time was right. It didn't pay to trifle with magicians.

Gregary and Brakkar approached, and Sandros shook his head from side to side quickly, as if to shed the severity of their exchange.

"I failed. I'm sorry I drove you all so hard to get here. I had to try," Gregary said, his voice heavy. "Now you can see it's no tale. Black Brook and Barleymore are gone, and now these creatures are spilling toward the south. If they're here, then the steads north of here will be the same. The Jannesses, the Wilmsoles, Old Salez and his wives, all must have shared the fate of the Mathiscenes. If the things keep spreading the way they are, the whole of western Joymont will be overrun. Without the west, Joymont will starve this winter."

Osolin tried to picture Old King Joymont starving and could not. They'd made her kneel before him to swear the oath, and Joymont had peered down from behind no fewer than three chins, scowling as if she were dung clinging to the royal wolfskin rug. She'd glared back at the wide throne he easily filled and wondered if he could even rise from it without aid. Then she'd spoken the false oath and cut her hand before the gathered yokels of the keep, same as the rest.

"You all swore to try and save Joymont. Now is the time to decide if you want to keep that oath. If you don't, we must part ways now. I will give you what food I can spare."

Osolin expected this to be directed at her, but no, Gregary was looking at Sandros. Brakkar stood by Gregary's side. It was clear the bloodpriest had already chosen.

"I want to save Joymont, same as you. But I don't think your plan will work," Sandros said. "He wants to sail to Aran and appeal to the King, ask him to send an army," he explained to the others.

"We're his nephews. He will help us."

"He's a king. We have nothing to offer him in return. When did you ever see Joymont do someone a favor out of the goodness of his heart?"

"Well, we certainly can't just do what you want. Fire doesn't solve everything."

"If they'd done what I wanted to begin with, this would have never happened! We should have burned the whole—"

"That time is past!" Gregary shouted, and for a moment the birds and grasshoppers were stilled.

Sandros clenched his jaw and balled his fists to keep from shouting back at Gregary. This was not a ploy, Osolin was sure. He truly looked like he wanted to scream.

"Why don't you fools just leave? This isn't even good land. Even without the monsters, it's cold and ugly. You're within stabbing distance of Urth'Wyrth, the Legion could stretch out its arms and knock over your little keep without even noticing," Osolin said with a dismissive flick of her wrist. "Why not just pack up that sad little castle and move elsewhere?"

"Sandros and I have spent our whole lives in the service of Joymont. We've been here since there was no keep, no real kingdom, just five farms around a wooden stockade. Kingdoms don't just spring from the earth, keeps don't build themselves. You have no idea how much work we all put into raising this place up."

The priest grunted.

"Open your eyes, boy. It's nothing. Just some stones and some fools sitting atop a hill. I've been to many a town and many a city, and this is nothing but a pissing post on the side of the road to nowhere. They don't even have a temple to the Red Giant."

29

"You swore an oath, Brakkar."

"True, I swore and I won't give lie to my blood. I'll do what I can to save the flock of fools. But your teary-eyed brother is right. The King of Aran is a coward and a fool. I think we should go to Iltran."

"Why would we possibly want to go to Iltran? It's a ruin in the middle of nowhere!" scoffed Sandros.

"For favor. Hidden within Iltran is the Great Cauldron, a cavern where the stones bleed and the water burns. It is holy. Surely a prayer spoken within by the truly devout will not be ignored. A pilgrimage is your answer. With the favor of the Bloodstar, all things are possible. Perhaps the Giant himself will walk the Arc and smite these beasts, save your pissant little hamlet. Imagine it!"

"Oh, are we imagining things now? Perhaps pigs will take wing and fly into battle against the manticores. We can simply find an inn and wait for the porcine valkyries to save the day," Sandros scoffed.

Brakkar turned his head at the magician's contemptuous tone. A cold stillness came over him, and Sandros took a step back, his eyes a little wide. It was plain on his face, he knew he'd gone too far.

"Do you liken the Red Giant to a pig?" Brakkar asked, taking a step forward.

"No! It was merely a joke."

"IS THE RED GIANT A JOKE?" Brakkar roared, and he surged forward, his big crushing hands wide.

Osolin saw that Brakkar had eyes only for Sandros. She stuck out a foot and tripped him, and the priest slammed face-first into the ground, sending a cloud of ash rising. Sandros stood open-mouthed as Brakkar scrambled to rise.

"Run, idiot," Osolin said, taking a step backward as Gregary charged in. Gregary hit Brakkar in the side with his shoulder, knocking him over once more, and the two were suddenly entangled, soot puffing around them as they wrestled.

It was over swiftly. Brakkar rose, yanked Gregary off him, and flung him aside as if he were made of hay. Gregary landed on his back with a heavy thud, the wind driven out of him. He lay hacking and gasping in the rising dust.

Sandros was sprinting, and the bloodpriest charged after him. At first, it looked like Brakkar's long strides would win the day, but Sandros bolted through the tall grass like a hare. It became clear that Brakkar could never catch the mage, but still he flew after him, roaring challenges. Osolin offered Gregary a hand and pulled him to his feet. He looked like a corpse, his face covered with ashes, his fine clothes dark with soot.

"I've seen this game before," Gregary said, grinning despite the filth.

"That idiot will never catch him. See how he runs. Wait, why is that fool turning around? Run, you dolt!"

"Turn away. Quick!"

"What?" she asked, but when she saw Gregary turn and cover his eyes with his hands she swiftly did the same. There was a loud crack, and she could see a flash of brilliant light, even through her hands.

"AUUUGHHHHH!"

The bloodpriest's scream split the air. Turning back to look, they saw he'd drawn his mace and was swinging it around wildly at nothing.

"I'M BLIND!" Brakkar cried, and he swung himself off balance and fell. "Giant! Save me!"

Sandros had resumed running. He looped around and ran back up the hill to join Gregary and Osolin, bending over and wheezing as if he were about to die.

"Gods… did you see how he…" Sandros began, and he had to stop to catch his breath. "You saved me. Thank you."

"The debt is repaid," Osolin said. "Now we are even."

The three looked down at the big man as he continued to thrash against the grass and howl like an animal.

31

"It wears off," Gregary explained to Osolin. "Sandros did it to a legionnaire once when I wasn't expecting it, and I was blinded too. Took me about half a day to see right again."

"Should we tell him?" she asked, looking down at the pitiful sight.

"No. We should leave him there and go. He's trouble and we don't need him," Sandros said, looking quite satisfied with himself.

"I don't want to leave him behind." Gregary said.

"What! He's a madman! You saw how he came after me."

"Stop needling him about his god. He was perfectly fine until you started with your jibes."

"He wants us to go to Iltran! Iltran! It's a pile of rubble!"

"Of course we're not going to Iltran. Doesn't mean you have to set the man off. I believe he truly means to see his oath through, which is more than I can say for either of you. "

"What do you mean 'either of you'?" Osolin demanded.

"You don't care about the oath. You said as much."

"I'm no oathbreaker," she protested.

"That's a good one. I fully expect you to cut out the moment our backs are turned with whatever you can carry," Sandros kicked in.

"What! How dare you accuse me!" Osolin hissed, but both men could see the words had struck home.

"Never take up roke. You're an open book," Sandros said, pulling up the corners of his eyes with his fingertips. "Who will clean up after Sandros?" he mocked, his voice high and singsong.

Osolin watched him caper, pressing her bottom lip out with her tongue. Shaking her head with disgust, she began to turn away from the magician then swiftly turned back, ramming her fist into his chest with all her might.

Sandros' eyes bulged and he dropped to his knees, unable even to gasp. A strangled *hurk hurk hurk* was all he could manage.

"Thank you," Gregary said as Sandros curled into a ball on the ground. "I've been wanting to do that ever since they imprisoned us. He's been insufferable. You earned that, little Sandy."

"Don't… call me…" Sandros croaked, but he could not get any more words out.

Gregary turned to Osolin, ignoring his gasping brother.

"I don't understand why he insists on antagonizing everyone. Who cares what god Brakkar follows? Why shouldn't we trust you? You're in the same plight as us and worse. We should be working together."

"What do you mean, 'worse'?"

"Not to be rude, but your ears are notched. Anywhere you go, men will look at you and see a bounty. If you go alone, it's just a matter of time before you're captured and dragged back to Wyrth. If you're with us, at least it's a fight."

She hated to hear him say it, for it was true. It wasn't by choice she'd been skulking in the woods and sneaking in to plunder storehouses. Ten thousand times she'd run her fingers over the triangular notches, her stomach twisting with fury, imaging the notches she would give the ones who'd done this to her. She caught herself doing it again and her cheeks grew hot with embarrassment.

"You're free now. The past is gone."

How she hated this know-it-all shant! As if he could murmur a few platitudes and make everything alright! She burned with the desire to just take his offer, take the food and set off on her own, just to show him. But it was foolish, as foolish as the mage for taunting her, as foolish as Brakkar for chasing what he could not get.

"STAR! GIVE ME SIGHT SO THAT I MAY HAVE MY REVENGE!" Brakkar yelled. He was using his mace like a cane, stooped over and hobbling toward the sound of their voices.

"Brakkar! Hold! Your sight will return by the end of the day. No more fighting!" Gregary called out.

"He *blinded* me!"

33

"You started it. Sandros will not speak ill of the Bloodstar again, you have my word. If you are to travel with me, I must have yours: no more fighting. You as well, Osolin. Let this be the last violence among us."

"Fine," she said, uttering the word like a curse and glaring at Sandros.

Sandros had just managed to sit up and seemed to be trying to make up his mind whether or not to throw up.

"Fine, I agree. No more fighting. Now return my sight," Brakkar said, and he made his way to them, patted all around an area of ground to make sure there was nothing there, and slumped onto it.

"Look at us," Gregary said, gesturing around. They were all scuffed up and filthy and the day hadn't even begun.

"I can barely see you at all. All is glare and ghosts," Brakkar said unhappily.

"It will pass. We'll rest until you can see enough to walk. Then, unless someone has a better idea, I think we need to head south and try to find a ship."

"I do have a better idea," Sandros said. "Let's go west."

"Into the wilderness? What for?"

"We find the Doomsayer. The scholar of the Kalparcimex."

"We find him and then what, he tells us 'I told you so'? We were children when he came, he's probably dead. Even if he's alive, he would never help us. Joymont laughed in his face, told him to be gone before the sun set. The man was furious."

"Then we find his student, or another like him. He warned us this would happen! He told us the jungle was spreading. Now, ten years down the road, we find these beasts at our doorstep. It's no coincidence. Surely someone there knows what they are and how to get rid of them."

"That's more of a gamble than going to Aran. At least we have kin there."

"There is nothing surer than the wrath of the Red Giant," Brakkar rumbled. The trails of tears had dried onto his face.

"I think we should go to Tck'Hurr and bring the body of one of those manticores. The smiths there are clever, we'll find one who can make an arrowhead that can pierce it. If they can, we can return with a cartload of arrows and wipe them out," Osolin offered.

"We'd have to get an intact shell somehow. There's nothing left of the barn. And Tck'Hurr is halfway around the lake. By the time we get there, Joymont could be gone."

"Then at least we'll be somewhere warm. It's no stupider than any of your ideas."

"Well, we have to pick one. North to Iltran, east to Tck'Hurr, south to Aran, or west into the bughouse. I still think Aran is the best chance we have."

"How should we decide? We could draw lots."

"We should play roke for it," Sandros said. "We'll be half a day waiting anyway."

"Where are we going to get a set?" Osolin asked.

"I brought mine," Gregary said.

She could not keep from clicking her tongue and rolling her eyes. What else had these idiot shants brought in their giant packs? Changes of clothes, games… she fully expected Sandros to break out a full tea service with saucers and little silver spoons as they played.

"What? Do you not like roke?" he asked, not understanding. She only sighed.

"I cannot see the tiles to play. I think we should perform a divination," the priest grumbled.

"I feel certain any divination you perform would tell us to go to Iltran," Sandros said.

"Because it is right!"

"Here," Gregary said, reaching down into the grass and picking something up. At first the others thought it was a stick, but soon they saw it was a spine from one of the beasts, blackened by the fire. It was as long as Gregary's forearm, an inch thick at the base and tapered to a needle point. For a moment, each considered what it would be like to be struck by one. She saw Sandros' shoulders quaver.

"We go where it points, agreed?" Gregary offered.

"Agreed," Sandros said at once. The others shrugged and then nodded in agreement.

Gregary held his arm straight out and dropped the spike, spinning it with his wrist.

"Which way does it point?" Brakkar asked.

"West," Osolin said. The spine pointed dead west. She noticed Sandros withdrawing his hand into the sleeve of his robe. Had he done something? She looked at his face, but he was staring at the spine, the same as the rest of them.

"Then it is settled. We go to Ten. We'll bring the spike so we have something to show the Doomsayer, if he's still alive. Do you even remember his name?"

"Xan," Sandros said. He picked up the spine and pointed it at the mountains in the distance. Then the spine began to writhe in his hand, and near the tip, three hooked prongs extended, grasping at the air.

With a howl of surprise, Sandros flung the spine away as hard as he could.

"That's him right there."

The four of them grimaced as one. Out of the whole den of scum, that one was the strangest. It didn't pay to approach men who wore cowls in winesinks and sat drinking by themselves. Shunted off in a dark corner, the man was clearly here to converse only with the glass before him, but they'd come too far to turn back empty-handed. Gregary flipped a sun penny to the one who'd pointed out Xan, and the little man tilted his head and looked at the coin incredulously. "You keep that, and our thanks," Gregary said, swelling his chest a bit.

The little man seethed with anger, but Gregary and his companions had already turned their backs on him and were making for the cloaked man's corner. Furious, he seized the nearest thing at hand, a half-full flagon, and hurled it with a surprisingly good arm. The earthenware jug struck Gregary square in the back of the head and burst apart, showering him and his companions with sour rimebeer and shards of pottery. Gregary pitched forward and landed in a clatter of chainmail, blood welling from his scalp.

"Throw me a copper, you shant cunt! Throw me another copper, you pigfucking quilg! I can buy and sell the whole passel of you pissant city swine! I can buy your whole fuckin' families and put your mothers back to whoring where they belong! I'll have your fathers mucking the stalls with the lot of you chained up in a sty of your own shit! I'm rich, goddamnit!"

Silence swept the Red Queen Rises, and then the little man kicked over a table and put up his hands, circling his fists in a pugilist's stance. "Come on, you shits! I'll fight all four of ya!"

The cheering and laughing began at the same time. Men hooted and clapped their hands with delight, the whole tavern convulsing with expectant glee.

"Get 'em, Rorey!" the patrons cried, and bets were shouted across the tavern at once. It had happened so fast that the four foreigners had barely gotten Gregary to his feet before the little man advanced on them. Only five feet tall, with a thin beard, red hair, and a boyish, friendly face, Rorey Morey seemed like an unlikely opponent.

One against four, and still there were plenty who were crying out Rorey's name, raising fists full of coin. Rorey took a moment to argue with some of the odds being shouted, and laughter rang all around. Nearly all of the bets were on him, and the four foreigners were looking around, trying to figure out what the joke was. There was nothing to the little man.

A few liked their chances with the strangers. It had been a long way from Joymont, and the four had been in several fights along the way, collecting many scrapes and bruises, and scavenging the possessions of the dead until they all looked positively well-equipped. The bettors looked at the falcon-in-flight emblem on Gregary's cape clasp, marking him as a Knight of Aran. At his side, Sandros wore the red robes of the Ruby Citadel, his own clasp bore the Ignis Eterna, wrought in cut rubies. It was rare to see either emblem this far west, and there were a few cautious wagers yelled out by men who recognized their orders.

The Ibexian woman at Sandros' side had a crossbow strapped to her back over a red-on-white tabard emblazoned with a golden star that had clearly belonged to someone else. The bar's patrons saw two notches on either ear and two daggers at her belt. She stared back fiercely at the men sizing her up, and then looked down at the little man who'd challenged her, eyes narrowed with disdain. It was just another drunken brawl in another dusty little tavern.

Those three should have been enough for any one man, but it was the fourth that had people talking. A towering man with a thick red beard and arms that would shame a blacksmith, there was no mistaking the heavy, ornate mace Brakkar carried. He wore the raiments of the Bloodstar, and his eyes were alit at the prospect of a fight. More and more bets began to sway toward the four foreigners.

Sandros still looked confused, thinking the whole thing was some inside joke at the bar. The tiny man simply could not mean to fight all four of them. He glanced at Gregary, whose eyes seemed to have trouble focusing.

"Hold on, little one, we don't want—" Sandros had his palms up for peace. Mid-sentence, Rorey rammed a fist into his gut, folding him in half like a sheet of paper.

"Hands up and fight, ya fuckin' cunts!" Rorey cried. He dropped his head and went for the biggest target, charging for the war priest. Brakkar snorted. He was two feet taller than Rorey, and easily double his weight. He thrust a giant hand against Rorey Morey's forehead and held him at arm's length. Then he shouted with surprise and yanked his hand back. There was a bloody half-moon left by Rorey's teeth between thumb and forefinger. The little man rushed in and kicked him hard in the kneecap, toppling him.

Osolin clipped Rorey in the back of the head with the ham of her fist and followed with a succession of quick kidney punches that should have dropped him but didn't. Instead, he wheeled on her, grimacing, and made an obvious feint with his right. She was ready to dodge his left hook but then the right, which wasn't a feint at all, popped her square in the nose. The punch snapped her head back, and then his left hit her in the breast hard enough that she gasped and fell back.

"IS THAT ALL THERE IS TO YOU?" Rorey yelled, and the whole bar shouted it along with him, raising their glasses. This was nothing new to the patrons of the Red Queen. Gregary flew at him, tackling him to the ground with a crunch that made men wince. He tried to pin the little man, but Rorey banged away at the back of his head with his fists.

Gregary had to try to change up his grip to get his opponent's arms, but the beer and blood made him too slippery. The next thing he knew, Rorey was out from under him, wrenching his arm behind his back.

"Yield, you fuck!" Rorey shouted, cranking the arm for all he was worth. He knew what he was doing. In a moment, he would dislocate Gregary's arm. "Fuckin' say it!"

Sandros wiped the vomit from the corner of his mouth with the back of his hand and then began to chant. Wisps of smoke twisted about his fingers, and every candle in the place burned twice as bright. The fireplace roared to life, spitting out embers.

All the patrons shouted at once. At first, Sandros thought it was just superstitious fear, but instead they were all drawing weapons and screaming for his blood. The words of the spell choked in his throat.

"None of that bullshit. This was a fair fight. You lost." The cloaked man had drifted over from his perch, and quiet followed him. He spoke softly and everyone wanted to hear him. Sandros looked at Xan, who wore a mask that had been rolled up to the nose to let him drink. The mouth it exposed was nothing but hideous scars, as if he'd been burned nearly to death. His eyes were hidden behind dark lenses fixed to the mask.

"I YIELD!" Gregary cried at last, sure that his arm would break in another instant.

"Fuckin' RIGHT," Rorey yelled, leaping off of Gregary with his hands raised in triumph. "Who won money? Buy me another goddamn flagon!" the little man shouted, strutting up to the bar.

"You ain't worth a flagon no more. No kinda odds at all on ya, Rorey. Oughta take a couple of dives, get people bettin' again," said Stonegren the barkeep. Still, he was pouring one.

"Fuck diving. Get me a real fight! I remember this one time I got in a scrap with one of them Tck'Hurr fuckers, round Moresleeb..."

Attention turned to the little man at the bar and away from the four beaten foreigners. They stood there reeling and bleeding as the masked man they'd come to speak with looked them over. Whatever impression they'd meant to give him, this wasn't it.

"How..." Sandros began, looking at his three beaten companions.

"Rorey Morey, champion pit fighter of Urth'Wyrth. He does that from time to time." The man in the hood had rolled down his mask and his voice came muffled through slits backed with fine mesh. The cloak he wore caught the candlelight and twisted it back in a thousand iridescent shades. This close, they could see there were tens of thousands of beetle shells sewn onto it. A weird one, this Xan.

"You four were looking for me?"

They were picking themselves up, the wobbly mage holding a cloth against Gregary's head. Osolin had her head tilted back, trying to stop up her bleeding nose with a now-ruined silk handkerchief.

"I'm warning you now, if you're here to cause me grief, I'll make Rorey seem friendly," he said, looking at each of them through the lenses of his strange mask, and the breathing slits bent from the smile beneath them. The man spoke differently from the others in the bar. There was a studied, almost courtly correctness to his pronunciation. The four adventurers shook their heads.

"So then. I'm Xan. What do you want from the Kalparcimex?"

It took a few minutes for the bar to settle after the scuffle. Sandros the Sanguine was still a touch green from the gut punch, and the rest of his companions were angrily watching Rorey Morey as he strutted about the Red Queen like a rooster, cheered on by the whole bar. The little bastard even sauntered over with a flagon for their table, grinning like a fool and offering his hand.

"No hard feelings, you lot," Rorey said, his cheeks red and his words slurred.

Gregary and Brakkar could only stare murderously at him, and Osolin hid her own glare behind the kerchief.

"I said. No. Hard. Feelings." Rorey thrust his hand forward again, seeming to sober up with each word. Finally, Sandros shook it, certain that another beating would follow if they gave insult. This satisfied Rorey, who wobbled back to the bar. The little man could handle a fight better than a flagon.

"Don't drink that, by the way. He'll have pissed in it," Xan rasped, nodding at the flagon. Sure enough, Rorey and his chums kept glancing over at them from the bar, barely stifling giggles.

"Charming," Osolin said, withdrawing the handkerchief tentatively. The flow had stopped.

"Western hospitality," Xan shrugged. "So what's the word?"

"They say that you are the foremost—ah, authority on the insect jungle. We've been sent to speak with you on behalf of King Joymont," Sandros said.

"Joymont, eh? Did he mention that I'm also the foremost authority on large sacks of gold?"

The four looked at him, blinking.

"The things I know aren't free," Xan explained, slowly.

"But... this is a mission of mercy. The fields of Joy Mountain are overrun with monsters from the insect jungle, the beasts devour everything. If they aren't driven off, the farmers, all of Joymont, will starve come winter."

"Ah. I see." There was a long pause. The masked ranger was winding up for something. They waited, and he delivered.

"Alas. If only someone had gone to 'King' Joymont years ago and told him the Kalparcimex was spreading. That he ought to abandon his shitty little castle and his misguided quest to create a dynasty in land everyone else was too wise to settle and go back where he belongs. Perhaps this could all have been averted."

"Yes, and he gave your words much consideration. But in the end, you cannot uproot a whole realm on the word of one man. He consulted insect masters who thought you wrong. His advisors told him there was no danger," Sandros said, speaking rapidly, as if he could sweep away the whole thing with his words.

"Then perhaps they should advise him on how to deal with this problem as well," Xan said, and though Sandros could not see Xan's face, he could hear the righteous pique of an unheeded scholar behind the mask.

"King Joymont remembered you and your warning. When the insects came, he cursed his poor judgment and sent us to find you. It is said you are the greatest expert of this Kalparcimex in all the Arc. He begs you to aid the people of Joymont, and help us to drive these beasts back into the jungle whence they came. Surely you will be richly rewarded."

"Surely. I doubt that fat dolt said any such thing, and I'm certain he'd swindle me out of any reward the instant he thought my use was through."

"AN INSULT!" Gregary shouted, rising unsteadily from the table in a clatter of armor, and in a moment, Brakkar rose with him. Xan remained seated, looking up at the two, and it was up to Sandros to calm them down and get them back in their chairs as shouts to fight rang out from the bar.

"Don't let that insult stand! Duel him!" shouted Stonegren, pattering both hands on the bar like a drumroll.

"Your King is a coward and a fool. I was there when his whole 'kingdom' was three pig farms. It was a shitheap then and nothing has changed," Xan said, provoking the woozy knight.

Gregary's face grew redder and redder, but he remained in his chair, gripping the table so hard his hands shook.

"Remember your oath, dunce," Osolin hissed, her eyes darting around the room. It looked like the fool might get them all killed. Gregary nodded, his bottom lip crushing the top to keep words from escaping.

"So, in short, I'd sooner trust the piss in that flagon to turn to wine than him to make good on a promise."

"This freak is useless, he can't defeat the beasts. It's not too late to go to Tck'Hurr," Osolin sniffed. Her nose was stopped up with blood, she sounded like a salt pirate.

"What kind of beasts?" Xan asked, his curiosity finally getting the better of him.

"Manticores—foul, armored things that fling spikes from their tails that can pierce a breastplate of Wyrth steel at fifty paces. The spikes are poison, a single touch is death," Sandros said.

"What?"

"Here," Sandros reached into his pack and withdrew the blackened spine. He had scorched it until it stopped moving.

"Well, you've ruined the spine, you can throw that out. Manticores, ha! This is from a tink. Not poisonous in the least. Four of you and you can't handle a few tinks?"

"We tried, and lost a hundred men. Only Sandros and I survived. They've decimated our herds as well. There are hordes of them."

"Wait... herds... you let tinks get loose in your herds? Gods above, what fools."

"I can do nothing. There are so many, I'd have to burn down half the kingdom to root them all out," Sandros said, his eyes downcast.

"Well, it's no wonder you're in such a state, they'll be breeding in your cattle. You probably have a whole swarm of them by now. Might even have a few winks to contend with come winter."

"Winks?"

"Winks are a problem. Winks would be worth bothering me for. Not this nonsense."

"Nonsense? Sir, we've traveled over fifty leagues to get here, hoping against hope that you can help us. Better than a hundred good men are dead, and thousands will starve this winter, and you call this nonsense?"

"You, you're some kind of magician, right? And you can't figure out how to kill a bunch of tinks no smarter than dogs? They're going to wipe out your whole realm?"

"I... I haven't got a clue about tinks or winks or any of this. I've never heard of these monsters, I have no idea why they're so far from your accursed jungle. Perhaps this all seems a joke to you, but people are suffering. We've passed through half a dozen steads where everyone is dead, men, women, children. I'm relying on your decency here."

"Decency, huh? How much decency did you bring with you? Coin, I mean. All of it."

"What?"

"Everything you've got on you, the lot of you. On the table now, and I'll tell you how to get rid of the tinks."

"This one tries to rob us! Fool, you will tell us everything or I will smash you into paste!" Brakkar rumbled, pounding both his fists on the table and sending piss sloshing out of Rorey's flagon.

"I'm terrified. Please don't beat me like you beat Rorey," Xan said. Brakkar tried to stare him down, but it was useless through the dark lenses.

"I can't believe someone could be so cold, so unaffected. Care you nothing for the suffering of your fellows, sir?" asked Osolin, and this drew a muffled snort from behind Xan's mask.

"Do I look like I have a lot of fellows? I can't believe someone wearing the mark of an idiot guild of Ibexian thieves would talk of morals. If you want to advertise your idiocy, the notches are enough." He tapped the back of his left earlobe, indicating her tattoo. It was a faded blue scorpion no bigger than the nail of her littlest toe, hidden behind her ear. None of the others had even noticed it, but somehow Xan had and he dared to mock her for it.

She was halfway across the table with the silver-ringed dagger when he caught her wrist and sent the weapon clattering against the ground. The back of his other hand cracked her across the mouth and sent her down to join it.

"By the way, there are no scorpions in Aran. That guild has been a joke since its inception. Even the name is stupid," Xan added, salting the wound.

He was on his feet now, ready to fight, but the other three were beaten, and there were tears in Osolin's eyes as Gregary helped her to her feet.

"Filth," she muttered, blood pooling at the corner of her mouth. The blow had set her nose to bleeding anew. It had been a hard night for her.

"Gold," said Xan, behind his emotionless mask. "Gold or I walk."

They were miserable as they pooled their money on the table. Between them, they produced fifteen stars and some change.

"Now, the money you held back."

"That's all of it, goddamn it!" Gregary said, nearly shouting, but the mask shook back and forth, and at last Osolin coughed up the seven stars she'd held out. With a gloved hand, Xan swept the money off the table and into a pouch.

"Alright. Here's the secret to getting rid of the tinks. Do you need to write this down?" The eyes of the whole bar were on them, rapt.

"Memory is my trade," Sandros said, looking desperately unhappy. Fourteen of those stars had been his.

"Ok, here it is. Do nothing."

46

"What?"

"Tinks are territorial. They only reason they aren't fighting is there's an abundance of food. Once they eat that, they'll be killing each other off right and left. Then you only have to wait for winter, it's still too cold for them, they won't survive. Abracadabra, no more tinks. Meanwhile, I suggest you take this opportunity to uproot your doomed kingdom and move it far, far east. The Kalpa cometh. Thanks for the gold."

There was a whistle from the bar, and many heads shook.

"What!" Only Sandros could even get that out, the others were speechless. "We marched fifty leagues and spent all our gold to hear 'do nothing'?! That doesn't even help! The people will still starve!"

"Truly. The worst part is, you didn't even need to come to me. Anyone out here could have given you the same advice for nothing."

"Ya, it's just common sense," threw in Stonegren, whose famous gray smile was wide, watching the foreigners get fleeced. "You could of asked a child. Child woulda' known better than to let tinks get into his herd, too, that's just idiocy." In his hand was an iron rod that had clearly seen much use, and as the four travelers looked around the room, they could see knives protruding from sleeves, and a great number of daggers appeared from the ether.

"A curse, a curse on the whole lot of you thieves and curs. A curse neverending on this bar and everyone in it!" Sandros shouted, throwing back his chair and raising his hands high. They burst into flame, and again all the fire in the room rose in anticipation. There was a crazy light in the mage's eyes, an eagerness that never failed to put fear into the hearts of his foes. Except this time.

"Ain't you lot in the bar too?" Stonegren asked, still smiling. There was no fear in any of them. Sandros felt the point of something sharp and looked down to see Xan's dagger digging into his solar plexus.

47

"One more word and you will die. Your friends shortly after," Xan promised, and the fire died, smoke that smelled of burning hair trailing from Sandros' hands. "Now get gone, all of you. Welcome to the west."

"This isn't over!" Gregary shouted as they slumped out, surrounded on all sides by a gauntlet of blades.

"This isn't over!" Rorey Morey shouted, his voice high pitched and mocking, aping Gregary's walk and marching out behind them. At the doorway, Gregary was about to turn and shout something else when Rorey booted him in the ass and sent him flying out into the street.

"I'LL HAVE MY REVENGE!" Rorey shouted, and then he slammed the door on them. They could hear laughter roaring even through the door.

Outside, the wind kicked up and the sign of The Red Queen Rises squeaked on its hinges. The four beaten adventurers looked up at it in misery. Upon it was the image of a crimson centipede wearing a golden crown, bursting from a woman's bare chest in a nova of blood.

It began to rain.

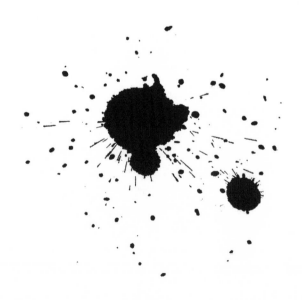

Bars, as a rule, tend to be dark places. This close to the Kalpar-cimex, wax was plentiful and candles were cheap, but of course, darkness was even cheaper. Even alongside the darkest, dankest winesinks of this land, where thunderclouds were ever-present and great swarms of insects blotted out the little light that slipped between them, Nod's Hole stood out as the blackest pit any of the exiles had ever entered. The hearth was just embers, and a screen had been set before it so they could barely see an inch in front of their faces as they stumbled in from the street through two sets of heavy black curtains. Still, somehow, the heat was sweltering.

Thick cane smoke swirled around them, and men clustered close around Ibexian-style sunken smoking pits whose embers barely gave light. The only other illumination within came from the bowls of the half-dozen pipes scattered around the room. The four travelers made their way to the bar with a great ruckus of banging their shins on chairs and their hips on tables.

People hissed at them as they drew too near, and they slunk toward what they hoped was the bar as carefully as they could. Even still, there was a squawk of protest as Brakkar tripped and landed on top of one of the smokers, nearly plunging both into one of the ember pits. A great warble of slurred angry voices rose at the outrage and there was a clatter of whispered apologies from all four until, finally, they found their way to the bar and their eyes began to adjust to the dim.

"We're looking for the Black Mage," Sandros said in a whisper. Still, his voice rang out in this place like a shout. In the confounding darkness, he could just make out the outline of a tall man behind the bar.

"Leave," the man said in a deep, slow voice. They could see the flash of teeth as he spoke. Two points of light sprang out above them—his eyes had opened.

"Is he here or not?"

"Now." The word seemed to roll out through the darkness, and there was a shift in the air. People were moving around them, but whether they were moving away or moving toward them, they could not say in this relentless dark.

"⊬⚡H!" Sandros shouted, and a ball of white-hot fire appeared in the palm of his hand.

He held it up and there were shrieks of pain. Smokers who had been creeping toward them fell back with their hands over their eyes. As if they'd shined a light into a nest of roaches, men scuttled away from them. There were many more people in this place than they'd thought.

Wretched people, their skin pale and purple-tinged, their arms thin as sticks and their eyes hugely dilated. Some clutched pipes close to their chests, terrified someone had come to take their smoke away. Some froze mid-copulation, others continued, unaware or uncaring. Only the man at the bar did not shrink from their light, and as Sandros' flaming orb shone on his face, he saw the man's eyes were totally white. He was blind.

In the light, Sandros saw that every surface in the place had been painted black, even the bottles behind the counter. There were no windows, and dusty black cloth hung from all of the walls. How they must hate the light!

There was whispering in the air under the cries of protest and pain, and the orb of fire began to flicker and dim. His companions had drawn their weapons, and Sandros concentrated his will, trying to hold his spell steady.

"This... is no place... for you... little light..."

The voice was soft, and it seemed to come from all around them. The fear worked against him, and his light faded away until he held nothing better than a candle flame. The situation was dire—if that were snuffed, the whole bar could rise against them. In his mind he saw himself being dragged down by a throng of mindless addicts, held down by a dozen hands as they began to devour him alive...

Terror set his thoughts in flight quickly, and he thought he must have light at all costs, light to keep these wretched things away from him, light to drive off the voice of the Black Mage. He looked up at the ceiling and began to invoke the most powerful spell he knew, a fiery tornado that would devour the ceiling and let the light of day shine down upon this nest of troglodytes.

"**OUT!**" came the voice of the blind barkeep. It was the third word he'd said, and the third was the charm. His voice slammed into them like a battering ram. They were lifted bodily and flung almost ten feet to crash onto men lying on the floor. Brakkar screamed. He'd landed on a pipe and shards of glass and bits of burning coals were embedded in his ass.

They needed no call to retreat, all four scrambled for the exit. As Sandros made for the door, a hand caught his sleeve and held him firm. He looked up, but there was only darkness.

"Would you really have called the Red Wind? There are people upstairs..." It was the same soft voice as before, only now it came from directly next to him.

Sandros' eyes were wide. In his terror, he'd forgotten there was another floor above them.

"No! I didn't know! I didn't mean to!"

"I see," said the voice, and he thought he could hear a hint of disappointment, but it was madness. He might have collapsed the whole building and killed the lot of them.

"Please! Let me go! I'll leave and never come back!"

"But you haven't gotten what you came for..." The voice was calm, almost teasing. There was no gravity to the things it said, it was sweet, almost childish. He could not tell if it belonged to man, woman, child, or beast. Sandros slowly became aware that he was pissing himself.

"Very well. Scuttle off, then."

The grip at his sleeve was released, and at the door his companions had both curtains pulled open, casting the pale light of day upon the smoke den, bringing fresh cries of pain from the smokers. Looking up, he could see the source of the shadow voice, a form dressed all in black, wearing a hood and veil.

"Sandros!" Gregary shouted from the door. "We have to get Sandros!"

"He's so rude," the veiled one said, and with a wave, the door and Gregary vanished, only blackness where they'd been. "I gave you leave."

Sandros rose, acutely aware he'd soiled himself, wanting nothing so badly as to be gone from Nod's Hole. But somehow, he found the strength to speak.

"We came to beg a favor from you," he said, surprising himself. His voice was shaky but he could get the words out at least.

"This is how you beg?" He could just make out the arm that gestured to the chaos within the smoke den. The smokers were clustering along the walls now, though more than a few were groping about on the floor, hoping to find fallen threads of cane.

"Please! They say you are powerful, the most powerful mage in the west!"

"They do?" the voice said, almost humming with pleasure. "Who said that?"

"Varagoi the Insect Master, and Resafust the Scribe. They said if anyone could help us, it was the Black Mage." Sandros gave the names easily, even knowing it might bring down the mage's wrath upon them.

"If Varagoi and Resafust say it, it must be true. They are very learned men. But please, only yokels call me the Black Mage. My name is Ink."

"I am Sandros." No Sandros the Red for this one, he was not about to brandish his title at one who'd seen him piss his pants. "Please, we have been sent from Joymont, where a great horde of insects is devouring everything in sight. They—"

"Oh, I know your tale. Everyone knows." Again, the hint of mirth.

"Varagoi said there is a type of insect that eats the tinks, deep within the Kalparcimex. Bashyskyla. He says that tinks hate and fear them, and will leave our land if we can bring one back to Joymont."

"A capital plan. I heard you asked Varagoi to take revenge on the ranger. They say he laughed at you."

"He did."

Isn't that interesting? A man the insect masters will not touch. Do you still want your revenge? For your money and your pride?" It was an offer.

"We were angry then... the mission is more important."

I see." Again, the hint of disappointment.

"Please, can you help us? I am sure you will be greatly rewarded."

"And no one else in town dares to venture so far into the Kalpa to capture a bashyskyla. Save the ranger, of course."

"Xan says we should just let the tinks live, that we should let our people starve."

"I hear Xan is very wise."

"I cannot let my people die."

"How noble." It was only a faint hint, but Sandros was sure he was being mocked. His eyes had adjusted and he could see the dark forms of addicts gaping open-mouthed at them. Nod, the unseeing bartender, was still rooted to his spot. Looking at Ink, Sandros could make out no features, just darkness.

What in the world am I getting into?

"I will assist you in your quest," Ink said, and extended an arm. Sandros groped for it, half-expecting the freezing cold touch of some demon or wraith, but the hand that found his was warm and uncalloused, smaller than his own. They shook.

"On the morn, I shall meet you wherever you are staying. Until then."

53

There was a crash and Gregary tumbled into the smoke den as the pitch black wall he'd been battering against disintegrated. Light from the street filtered in. Sandros looked around the room, but there was no sign of Ink. Hastily, they fled into the stinging light of the street.

"Are you alright?" Gregary asked, and Sandros nodded, looking down at his damp leggings with embarrassment.

"I hate the west," Gregary said, a miserable look on his face. "What happened in there?"

"The Black Mage—Ink—will help us. We're to meet tomorrow morning to venture into the insect jungle."

"Sandros... your hand," Osolin said. Glancing down, Sandros recoiled in alarm. For an instant, he thought his hand was drenched in blood, all the way up to the sleeve. But it was not blood, there was no pain. The mage's touch had stained his clothes and skin as black as night.

In the morning, the four travelers found the shadow waiting for them in the common room of Halley's Horse. The Horse was a small inn which just happened to be as far as one could get from The Red Queen Rises without actually leaving town. Her owner was a retired warrior who'd grudgingly given them free room and board when he learned Brakkar was one of the Bloodstar's chosen. If not for his charity, they would have been sleeping in an alley. The prices other inns had asked of them were so high they assumed they must be blackballed.

That corner seemed four shades darker than the rest of the inn, but as the black mage rose to meet them, Sandros saw that the darkness followed. Curious, Sandros murmured a few words and his eyes glinted blue as they drifted into the planes of magic. Yet he could see no lines of power, no glowing sigils, nor breaches where energy spilled from one plane into the next. Not a single sign to indicate the presence of magic. Then, with a startled yelp, he realized he could see nothing at all. He was blind!

"Sandros!" Ink's voice came through the black as he groped around for something, anything to hold on to. "How shameless!"

It was mock indignation, but he was truly blind, and he caught ahold of Gregary's sleeve, feeling the metal rings beneath the cloth.

"I can't see!" he said, and his companions made noises of alarm.

"What are you doing?!" Gregary's voice came through the dark. He'd put a hand on Sandros' shoulder to steady him, and the touch was the only thing separating the mage from total panic.

"He all but looked up my skirt, this one. Such nerve! The uncouth temerity!" Ink's voice brimmed with amusement under the feigned outrage.

"I didn't mean—I'm sorry!"

"A lady's secrets are her own, Sandros the Scribe. Remember that." All the sights of the world came back to him suddenly and they *hurt*. The headache came on hard, and it had all the trappings of a real floor-banger. Sandros pinched his upper lip hard between thumb and forefinger to dull the pain. He was wearing a glove to cover the black mark she'd left on his hand. The skin was raw from scrubbing, but the stain was as dark as ever.

"I didn't know, I beg your pardon. It won't happen again." He was reeling both with the burden of seeing and the knowledge that the black mage was apparently a woman. Who could tell behind that shapeless robe? He could not even see eyes beneath her veil.

"I should hope not. Shall we?" Leaning against the wall by the door was a long, thin scabbard. She picked it up and went for the door.

"What the hell did you do to her?" Osolin whispered as they moved to follow.

"I only looked for magic! Mages do it all the time when they meet, it's nothing!"

"Gods, you're like dogs sniffing at one another and she bit you. I can't believe that's a woman," Osolin whispered back, and the other two murmured in agreement.

"A woman with excellent hearing," Ink said at the door, her voice high and sweet. Osolin's eyebrows shot up in embarrassment. For an instant, it seemed as though Ink was drawing a sword, and Osolin's hand leapt to the dagger at her side in readiness. Without flinching, the black mage unfolded the black parasol Osolin had mistaken for a scabbard and stepped outside. It was so overcast they could barely see a hint of the sun, yet still she walked along with it held low, hiding her veiled face.

The four adventurers followed her through town, and it seemed that everyone in Ten had time to gawk out their windows at them. There were more than a few sniggers from those who'd heard of their beating at the hands of Rorey Morey, and a few more who'd heard of the fracas at Nod's Hole.

The town of Ten was built on an island nestled in the caldera of Roanoa, a dormant volcano at the easternmost edge of the Kalparcimex. Even at the very edge of the insect jungle, it was impossible for men to live, but the altitude of Roanoa kept all but the hardiest insects at bay.

The water of the caldera was the next obstacle. It was pitch black and almost hot enough to cook with. Boatmen made their way to and from Ten following currents of cooler water that came from springs on the island. It was an unlikely place for a town, but not impossible, and there was a profit to be had.

The greatest insect masters in the Arc made their homes here, gathering all varieties of invertebrates and sending them along the perilous highland trade route that wound through the mountains in the east. From the Kalparcimex came wondrous medicines, fabulous dyes, resins and secretions for countless uses, and of course, the dreaded living weapons. Year ticks, crotch mites, bore locusts, and adder wasps, endless varieties of many-legged havoc were at their disposal. Only a great fool would cross a master, for their revenge was legendary.

The group made its way past the gawkers and gazers to the misty western harbor, which wasn't much to speak of. Two boats bobbed lightly on a rickety dock of snake cypress pitted and stained a purplish black by the caldera water. Beside the boat dock was a larger, better-kept dock for the cargo barge. The docks were set on a river where the cool water of the city spring met the searing water of the lake in a great wall of billowing fog

Three men in cloaks sat at the end of the dock holding poles, still as monks. They were actually fishing in that scalding soup.

Two were short and one was tall, and the tall one's cloak glint-ed in the half-light of the early morning. The four adventurers hoped in vain that beetle-shell cloaks were just the fashion in Ten.

"You're on the wrong dock," Xan called to them, though he hadn't turned to see them. A million tiny drops of water glistened on the shells of his cloak. "You want the east dock, boat to the high road is at noon."

"We aren't going to the high road."

At this, Xan cocked his head and turned around to look them over.

"Watch this for me, will you, Ahel?"

"Yeh," said the fat man at his side without looking up from his own bobber.

Xan set his pole into a hole bored in the dock and rose, the light glittering off his cloak as he turned to them.

"You're going into the Kalpa."

"Yes. You left us no choice," Sandros said.

"You're going into the Kalpa dressed like that. With this one." Xan did not point at the sorceress, instead indicating her with a tilt of his head.

"My name is Ink, Xanadros," the black mage said, saying both names with emphasis. The masked man's lenses and the dark cowl of the mage met in a curious staredown where neither could see the eyes of the other. Quickly, Xan saw the futility of it and ig-nored her.

"She's leading you to your deaths," Xan said quickly. "She's going to take you out into the Kalpa and leave you there because she thinks it's funny. What the hell do you think you can get out there anyway?"

"Bashyskyla. To kill the tinks."

There was a snort from beneath the mask. "Who put you onto this? Was it Raysson? Malks? Oh gods, it must have been Varagoi. He thinks he's doing me a favor, getting you killed."

"This one lies," Brakkar growled. The whole time, he'd never taken his gaze off Xan, or his hand off the handle of his mace.

"If you think you can swindle us a second time, you're mistaken. Sir! We need a boat," called Sandros.

"Yeh, busy," Ahel grunted. He'd set his own pole into the dock and was busy wrestling with Xan's.

"What the hell are you fishing for in that awful water?" Gregary asked, finally unable to contain his curiosity.

"Whatever's biting. Scribe, squire: Look at me. Look at what I'm wearing." Xan pointed to his get-up. Beneath the shimmering cloak, he wore a suit of oily black leather that covered his entire body. Sewn onto it were plates of hard translucent shell, protecting his vitals. Gregary wore a breastplate and coat of mail, and he did not envy the ranger. How he must sweat!

"This is what it takes to survive down there. You don't have the equipment or the faintest idea how to proceed in the Kalparcimex. Varagoi sent you to die."

"So you say."

"I do say. Do you four have any clue what a bashyskyla is? What it would do to your little hog town?"

"They eat tinks. If we can get one and lead it back, it will wipe them out. It's been done before," Sandros said.

"It's been done before in a fairy tale. Rill the Rang leads a bashyskyla over the mountain pass to lay siege to the wicked black tower of Horth'Wyrth and save the princess. Varagoi told you a children's bedtime story and you are following it to your idiot rube deaths. Do you know what bashyskyla really eat?"

No one replied.

"Everything. They eat EVERYTHING because they are the apex predator of the outer Kalparcimex. Does that mean anything to you?"

From the looks on their faces, Xan could see his words meant nothing to them. He'd soaked them for their gold, and they thought this just another hustle.

"Please, Xan, you're embarrassing yourself. Everything will be fine. We'll just be in and out," Ink said, twirling her parasol between two gloved palms. Again, he ignored her.

"Ahel," Xan said.

"Yeh, one second!" Ahel said, sweating with effort. He'd dropped the pole to take the heavy line in both hands, tugging it in. The line jerked back hard enough that it seemed he would go flying into the water after it, but Ahel turned and slung it over his shoulder, leaning his full weight into it. At once, Xan and the short man who'd been sitting beside Ahel rushed over and grabbed the line with him.

Grunting with effort, the three men pulled a flattened eyeless creature that was nearly fifteen feet long onto the dock. The four adventurers backed away cautiously. It had a wedge-shaped head like an adder, and the wire-wrapped fishing rope disappeared into row upon row of vicious, in-curving teeth. Its body was long and segmented, with dozens of legs like a centipede which curled under as they pulled it onto the docks.

The catch glittered in the dim light. Its armor was smoky and dark, like volcanic glass, edges sharp as the facets of a jewel. Through the crystalline exoskeleton, they could see its organs still pulsating, and at the end of its length, dozens of eggs gave off a faint red light. Once the creature was fully on the dock with all its legs folded under, it became perfectly still and its insides slowly stopped pumping. It had begun to die the instant it left the water.

"Gods. Big. An' she's full, chock full. Yer rich, Xan."

"You two pulled it in. We'll split it."

"Was yer pole," the fat fisherman said. The other man who'd helped pull in the beast was his twin, Yamel, and he nodded solemnly as Ahel spoke.

"I said we'll split it."

Ahel frowned and shrugged for show, and there was no change to his jowled expression, but a sudden spring in his step betrayed him. Yamel grinned ear to ear, his feet shuffling as if threatening to break into a jig at any moment.

60

"What is that thing?" Sandros asked, eyeing the gleaming length of it.

"Black queen," the twin, Yamel, said.

"She's beautiful," Ink murmured, stepping close for a look at the black queen's strange, glassy carapace. Threads of minuscule black dots began at the clear edges of the armor plates, coalescing into intricate swirling patterns at their centers. The four adventurers looked at her strangely, but the ranger's mask gave a quick nod of agreement.

"What's it for?"

"Not eatin'," Yamel said with a grin. "A rare catch. Stars, there must be forty reds in her. Forty reds!"

"Take it to Varagoi, tell him I said a thousand for the whole thing and if he offers you a copper less, tell him to go fuck himself and go to Gotty. Tell him I said that too, neither of us wants Gotty getting his hands on this one. And then tell him I don't owe him a favor for sending these idiots off to die. They're nothing to me."

"Thousand. Gotty. Fuck himself, idiots. Got it. I'll get the sledge," Yamel said happily.

"A thou... a thousand stars for that thing? For a bug you pulled off a dock?" Osolin asked, clearly astonished.

"Damn near pulled us off instead," Ahel said. "That's wholesale, girl. Thing's worth ten times that in the right market for the reds alone, shell's worth a pretty penny, too. Not a bad morning." Osolin glowered at Ahel when he called her "girl" but he was unfazed, nodding to the thing at his feet. *If I'm not afraid of this, what makes you think I'm afraid of you?*

"I can't believe it," Osolin said. She could not take her eyes off the black queen, couldn't stop sizing up her chances of taking on the ranger and the twins and making off with their catch. A thousand stars!

"Why do you think we're all out here? For our health? This is the west. Whatever you are back where you came from, it doesn't matter here. That money I took from you? Pocket change," Xan said.

"Then give it back," Gregary threw in.

"I only took it so you would leave. I'll give it back to you right now if you get on the noon boat east and go back to where you belong. You four are out of your depth," Xan said, and he reached into a pouch and pulled out a fistful of stars.

"We're here on a mission, and we're not leaving until it's complete," Gregary declared, his posture straightening, and the others nodded in agreement. Xan shrugged and put the coins back in his pouch.

"Keep the money, thief. When I am through with this, I will feed it to you," Brakkar growled, but no one paid him any mind.

"Hey, Ahel, you see these four? They coming back alive?"

"Not getting a return fare from these lot. Not that it matters to a wealthy man such as myself. Gods, Xan, the luck on you. Forty reds. Finger of the Laughing Star on this one and no foolin."

Xan just shook his head, the sides of his mask creased with his grin.

At last, Ahel looked at the four, then indicated his boat with a thick stubby thumb.

"Welp, day's burnin. Gotta get if we're gonna. Cost's ten a head, there and back, but five each for you should do it."

"Twenty stars?! For a ferry?"

"There's always swimming," Ahel said, and they saw the first sign of a grin between those great jowls. "Anyhow, it's thirty by my count, and I won't take nothin that comes from her, nothin she's handled. Nothin personal, Miss Ink. Call me superstitious."

"How do you figure thirty? There are five of us. Five each," Sandros said

"Ten for her, five for the rest. She'll come back."

As they cast their glances among themselves, Xan gave Ahel ten stars from the money he'd taken from them in the Red Queen Rises and climbed down into the boat.

"Wait! What are you doing, you can't come with us!" Osolin protested.

"Nor would I. Why do you think I'm on the dock? I'm going to work. This is the only boat to the Kalpa. You have no idea how lucky you are that you can't afford the fare."

The four adventurers looked at each other, then at the wall of fog. Finally, Osolin counted out thirty stars, shaking her head at the extravagance. In Joymont, a family of four could eat for a year on thirty stars.

"You held out on me?" Xan asked.

"I didn't have this when we met," Osolin said, unable to hide her grin. "Easy wealth is easily lost."

"Thieves and sorceresses, what have I got myself into?" Ahel wondered as they all climbed into the boat.

"What have I ever done to you, Ahel?" Ink asked, sounding hurt.

"Nothin. Like to keep it that way. Don't truck with wizards and such."

"Sandros is a mage, too," Ink protested.

"Not like you, he ain't."

They followed the cool current east through the wall of steam, sweating and panting. Ahel worked a pair of oars at the bow, rowing with a slow, patient grace so the boat slid through the glassy black water with barely a ripple. Xan sat closest to him, peering out at the jungle's edge. Ink sat at the stern, peering into the water, transfixed, as the four adventurers crowded into the middle of the boat, trying keep their distance from both Xan and Ink.

"I wish I could swim in it. Just slip beneath the surface, drift in that darkness, so warm my bones would glow like coals," Ink said longingly, and the four adventurers looked at her with a kind of worried horror while Xan peered at her through his lenses.

"Go ahead, I'll wait for you here," Ahel gruffed, never missing a stroke with the oars.

"Ahel, you are a horrible little man."

"Big where it counts."

"If you can only count to three," Ink said, holding up fingers, one, two, three. Osolin laughed, while Brakkar's eyebrows were up in confusion one moment and crossed in disapproval the next.

"Hush now, I'm rowin," Ahel said, not liking his chances of coming out ahead bandying words with the sorceress. For a while, the boat glided silently across the water while they sweated and looked tensely at the far shore.

"How deep is the caldera?" Gregary asked at last. Out in the middle of the lake, the expanse of still black water gave him a strange, shrinking vertigo. If the boat should tip, they would all die. His hands ached from clenching the plank he sat on. He was afraid the others would remark on it, but even more afraid of pitching into that black fathomless murk in his armor.

"Deeper'n any rope. You want to know, you'll have to swim down there with Miss Ink. Now hush all of you, there's things in there can swallow this boat whole, yeh don't want to wake 'em."

Mouths clapped shut. Perhaps it was a lie to keep them quiet, but it was a good one. It was easy to imagine the thing they'd pulled up onto the dock ten times as big, those inward-hooking teeth breaking the oily surface, rising around the boat in a ring...

As the boat drew closer to the edge of the jungle, a great droning filled the air: a thousand kinds of humming, chirping, and buzzing, all layered into an unending dirge. There was no shore, only a cliff that rose thirty feet from the water's surface, latticed with vines. Above the wall, the vines ran riot, blooming in great explosions of purple and red flowers, crawling all over a line of spindly white trees.

Then one of the trees began to move, and the passengers saw that it was no tree but an enormous stick insect nearly fifteen feet tall, its forelegs huge scythed claws as long as greatswords. It made its way down the cliff face directly toward their boat, chittering at them, cocking its head to look at them with thousand-faceted maroon eyes. The boat was only twenty feet from the wall. In an instant, that great beast could spring upon them and kill them all. Yet Ahel still rowed toward the wall.

"What are you doing! Take us away from that thing!" Gregary cried, the terror in his voice plain. Ahel paid him no mind. The warrior scrambled for his sword when the boat slid up to the wall of vines, so close the great insect could simply reach out a claw and cleave them in half.

"Here ya go, Emma," Ahel said, reaching into his pocket and tossing a plum up to the insect. The plum vanished in a flash of mandibles and the chittering stopped. For a moment there was a massive head-splitting chirp of two legs rubbing together, then the stick insect swiveled and climbed back up the cliff, apparently satisfied.

"You oughta stop feeding her, Ahel, she's getting fat," Xan said.

"Wish I could, plums are dear this time of year. But it's her dock, I gotta pay the toll."

"Truly. Safe return, Ah," Xan clapped the short man on the shoulder, then leapt from the boat onto the vines, scaling the cliff swiftly.

"Same," Ahel said as Xan disappeared over the top. A moment later, they heard him shout, "I don't have a plum! Leave me be!" followed by another monstrously loud chirp. Then it was just the adventurers, the boatman, and the black mage.

"He wasn't lying. You four will die in there. I'll take ye back right now, and I won't charge ye a thing more. Last chance." Ahel's voice was quiet now, stripped of its gruffness. "No offense to whatever game it is yer playin, Miss Ink, but I gotta live with myself."

The four adventurers looked up at the cliff, and then back across the caldera at the mist-shrouded town, then at Ink, who was collapsing her parasol. She said nothing.

"For the oath… for Joymont, we must," Gregary said, and he was afraid the others could hear the fear in his voice and would not follow him.

65

But it was because they heard the fear that they followed, for they were just as afraid. The others slowly nodded with him, stacking their palms one over the other, then they began the climb into the Kalparcimex while Ink kept staring into the lake.

When they reached the top, Ink was waiting for them there, twirling her parasol absently. Eyes widened, and Brakkar even looked back over the cliff to make sure this wasn't some other veiled figure, but only Ahel remained in the boat.

The boatman shook his head, drawing in a slow breath. He began to row back to town.

At the top of the cliff, Emma the stick insect was nowhere to be seen, and the drone they'd heard in the boat had grown into an intolerable cacophony. None of the travelers could hear their own thoughts, and they understood at once that the principal danger of the Kalparcimex was madness.

Osolin had both hands over her ears, and she cried out as a stirge the size of a small bird landed on her shoulder and stuck her with its needle-like proboscis. She slapped at it but it was already gone, and another took its place, piercing the thick leather of her jerkin. Gregary swiped at it with his hand but it flew away easily, and a trickle of blood welled from the bite. With blood in the air, the buzzing of wings around them became a great roar. Boiling from the undergrowth, a whole swarm of stirges darted at Osolin, a hundred needle-mouths seeking blood.

Yelping in panic, she ripped her daggers from their sheaths and sliced wildly at the swarm. She caught few of them and cut them apart, yet the others were not deterred. They darted past her swings and sunk their needles in, drinking eagerly. Osolin screamed in pain, pierced in a dozen places, but her companions dared not approach her while she was flailing with the daggers.

There were a dozen stirges feeding on her when Ink lifted a hand. Time shifted, the moment doubled, and doubled again, expanding around them. The air grew thick as sap, and every motion drew out seemingly for an eternity. Every stirge froze perfectly still, and then the entire swarm fell to the ground, leaving trails of shadowy images behind them.

The insects darkened as they fell, and by the time they hit the ground, they were pitch black husks littering the moss underfoot. With a flick of her wrist, the black mage released the spell and the world came roaring back to speed, the pitch of the sounds around them bending back to true.

Sandros stood open-mouthed at the display. It was like nothing he'd ever seen. He'd been searching his brains for a spell that could help without burning the thief alive, yet here Ink had done it with a flick of her hand. Osolin sobbed, her hands probing the places she'd been bitten, where angry welts had begun to rise.

"You owe me your life," the sorceress said, and there was an uncomfortable weight to her words, as if some pact had been made between them. "You four didn't bring banes? Varagoi didn't tell you?"

She could see they had no idea what she meant. The cowl shook from side to side, and Ink sighed. She reached out a black glove and it slipped into a rift in the air, then she drew it back.

"Children. Carry one," Ink said. In the velvet palm of her glove were four fire opals the size of birds' eggs, each graven with minute lines of arcane sigils. "Each of you. Lose them and die. Mar the runes and die." There was no humor in her voice, for once.

Sandros looked at the opals resting in the sorceress's black glove, and he thought of the stain on his hand that he couldn't scrub off. *What if it never fades?*

"What are they?" he asked. Accepting an unknown object from a black-robed mage was one of those classical blunders, like wagering with a demon or challenging a Tck'Hurr to a duel over a woman. Some things never went well.

"A charm. It will protect you from the little ones. For a while."

Sandros wanted badly to peer through the planes to see just what magics the banes might contain, but his head still ached from earlier. He felt certain if he tried it again, his sight would not return.

"Are there any other effects?" he asked instead.

"There's the effect of not having one," Ink said, her voice through the veil tinged with annoyance. She indicated Osolin, and the thief was a sorry sight. One of her eyes was nearly swollen shut, her upper lip twice as big as her lower one, and her face glistened with tears.

It was a wrenching thing to see. She looked half-dead when they'd barely set foot in the jungle. Osolin took a charm eagerly, tucking it into her pocket, and when she did not immediately fall to the ground blackened like the stirges, the others cautiously took one for themselves. Everyone was careful not to let them touch bare skin, they'd all seen the red mage's hand.

"You were fortunate, actually. At least stirges don't lay eggs when they bite. Come along," Ink said.

A look of pure horror crossed Osolin's face, wildly distorted by the swelling, and she turned back in the direction of the boat. For a moment it looked like she would make a dash for the cliff to try and call the boatman back.

"Wait," Brakkar grunted. The big priest removed one of his barbed gauntlets and set a scarred hand on top of the thief's head, murmuring.

"Thy blood be PURGED!" he cried, and clapped the back of her head hard enough that she pitched forward onto her hands and knees. She immediately began to throw up. When she rose, she was pale and unsteady, but the swelling was going down. Sandros tried to look away as the sounds of retching pulled at his own guts, but out of the corner of his eye he saw that the vomit was bright red with blood. Osolin wiped her mouth, swigged from her canteen, and then spat it out.

"A miraculous healing," Ink said, and Brakkar scowled at her tone.

"But we really must be moving. Night here will not be kind to you." The black mage ignored Brakkar's glower and walked off, twirling her parasol, along a narrow path through the brush. They could do little but follow.

The day was more than half gone before Sandros summoned the courage to speak to Ink.

"The ranger seemed sincere. I think he really would have given us our money back if we'd gone home. You can see how that would be a worry to me."

"He was sincere, just misguided. He knows not the magics I can work."

Sandros thought of the bane in his pocket, of the stirges falling blackened to the earth, and of the black handprint inked onto his palm. Since they'd taken her charms, he hadn't felt a single bite.

"Nor do I. I've never seen magic like this."

"How would you have, Sandros the Scribe? Darkness isn't something you see. It's something you don't see."

He was quiet at that, and they kept traveling up the narrow path that wove between two thick walls of cane. Lines of brilliant red caterpillars spiraled up some of the stalks, inching along head to tail, their movements synchronized so that Sandros could watch a wave of motion ripple across the line, disappear behind the cane, and return on the other side. It was mesmerizing. Following the line up one stalk, he saw it end abruptly. A jade green beetle the size of a small dog gripped the cane in its six legs and gobbled the caterpillars up one by one as they marched blindly into its maw.

"The red ones are deadly poison. If one falls on you, do not crush it, brush it away carefully," Ink warned. Soon a gentle rain of insects was falling and Ink hummed along as they bounced off her parasol. Her companions were careful to do as she said.

The path they were on wound in a seemingly senseless way, with many forks and intersections with other paths, until it seemed they were in a great labyrinth of cane. Ink led them forward, never hesitating, as if she'd come this way many times, but it was impossible to escape the feeling that they wandered in circles. If Ink truly meant to leave them out here, Sandros had no idea how they would find their way back.

At one place where the path split in three, Ink turned right, and Sandros glanced up the left path and saw something huge shamble across the narrow strip of beaten earth and disappear into the cane. His legs locked up. Whatever it was walked on two feet and was bigger than a wagon, taller than three men. It was a behemoth with a shell of glistening green chitin. Sandros could feel the ground shake with every step it took, could hear the canes snapping as it plowed its way through. The others had already moved ahead and he hastened after them. The thought of being left behind in this maze was terrifying

"I am Sandros the Red, I wield the Fire of Heaven. I am Sandros the Red, I wield the Fire of Heaven. I am Sandros the Red, I wield the Fire of Heaven."

Again and again he said the words beneath his breath, milking them for every shred of reassurance they could give. Hadn't he been first in flame among the Scourer's apprentices? Quicker of wit, faster to make out the arcane truths hidden in the ancient one's mumblings? None had embraced the fire so swiftly as he.

"I have seen demons and wielded the fire that eats legions. I have eaten the black leaf and glimpsed the searing faces of God. I am more than this place, greater than this danger." Beneath his breath, the words swelled to great proportions in his mind.

He thought of deeds he'd done and more to come, of the glory this quest would bring, farmers clasping his hand and weeping with joy, women in bars tugging at his robe to ask if he were *the* Sandros, their eyes glittering with awe.

He tried to convince himself, but always...

It was as big as a house and walked on two legs like a man.

The party walked a long way, until they'd combed the cane maze so thoroughly that even Sandros thought he was getting to know his way around it. They saw shimmering dragonflies with wings of stained glass and mouths of razor teeth, armored spiders that lurked on branches and lassoed flying insects with their webs, vast colonies of ants as long as their forearms. Everything kept a careful distance, approaching no closer than arm's reach. Whatever else Ink's charms did, they kept insects at bay.

Finally, as the light faded, they were surrounded by cat-sized beady-eyed blackball beetles that ran around them in excited circles. They would scuttle with incredible speed, then leap into the air and ball up mid-jump, rolling wildly away. Then they would spring up again and run back to do it again and again, seemingly inexhaustible. They made little squeaks, somewhere between mice and pigs. Their little eyes were fringed with white, and always seemed to point in different directions, as if they were dizzy from all the dashing about. Even Brakkar could not help but smile at their antics.

"They are like pups," he said, grinning for the first time since they'd come to Ten.

"I bet they'd be worth a pretty penny if we brought one back to court. Such capering!" Gregary said, wondering at the logistics of it. What would a noblewoman pay to be the talk of town, to have such a cute little imp scampering about, bouncing off walls and delighting guests? Quite a bit, he guessed.

"They get bigger," Ink said, frowning beneath the veil. They could tell only from her voice, the way she held her head, but Ink was becoming increasingly annoyed as the day burned away. She kept the parasol low over her face as they walked.

"How much bigger?" Gregary asked. If they got as big as, say, a sheep, even better, they'd make for fantastic circus beasts. What if they could be trained!

"Much, much bigger. And meaner. They are like this only for a few months and then they start tearing everything to pieces, chattering like madmen. Whoever brought these to a court had better not return there."

"How do you know so much of these beasts? Do you come into the jungle often?" Osolin asked. Since Ink had saved her from the stirges, she had been casting long glances at the sorceress, paying close attention when she spoke. A wary look passed between Gregary and Sandros. They'd never seen Osolin act this way before.

"I've been known to wander about a bit. But truly, these things are elementary to one who lives near the Kalpa. Compared to, say, a gatherer who works for one of the insect masters, I know very little."

"What about the ranger?"

"Compared to Xan, I know nothing. The man lives and breathes this jungle. He goes deeper than any other man dares. He has seen things, done things that no other man or woman on the Arc has. Ichor runs in his veins and he beds she-mantises."

They all looked at her curiously—it seemed like a joke, but who knew? A sigh came from beneath her veil, and her companions had the strong sense that beneath it, she was rolling her eyes.

"Anyhow, it is a shame he's against you on this, because we could really use him. We should have come across a bashyskyla by now. It will be night soon."

"How will we find one in all of this?"

"They sing."

Again they looked at her, dumbfounded.

73

"Beautifully," she added. "We should have heard one by now. We've gone far enough."

"Perhaps something killed it?"

"Nothing at the Kalpa's edge kills bashyskyla."

"What of the beast I saw earlier?" Sandros asked. The image of the lumbering emerald giant had never been far from his mind as they walked.

"A shives. Bashyskyla eat them."

"But it was as big as a barn. What in the light of God can eat that?"

"Something very hungry."

Sandros paused. This was all starting to seem ridiculous. Dire warnings every step of the way, and now they were meant to believe that their quarry was a beast that ate behemoths in between songs. It felt more and more like a snipe hunt.

"So this giant-eater, we're somehow supposed to bring this thing back fifty leagues to Joymont and cut it loose on these 'tinks' and hope it decides to stop there? That cursed Varagoi really was trying to get us killed. Why did you let us come out here, knowing that?" Sandros asked.

"To save the common folk," Ink said, her voice flat.

"We must, no sacrifice is too great. We are but five, if there is even the slightest chance we can save Joymont, we must try!" Gregary chimed in, not hearing the mockery. Sandros could not be sure he had hadn't mistaken her tone. If only he could see her face!

"Night soon, and danger," Ink said, and she folded up her parasol and returned it to its sheath. The jungle grew darker by the moment.

"What's changed? All day we have faced danger," Brakkar threw in. For the last few hours, he'd been fiddling with his great mace, clearly itching for something to pulverize.

"All day, you have faced gatherers. Night is for the hunters."

They hastened to find shelter.

12

The night rain came, cold and driving, bringing some respite from the infernal din. The four adventurers were huddled together, shivering beneath the yellowed husk of a giant beetle. Vines wound up the legs and its back was host to a colony of mushrooms and the scuttling, hundred-legged spiders that tended them. Beneath the great shell was probably the only dry spot aboveground for a league in any direction.

"You should be safe here. Don't make a fire," Ink had said, and she'd turned into the rain. The parasol, which had seemed so eccentric before, became more useful all the time.

"What! You're leaving us?" Gregary was the one who asked, though even Brakkar looked alarmed.

"I can think of better things to do with a night than shivering in a pack of unwashed wanderers under a beetle's shell. Remember, the charms only work on the little ones. If anything big comes after you, fight back."

All four began to protest at once, but Ink simply melted into the rain and left them. Without the moon, the darkness was broken only by the occasional flash of lightning.

"How can we keep a watch in this shit? One of the big ones could walk right up to us and we'd be half-eaten before we even knew!" Gregary cursed, and they looked to Sandros for an answer.

He thought for a while, then rummaged in his pack for a bit before he found a sack of marbles, spheres of Khemerian glass swirled with color and glittering dust. One by one, he spun crooked words over the marbles, and in each of them a golden light smoldered and then faded away. He walked about in the rain, placing them in a perimeter around the beetle's shell.

"If something comes, we will know," he announced, soaked to the skin but pleased with himself. "The circle is fifty paces out from the shell, so don't wander too far if you need to take a leak."

Sandros whispered more twisted words and steam began to rise from his clothes as he dried out. When he was mostly dry, he ended the spell and joined the others.

Now they sat back to back, huddled beneath bedrolls that were no proof against the wet air of the jungle night. The air that had been so enervating and humid in the day was suddenly a seeping cold that sank into their bones.

"Jungles should be hot. Volcanoes should be hot. Yet we sit on the side of a volcano in the depths of a jungle and I am freezing!" Osolin sulked.

"You would be freezing if you laid in a bonfire. Why are women always cold?" Brakkar groused, though the big man was shivering the same as the rest of them.

"Cold to you, maybe," Gregary chimed in, and an elbow poked him in the ribs.

"Bah, what little you know. In Urth'Wyrth, no woman does not know of Brakkar the Big."

"Brakkar the Bashful is the way I heard it," the thief retorted, drawing snickers from Sandros and Gregary. Brakkar's throat rumbled, and the moment was tense.

"How did you come to follow the Bloodstar in Wyrth? I thought they all worshipped that big volcano," Gregary asked, trying to break the tension. They could ill afford to get into a brawl out here.

It was a wise thing to ask. Brakkar started on his tale eagerly, as if he'd been waiting days for someone to ask.

"Once, I too believed in the false promises of Urth'Wyrth. I joined his legion and paved his smoldering sides with heretic skulls. I wore the burned plate and I awaited the Great Doom eagerly, like any other Wyrth fool. For five seasons I fought, and few are the ones who've seen five seasons in the burning mountain's service and lived. I was an elite, and roamed with others thus tested. Without number the men I slew, the villages I put to the torch, without limit the destruction I wrought. Yet it was all in the service of falseness."

"When my time came to die, it was at the hands of a demon, pulled from the ether by a Yarlee magus, a spindly little thing I could break between two fingers. But the infernal Yarlee surprised us in the dead of night, his sorcery stole our strength, and the magic of the demon held us fast. I watched as the weakling smote my brothers in steel one by one, while the demon devoured their spirits."

"What kind of demon?" Sandros asked, his voice low.

"An awful thing, an unblinking eye that hung in the air and bent time into wax. Each man's suffering went on forever, each spent an eternity awaiting his turn. The Yarlee deviant took his time, each man suffered the worst indignities, the greatest pain. All night long he had his fun. I was the last. Time and time again, I called out for Urth'Wyrth to break the spell, to loose me so that I might die in battle, not frozen in place like a greenling spearboy. But the false god did not answer, and that Yarlee weakling laughed at my last words and kicked me in the back, so I fell facefirst into the entrails of my sergeant."

"This was his great error, for with my eyes, my nose full of blood, the truth was revealed to me. The Bloodstar spoke to me as dawn broke, filled my veins with thunder, and I rose, streaked with gore, and ripped the Yarlee's throat out with my teeth, spilling his tainted lifeblood upon the earth. The demon too, I ended. With the fury of the Star upon me, the dark one's sorcery could find no purchase, and I tore him from the sky and ripped him to pieces. The thing that slew twelve legionnaires, and nearly Brakkar the Bloody, came apart in my hands like wet parchment.

To think that I could have died in thrall to such a thing had the Star not willed otherwise..."

Brakkar paused for a moment, his voice thick.

"But by the will of Tyrias, here I sit. I took a pilgrimage to the Sangispire, and from the priests there I learned the truth of Urth'Wyrth. Under their guidance, I learned how to worship the Bloodstar, and when I was ready, I cast off the armor of the Legion, broke the collar of service from about my neck. Never again will I return to Wyrth, until the reckoning comes. The grand army shall be led against the demon who slumbers within the mountain, calling himself a god. He shall be cast down and the Great Doom foretold shall be as naught beneath the crimson light of the true Star."

The three others were watching him closely, but Osolin's eyes seemed to gleam especially bright, her brows high with interest.

"When we have succeeded here, and I do not doubt we will succeed, for I am the Red Giant's chosen, you should all think of taking up his service. What good is it to save your little kingdom if Urth'Wyrth rises and chokes the Arc with his black breath? Only the Bloodstar can break the fire mountain, and the hour grows late."

"I have had much time to think, rotting in that cell, marching to this place. When the oath is through, I plan to begin assembling the holy army to crush Urth'Wyrth once and for all. Perhaps we can lead the beasts of this place upon them. If this bashyskyla can slay all the tinks in Joymont, what can it do to the Legion? Can you see how this is all part of His great plan? Imagine yourself, a hero fit for the Gates of Grimbalgon. Imagine the whole of the North freed from the threat of the Wyrth, united beneath the Red Giant as a single empire. That kind of might can drive back this infernal jungle, tear it all down and plow it beneath the earth. That kind of might can wipe out the Yarlee filth once and for all, can drive the hordes back across the Malskernorr. A red empire to sweep the Arc!"

The others were silent in the face of Brakkar's audacity. The zealot truly believed he could conquer the arc. Each of them withdrew into their thoughts. In the pitch black of the jungle storm, it was easy to envision the eternal darkness of the Wyrth doom. One by one, they fell into a miserable half-sleep.

"What! No, you can't eat me. I would destroy you utterly. Not even a filament of your spirit would remain."

The hroradrora flattened its antennae against its sleek tapered skull and made a sound like two bells ringing in tune. *Jing-jing.* As it barked, she could see fangs protrude from beneath its hooked beak, removing all uncertainty as to what the beast meant. It was upset.

She eyed the beast appreciatively. It was a beautiful engine of death, all smooth lines and sharp, wicked points. This one stood nearly seven feet tall, changing its color like a chameleon so that it was all but invisible. They hunted like that, standing in one place for days until prey got too close, and then *jing-jing!* Death.

Once, Ink had heard a group of hunters argue drunkenly in the Red Queen Rises about how long a hroradrora could wait without moving. One man said two days, another said three, one said a week, and the drunkest claimed they could stand still forever, that they turned to stone and could unpetrify themselves whenever they liked in the blink of an eye. Back and forth they bickered, and then they began to make bets, and the whole tavern got in on it. At last they'd crept up to Xan as nervous as schoolboys, hats in their hands, for an answer.

"As far as I know, it is forever. I've seen one standing in place for at least a month. Eventually they always get something, or something gets them," Xan said, to the groans of everyone but the drunkard.

The other three hunters began to argue with Xan and he'd told them to go watch one themselves if they didn't believe him. It had turned into a fight and not a good one. All that could be said for the hunters was that they didn't suffer long. Ink couldn't understand why people were forever approaching Xan, it never ended well for any of them.

Jing-jing! chimed the hroradrora.

"Are you mad because I could see you? Is that it?"

The hroradrora grew perfectly still and shut its eyes, trying to vanish, its skin striving to find a deeper shade of black. But none were so deep as Ink's gaze.

"I can still see you, give it up."

From the trees, the ranger's mask shook from side to side, wondering why the thing hadn't already killed her. To hear the bell bark of the hroradrora was death, yet the mage still taunted the beast. In the blink of an eye, it could all be over. He'd seen a single hroradrora female kill a party of five armed men before a single one could ready a weapon. Five lives claimed in a frenzy of blood and shouts of alarm that died in sliced-open throats, swords that tumbled from severed arms, and then the *jing-jing* of triumph. It was the kind of thing you don't easily forget.

The hroradrora's eyes slit open for an instant and he knew it was all over. It pounced on Ink, so fluid it seemed like it had been poured from one space into another, so swift he hadn't time to cry a warning or fire a shot. Yet there was no spray of blood, no strangled cry. Instead, the hroradrora gave a single startled note and began to thrash about. The mage had broken apart into a thousand black lines and the beast was caught in them like a net.

"You see? I wasn't even there, this whole time. You have a lot to learn about stealth."

Ink stood ten paces away from the hroradrora, untouched.

"You too, Xanadros!" she shouted up at his perch, and his eyebrows raised at this. He wondered how the hell she'd seen him. It didn't pay to underestimate the black mage.

The hroradrora was caught fast now. It could not move its legs or either set of claws, and it fell on its back, desperately trying to wriggle free. At last, it stopped struggling and made a sad tinkling noise. The great predator brought low by sorcerous tricks.

"Now, if I let you go, will you leave me alone?"

No, it will carve you in two, Xan thought, readying his bow. The hroradrora kept up its sad little jingle, getting louder and more panicked all the time. Xan hoped to hell she would have the good sense to just kill the thing and get out of there. Then the hroradrora gave three sharp cries in succession.

"Good! Tell your friends, I don't want to have to go through this nonsense again," Ink said glibly, and with a wave of her hand, the web of shadows melted away. The hroradrora was on its feet in a second, and Xan thought for certain it would pounce on her, but instead it bolted, heading for the trees, galloping away on its six claws in a way he'd never seen.

"You see, Xan? They're not as bad as people say," Ink called up to his perch. Looking upward, she saw that he had an arrow nocked and pointed at her, and she was stunned. She hadn't expected Xan to try and kill her yet. Her mouth was still open in surprise beneath her veil when the bowstring twanged. A spell came to mind but it was too late to get it out.

The arrow flew over her head, close enough to feel the wind of it, and there was a loud crack behind her. It snapped her from her trance and she leapt aside a moment before five hundred pounds of pointy chitin crashed to the ground where she'd been.

It was another hroradrora, but this one was far bigger than the other, and its fangs did not protrude past its beak. Another key difference, the other hadn't had one of Xan's arrows through its eye. Somehow, the big hroradrora had slipped through her wards, and she hadn't had the faintest clue it was stalking her. Troubling.

The new one was busy dying, its shell running through every color one last time in a riot of scintillating waves. Then, at last, it faded to a milky translucence and the beast was still.

Ink was fascinated by the display and hadn't noticed Xan drop down to join her until the death-shimmer was done.

"Juvenile male," the ranger said, pointing in the direction the first hroradrora had run off.

"Adult female," he finished, sweeping his pointed finger to the milk-white corpse.

"I see," Ink said.

"I want you to stop toying with the Kalparcimex. I want you to stop leading those four to their deaths and go home. I want you—"

"Do you really?" the voice whispered from around him, from every direction.

81

Xan stopped mid-admonishment. Ink was gone, vanished in a puff of darkness right before his eyes.

"Magicians." The ranger spat the word like a curse.

With a sigh, he bent over the hroradrora with his knife to see if there were any eggs in her.

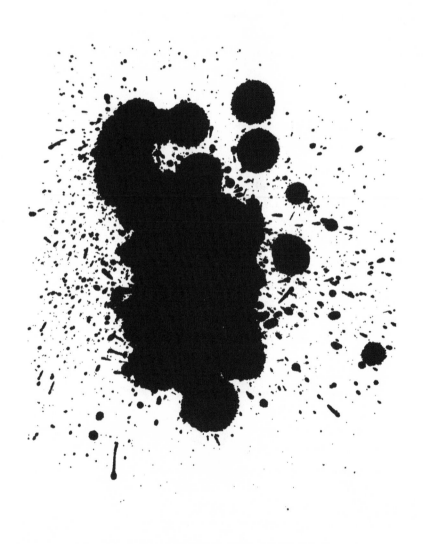

"Three priests. Give me the dice."

"Of all the stars in the sky, how in the hell has she got three priests?"

"I've been buying them the whole game."

"You've been buying them just in case someone pulls the demigod, and you just happen to have all three when they do?"

"Priests are underrated. You could have saved your archmage if you'd bought one instead of all those fireballs."

"That's not how a burn deck works... oh gods, roll and get it over with. Three priests on a demigod, I swear she's rigged the deck."

"Look at that, seven stars. So long, demigod. That's game." Brakkar and Gregary groaned now, too. Brakkar had thought he'd had a chance to buy the throne with his three chalices, a rogue, and a hoard. Gregary had been lagging behind, his only consolation that he wasn't dead last, but then Osolin had backdoored her way right into the lead.

"I can't believe it. Look at this shit," Sandros fanned out four fireballs and the last archmage, an incredible hand. The demigod would have been his next turn. "Three priests."

"I never go for mages myself. Too vulnerable." Everyone leapt a foot. Somehow, Ink had gotten right behind them without anyone noticing as they agonized over the final hand of roke.

"Mages are just fine if you don't get done up the ass by three priests the hand before you win. Gods piss on me from above!"

"My condolences to your ass, Sandros the Scribe," Ink said. Osolin was grinning broadly. Sandros did not reply, for he knew he acted the fool.

They'd been playing since dawn, waiting for Ink to return. The game had kept their minds off the possibility that she might not. Twice in the night, an explosion of light and sound had woken them, twice they'd jolted awake into battle-readiness. Both times, whatever had planned on eating them had been scared off, leaving them jittery for half an hour while their nerves settled enough to get to something like sleep.

"The bashyskyla are gone. I've been traveling all night, and I haven't heard or seen a single one."

"Do they migrate? Or have a mating season? Perhaps we've just timed our foray poorly."

"Our friend the ranger could tell us. I ran into him. He sends his regards."

He hadn't.

"But as for me, I haven't a clue. It feels wrong. It all feels different than I expected it to." Ink seemed distant. Veil or not, they could see she was troubled.

"How much water have you four got left?" she asked at last.

"Couple days," said Gregary. "But there's plenty of rain."

"I wouldn't," Ink cautioned. They all looked at her curiously. She'd brought nothing with her but the parasol. They had never seen her eat, drink, or eliminate.

"Drink nothing that isn't gathered from the treetops, and boil that twice. I want you four to stay put for the day. Play cards, keep a close watch. I can cover more ground without you. If I find one, I shall return. Have your scribe put down better wards."

"But... I didn't come all the way out here to hide under some beetle's shell and play cards," Gregary said, bitterness leaking into his words.

"If I'm not back by tomorrow morning, go back to where Ahel left us. Have your scribe light up the sky, draw the boatman's eye. There's mercy in that little man, he will return for you."

All four of them wondered if they could even get back to where they'd started. There had been so many twists, so much weaving through the cane maze, so many forked trails and switchbacks. But Ink was already walking away. There was nothing left to do but gather the tiles, shuffle the cards, and grouse on about the three priests that had stolen the last game.

The song of the Kalparcimex is unending noise, a billion voices crying out to be heard, from legs bowed like fiddles, wings that trembled against the air like reeds, demands, warnings, and lures bellowed from a billion mouths. Wherever there is room in the air for a note to hang, something screams into it, demanding a place in the mad orchestra.

The sound alone could shatter a man. The din wears at the spirit with the timeless persistence of water, working its way into every tiny crack in the mind and freezing sound into that place. The drone of antmaster beetles, the incessant babble of lieflies, the unforgettable ringing cry of a hroradrora, they stick in craws and refuse to shake free, a hundred little tunes snagged in the mind like burrs until there's no room left for anything but madness.

Back in Ten, there were more than a few used-up collectors mucking stalls or toting bales. Deep in their cups, the men would whisper to each other of the time the jungle had finally spoken to them. Each swore that the voice made of a billion singing insects had tried to teach them a great mystery, and they compared notes and argued bitterly as to what it all might mean. Their only consensus: whatever the secret was, it was too much for a man to bear. They were the lucky ones, who could still work after the jungle broke them. Most fell into the spiraling dark of Nod's Hole and its economy of slow, withering debasement. For those who could not bear that, there was always the rope.

A man who could take the endless drone, who could manage to work within the Kalpa for a year without losing his wits or his life could call himself a ranger, and no one in a bar would call him out on it, though they might raise an eyebrow. Some who'd made it two, or even three, might get called that by the younger gatherers, but only if Xan wasn't around. There were rangers and there was The Ranger. Perhaps there might have been another rank for other rangers like Xan who'd been roaming the Kalparcimex for five years or more, but there were none. They retired or the jungle got them.

Every one of them came to Xanadros at some point, making their case to become his apprentice and learn his secrets. Some brought tributes of rare insects, some tried to prove their skill or knowledge, and all were refused. Once every few years, some fool would get the idea to just attack him, thinking they could win his respect by besting him or just cracking from frustration. The Ranger made their ends gruesome enough that it would be another few years before another fool dared to try his luck.

Whispers said it was Xan himself preying on the other gatherers. Some thought it was pride, that he could not suffer another to approach his lofty perch of mastery. Others thought he had betrayed his own kind, striking a pact with the masters of the inner Kalpa, that he culled all those who might grow strong enough to learn their secrets. A few drunks even claimed he was a vampire, that he would live forever so long as he fed on the heart's blood of his rivals. You could say any crazy thing about Xan and it would stick. If people didn't see him walking the streets to sell his quarry and drink at The Red Queen Rises, they would probably believe he was ten feet tall.

The ones who could hack it were in the jungle now, insect masters and gatherers moving about the outer Kalpa. Veterans who did not have to stuff up their ears with bits of wax like the four adventurers from the east. Hunters who could tilt their heads at the din and feel that something was missing, that something was wrong. They padded along their careful paths, wary of crossing into another's territory, trying to ferret out the disturbance. As they tracked, they came across fallen beasts that were just blackened husks, and their shoulders quavered with the lingering feeling of sorcery. They craned their heads at the off-key din, and wondered at tracks that made no sense.

Something strange moved through the jungle, a foreign body that had everything up in arms. Insects that should be docile reared up in aggressive displays of beating wings and bared fangs. Great beasts roamed where they should not be, and where their paths crossed, there were wide swaths of jungle broken by their battles. Tree trunks were snapped and undergrowth was flattened and uprooted, and sometimes the corpse of a huge insect lay among the ruin, beset by scavengers.

One by one, the rangers made up their minds to leave, and quarries were abandoned, spawnings that had been carefully charted and awaited were sacrificed, whole runs of traps went unchecked, curiosity was squelched. A whole pack of men sifted from the edges of the outer Kalpa and gathered on the cliffs, building a great bonfire to call Ahel and Yamel. It was a strange meeting of solitary men from many parts of the lake. They spoke many different tongues and trusted each other little. Yet here they all were, glad for the company, glad to know that it wasn't just the onset of jungle madness. All felt the coming storm.

Beneath the beetle's shell, the four from the east sat, still playing roke, deaf to the change in the air. Sandros had carved wards into stones and placed them all around the perimeter of their camp, collecting his little glass spheres whose magic had dwindled. Everything outside the wards seemed leagues away, and they had only to contend with the noise of the insects within their camp. The effect on their morale had been enormous. They were sick of shouting at each other, sick of plugging up their ears with wax.

Osolin tried the same spoiler priests strategy in the next game, but this time, Sandros had played more conservatively and blocked her, hedging his mages with a priest that was always timely in the draw, building a nice little lead for himself. When the tolling came, it was Gregary who stole it away from them. He'd built his footmen into a phalanx led by a hero and swept three tiles with them in a single turn without rolling a single loss, and in the final hoard, he drew the scepter and a portal. Not even the demigod could halt such a lead, and once more, Brakkar was left with a hand that could buy the throne a turn too late.

After such a hand, no one was anxious to play again. The three losers were disgusted, the best sign of a good game. Gregary won so rarely that he wanted time to bask in the victory. They sat beneath the great shell, fighting the oldest and most persistent of their enemies, boredom. There was a great wind in the canopy, and it roared down through the legs of the dead beetle from time to time. They put the game away in its leather case before the cards could blow away.

"Play us a song, Sandros," Osolin said. The way she said it was just slightly more than a request, and slightly less than a direct order, so that he hesitated. He did not want Gregary and Brakkar to see him as doing her bidding, but neither did he wish to seem contrary to the wishes of his companions. Instead, he gave her a sidelong glance with his eyebrows raised, but then he shrugged and slipped the flute from his pack. In truth, he would take any excuse to play, and didn't mind being told what to do by a woman either. But appearances must be kept up.

"Your hand... it's still black," Osolin said. Sandros had taken off his gloves to play, and the mark of Ink's hand was still on his, it had not faded in the slightest. He said nothing. What was there to say?

"What if it stays that way forever?"

Again, he shrugged. What could he do? The mark, the fact that it was still on him despite all his efforts to remove it, just showed that Ink was more powerful than him. He did not want to think about it, and instead he rolled the flute between his hands.

It was a good flute, carved of the tough, resonant wood of the redbay tree, varnished so that the reddish-black whorls of the grain would glint in candlelight. Good but not great. His great flutes were back home in Joymont. A longflute carved from a mammoth's tusk, a medium one of polished Yarlee silver that gave notes so sweet they hurt, and even a short flute of black yohl that was cut to the Amechee scale which he seldom played, for it always filled those who heard it with a strange dread they could not put words to. Only blood could buy yohl.

Sandros had the long, deft fingers and natural ear of a born player. If King Joymont had not sent him off to the Ruby Citadel he would surely have become a great musician. Or so he'd always thought. How bitterly he had resented the old man when he learned he would be sent off to apprentice to the Scourer. How he'd hated the ancient one when the archmage caught him sneaking off to the rooftop to play and snapped in twain the wooden flute he'd spent hours secretly carving.

The years lost, gray and tiresome, without so much as a note to keep him company. Even whistling could earn you a whipping in the tower of the Scourer. The mumbling old madman couldn't hear a word unless you shouted it at him, but he could hear a twelve-year-old boy humming beneath his breath from three floors up and across a courtyard. Just the memory made his shoulders ache.

But that was all done now. When he'd returned from his studies, Joymont had given him a fat purse for whoring and carousing and he'd spent the whole bundle on the silver Yarlee flute his fingers ached for even now. He'd spent a week away, and his uncle feared that he'd gone on such a bender that he'd died in a ditch somewhere. The whole time, he'd sat on a rock in the Flinderwood dipping his toes in a secluded pond like a naiad and trying to coax the nimbleness back into his fingers. Trying to make up for the years of lost practice. Those were his happiest days, and when he returned home, he'd made a show of looking ashamed and staring at his boots, smiling to himself the whole time.

Beneath the shell of the great beetle, he brought the redbay campaigning flute to his lips and blew the secret song of the boy who'd spent his graduation purse to hide in the woods fluting. The clearing rang with his tune, and his three companions were silent for a time listening to him. They shut their eyes and chased after the hidden thing behind Sandros' notes that seemed always to dance ahead of them.

His heart stirred with pride when he saw them so entranced, for who among the other three had this secret within them? Not his brother Gregary, who was just what he appeared. Gregary was given the same purse when he came back from the academy knighted. He had spent his purse whoring and drinking as he ought, and came back bow-legged and green-faced after four days, pleading for a healer.

Nor was there art in the Bloodpriest, who kindled only with zeal for his war god. There was more beauty in a pigsty than in his soul. Perhaps in the thief... but even now she spoke and broke the spell, and he sank from the lofty heights he'd reached. The song became just a song, the player became just a scribe.

"What do we do if we can't find this bug?" She was forever bringing up the exact question the rest of them were trying to ignore.

Sandros lifted the flute from his lips and looked sadly into the distance, as if he could see the notes fleeing.

"We try and beg that ranger one more time to deal with the tinks for us, and if he refuses, we'll go back and I'll burn them out. Assuming the black mage isn't really planning to kill us the way he claims."

"She's not planning to kill us. Why would she have saved my life? Why give us charms to protect us? And why in the Void did we come out to this miserable place if you can just burn them out?"

"Because I can start the fire, but I can't stop it." That shut her up. She had seen Sandros' handiwork.

90

"I'd have to burn out the fields, and chase them into the Smilewood and the Flinderwood. All those pigpines, the whole forest, would go up like tinder. It would blacken the realm. Then we'd lose not just the fields but the timber too. The whole of the west would be ashes. But we can't just leave the things be, let them kill themselves off, because then the peasants will revolt." He had given it much thought.

"I don't understand you northerners, always up in arms over something. Why would they rise against you? You didn't bring the fucking things to them."

"If they see us doing nothing while they starve, they will rise. With the army out east fighting the Wyrth and the ones we've lost trying to wipe out the tinks, they can take Joymont. The stores there aren't enough to feed one in ten, but they don't know that. Peasants always assume their lords feast every night, astride a pile of gold," Gregary said, nodding at his brother. Their royal uncle was well aware that his people did not love him, and the two had been brought up to understand they could live in their castle and wear their fine clothes only so long as the little people could be kept in check.

"I should have taken my chances on the road," Osolin said. "I still think we should have gone to Tck'Hurr."

The air began to fill with butterflies, tiny blue ones with wings that shone like oiled velvet. Their numbers increased, and finally, a great swarm of them roiled past, the center mass of their mating frenzy so thick the adventurers could not see through it. Ink's charms kept the storm of butterflies at bay, but the adventurers could still smell the weird flowery scent blown onto them by countless little wings. The light caught the fluttering insects and it was mesmerizing, like a fog of liquid sapphire swirling through the air. They were gone as quickly as they'd come, and the air seemed too still without them.

Sandros had put his flute away, and he laid out the tiles on the flat rock. For a long time everyone ignored them, still holding onto the image of a million blue butterflies. Finally, it began to rain, and Gregary looked out at the water pissing down around them and picked up his hand, shaking his head. The others had to follow suit. Roke wasn't worth a damn with two.

Inhale. Draw in the curious spice of the jungle, the musk of flowers and decay; the raindrops subliming on every surface; the searing, alien scent of the quarry. Exhale. Cut loose the ever-nagging fear, the black glimpse of death, the pain ringing out from every joint. Again. Become one. Become one. Become one.

When Xan let the arrow fly, he was fully alive. The veil was lifted, and every one of his senses roared on unfiltered, disregarding nothing, taking in everything. There was no way to pretend this was anything but what it was.

The quarry was old, he knew the sound of a bow, he knew what it meant, and the arrow was still in flight when he lifted his head to return fire, a gout of acid. But Xan, in the fullness of the moment, had dropped from the tree, feeling that his prey would do just that. His perch was annihilated, the leaves withered in an instant, the sturdy limb that had held his weight devoured by the caustic spit, and all the trees around it swayed, distributing its weight through the network of vines. Flighted insects startled by the disturbance shot off in every direction.

Xan didn't run. Either he'd made the shot or he would die. The old one was faster than him, and a better shot, he would not miss again. Still, it didn't pay to take chances, and he crept behind a tree and stuck his quiver out. When no volley of acid annihilated it, he crept forward to his target.

The bashyskyla lay still, Xan's arrow had taken it right in the chink. Behind the great horned head, with its triangle of three compound ruby eyes, was a single vulnerable spot which was revealed only when the beast's head was lowered. "Vulnerable" was not quite the word either, for a normal arrow would do nothing but enrage the beast and cost the lives of everything within half a league. Xan hadn't used a normal arrow.

The ranger had a whole quiver of tink spines bound to fletched shafts. The tink larvae were born to punch through armor, stronger than steel and far deadlier. There was some irony here, as the bashyskyla was a great eater of tinks; a single adult male a quarter the size of this ancient one could eat twenty tinks at a time, sniping them with its spit and devouring the remains. Yet their spines were the only way Xan knew to bring a venerable bashyskyla down.

Even now, the tink larva was digging into the great beast—the instant it tasted blood it had unfolded its razor sharp legs and gone into a frenzy. Tinks flung their spine-larvae from their tails. When one struck a host, it would burrow inside, kill it, and gestate in its corpse. The bigger the corpse, the bigger the tink, generally, and this bashyskyla was huge. Yet there would be no happy ending for Xan's arrow. Even now, the bashyskyla's acid blood was killing it.

Xan would not profit from this either. A fortune in acid would go to waste with no one to harvest it, and he didn't have the equipment to hack through its carapace to get at the glands alchemists would sell their souls to for. A bashyskyla this big... there was no telling how old it was. A hundred years, a thousand, ten thousand. Men did not keep records of such things, and the beasts simply did not die after the juvenile stage. At the edge of the jungle, nothing could kill them. A great waste.

"I am sorry, old man," Xan said, and at his words, the great horned head lifted and Xan's heart nearly burst. The three ruby red eyes beheld him and Xan knew he was doomed, somehow it hadn't died. In an instant, he would melt in a barrage of the most caustic acid on the Arc.

But the ruby eyes darkened to black, and Xan leapt to the side an instant ahead of the acid. At once, he heard the hiss of withering vegetation. The bashyskyla had missed! Lying against the ground, he felt the thump as the thing's head slumped to the ground, and he patted his body, sure that he would find a great poisoned hole eaten into his armor. Yet he was whole. The old one had missed! It was impossible, at that range, even half-dead there was no way...

"Oh."

The shadow stood at the other side of the clearing, her hand still pointed at the great beast.

"So. This is why we couldn't find any bashyskyla."

Xan nodded. "The others I sent into the inner, but this one was too old to listen to reason. I gather from the others he's been something of a tyrant. Still, a shame."

"You would slay the beast rather than let us have him?"

"Have him? He would have had you, you would all have died trying to take him. And if you hadn't, the bashyskyla would have done for you down the road when he broke whatever spell you planned to leash him with. If you made it out to Joymont, it would be even worse. Once the tinks were gone, the bashyskyla would devour the whole realm. If those rubes can't stop a few tinks, what can they do to a great bashyskyla?"

"You worry like an old woman, Xan. It would be fine."

"In a generation, all that would be left of Joymont would be savages bringing the bashyskyla offerings and worshipping him like a god. And then the land... It is one of life's great mercies that bashyskyla do not often venture from the Kalpa. To lure one out is an incredible sin. Even for you."

When she did not deny it, when she stared deeply at him from behind the black veil, he felt certain that this was her plan. Just like the bashyskyla, it was a great mercy that Ink seldom left the suffocating dark of Nod's Hole. Now these idiot adventurers had roused her, and a price would be paid.

"I've won. There are no more of them out here, and you aren't going into the inner. Just kill your four fools, or sell them to a demon, or whatever you planned, and leave the Kalparcimex be. You've upset the order enough."

"I've upset it? I'm not the one killing ancients and driving monsters into places where they have no business." Beneath the mask, he was thinking, "They aren't monsters!" She was sure of it. But he did not retort. Slaying the great bashyskyla weighed heavily on the man. How he loved his poison forest.

"I'm here to help these brave adventurers. Doing a good deed. You should try it sometime."

Xan scoffed at her. "You could simply go there and wipe out the tinks yourself, if you cared so much for these villagers you've never met. You don't need to bring a bashyskyla down upon them. What are you really here for?"

"I was bored. The fools begged me, so why not? It isn't as if you couldn't do the same, ride in like a hero, slay the evil scourge. It wouldn't even take you a month. You'd probably turn a profit, even if that fat fake king gypped you."

Xan did not reply.

"You owe me your life, Xanadros," Ink said at last.

"And me yours, Insolade," Xan returned, dusting the earth from his leathers.

For a moment, the two masks stared at each other. Behind the black mage's veil, her jaw hung open in surprise.

"How... how did you learn my name?" Ink asked, and her voice was tiny, the voice of a girl, not a sorceress. The breathing slits on his mask creased with the ranger's silent smile. He turned away in a shimmer of his opalescent cloak, slinking off toward the jungle.

"ANSWER ME!" she shouted after him, shaking a gloved fist. "DON'T YOU WALK AWAY FROM ME!"

Her voice rang across the clearing, and he slid behind a tree and was gone before she could compose herself enough to destroy him. She was not the only one who knew how to vanish.

Insolade kicked a clod of dirt at the dead bashyskyla, her breath coming in little angry sobs.

Sandros had just fallen into Osolin's trap when a quilg fell into his.

Osolin's trap was a rogue she'd put beneath a tile. Sandros had thought it a bluff and tried to move his party through, and once more, he was about to lose his archmage.

Sandros' trap was a flat stone as big as a dinner plate. He had scratched three ring-within-ring groupings of runic script onto its surface with a steel point and imbued it with power. The quilg's tentacles flitted over the flat rock, tasting the air, mulling over the human scent, and at last it decided it did not mean danger. Little in the outer Kalparcimex threatened a quilg. It was three yards long, and its glistening skin was covered in spikes as long as a parrying dagger, encircled with bands of brilliant yellow, pink, and orange coloration meant to convey that it was quite poisonous.

The quilg inched forward on two sets of four legs. It passed over Sandros' trapstone and crawled toward the beetle's shell, wondering if perhaps the four card players were something good to eat. With a hiss, the runes burnt away and the trapstone grew white hot, and then with a tremendous crack it exploded, blasting shards of molten rock into the quilg's underbelly.

It had nothing to protect it from the burning rock, and the trap burnt it nearly in half. The quilg gave an awful raspberry death cry, a high-pitched scream with its mouthful of slimy tendrils all convulsing against each other.

Perhaps at some point in history, another man had made the awful mistake of burning a quilg, but if so, his hard-earned wisdom had not survived to instruct the four adventurers. When acrid yellow fumes began to rise from the still-writhing bulk of the beast, the four did not run in the opposite direction as they should have. Sandros even began to move toward the quilg, thinking to finish it off with another spell.

Three steps toward the beast, he stopped mid-stride as his eyes began to water. When the smell hit him, his gut seized, threatening to give up all it contained and more. As he turned to run, the others saw the panic in his tear-streaked face and began grabbing their bags. Sandros bent to the side and vomit shot from his mouth in a torrent. He raised a desperate hand, waving his palm at them.

"The traps!" he managed to get out between heaves. There were more of the exploding stones all around the clearing. If they tried to flee, they would share the quilg's fate. Sandros could not speak the words to disarm them, he was on his knees, and then his legs gave out and he lay cheek-down in the carpet of rotting vegetation, gagging again and again.

The other three could not escape. The stink rolled over them like a storm front and soon they were curled into the same fetal balls. None of them had ever encountered anything like this. The stench was like some putrid yellow-green fire smoldering beneath their faces, stoked with rotting meat and chicken shit, burning up everything that was good in the world. They lay on the earth, helpless as newborns, strength gone from their arms, eyes blind with tears, no sound but heaving and weeping misery.

Finally, it began to rain, and if they'd had anything left, they would have wept at the mercy of the sky. It began slowly, a fine mist filtering down onto them from the canopy, and then it built, from drizzle to hard rain to torrent, washing away the unforgivable sin of setting a quilg ablaze. Gregary was under the beetle's shell when the rain began, but he crawled, dragging his armored body through the mud and undergrowth, to get beneath the rain—anything to wash the god awful stink off him.

They all lay in the rain for a long time, and when it was through, they were soaked and shivering, and glad of it. They would have bathed in a rain of fire to get free of the dead quilg's revenge.

"We must. Out. Sandros," Gregary said, not trusting his mouth to form more than a few words. The rain had only blunted the smell. Somehow, the stink of the thing had gotten onto his tongue, and he spat again and again, trying to get it off. Sandros spoke a few twisted syllables and gestured to what he thought was west. It was directly away from the quilg and that was all that mattered. Sparks drifted up from his stones and died on the wind.

"It's safe now," the mage croaked, and then he grabbed his pack and began to trudge that way. The rest followed, more than willing to let him be the one to find out if the spell was truly broken. Each lifted their pack and squelched after him, but the roke set remained on the stone, and no one moved to pick it up.

"Gregary, your set," Osolin said when it was clear he meant to leave it.

"I never want to play another hand of roke as long as I live," Gregary said, hoisting his pack and walking shakily after his brother.

The knight took pains not to flaunt his wealth, but in these little gestures, she saw just another shant. He could throw his little fit and simply buy another set. Someone who'd had to carve their own tiles and paint wooden slats in place of cards wouldn't dream of abandoning theirs. There were plenty of men who'd dashed into burning houses to retrieve their homemade roke boxes. How many sets like that had she played on in Fang? For the thousandth time she was glad she hadn't slept with Gregary on that boozy night at the Seventh Scion tavern three days west of the Mathiscene stead. Instead, she'd chosen Sandros the Scribe, whose quill would not rise, no matter how she wielded it.

Frowning at the memory, Osolin went to pick up the set, but the stink of the quilg hung heavy in the air. It would be on the cards, and they couldn't be washed. She shook her head at her final hand, then hastened after the others. Fanned facedown on the flat rock were her three priests.

If not for the quilg's lingering curse, they would have smelled the hot springs long before they came upon them. The mists drifting through the trees reeked of brimstone, and beneath that there was a salty, mineral tang to the air. As they drew closer, they marked how moisture beaded everything and plants low to the ground became withered and yellowed. There were fewer insects on the wing here, and the air grew warmer with every step, driving away the chill of night.

The springs were a hundred yards across, overlapping pools of clear, clean water with raised rims, surrounding a giant crater. The endless flow of water had washed away the soil and laid bare the bones of the earth: pink banded stone, polished by millennia. At the water's edge, a whitish crust of minerals had built up.

"I dub thee Saltbeef Springs," Sandros chirped, and the others nodded. Once said, it was impossible not to see it. The scribe had a way with names.

"Would that they were. I tire of biscuits. If only there were something to hunt in this cursed jungle!" Brakkar's gut had been rumbling for some time. His eyes had taken to lingering danger-ously on the strange fruits dangling from the trees and the creepers as they passed.

"The something is us. Night is for the hunters, she said," Sandros was looking through the trees at the edge of the clearing, searching for threats.

"Bah! Let them come. I'm sick of games and waiting. I want something to fight!"

"You had your chance back in Ten with little Rorey Morey."

"The mutant caught me unawares. If I catch him again, things will be different."

"You go right ahead, I'll watch," Sandros jibed.

"Same as it was, right? Never even raised your hands and the little man finished you in one punch." Brakkar puffed out his cheeks and stuck out his tongue, both hands over his stomach in mockery.

"I'm a lover, not a fighter," Sandros said with a sheepish tilt of his head.

Osolin snorted and Sandros shot her a swift look of warning. She rolled her eyes and looked around the spring. Slipping off her boots and leaving them on a flat rock, she found the water was was almost too hot to bear, the stone worn as smooth as marble beneath her toes.

"Ahhhhhh…" she moaned with contentment. Her eyes turned skyward. How good the warm water felt on her battered feet! She shucked off her pack and stepped over a white mineral fringe between two paddies, hoping to find a pool deep enough to bathe in.

"Stars! Look at the size of that thing! I thought it was part of the spring," Osolin called, pointing.

The central spring was a huge pool, thirty yards across, water cascading down from a raised lip of what she'd thought was stone. But now that she was close, she could see the ring was made of husks, the cast-off shells of huge centipedes that encircled the entire pool. As she crept closer, she could see that the closest shell still had a centipede in it. Sandros had taken off his own boots to join her.

"They must come here to molt. Gods, it must be a hundred feet long," the scribe said with a wary eye on the dark form beneath the husks. "And look, the other rings, beneath the salt they're shells as well." He nudged a crust with his toe and beneath it were rings and rings of centipede husks.

Osolin did a circuit of the springs, keeping a wary distance from the sleeping centipede at the center, and then joined the three men back at the flat rock. All three had removed their boots to sit with their feet soaking in the hot water.

"I wonder if it would wake up if I climbed over it," Osolin mused, eyeing the big ring.

"Why on the Arc would you do that?"

"I want a bath. It's too shallow here."

The three men exchanged dumbfounded looks.

"I want the stink off me too, but no chance in hell I'm getting near that centipede. Look at the size of it! We can just wash up here where it's safe."

Shrugging, Osolin turned and started investigating as the three men began taking off their gear, setting everything on the dry ridge. Sandros watched her curiously, and at last she found a large rock that must have weighed fifty pounds or better.

"Have a care."

Osolin heaved the stone at the giant centipede's husk. It hit the shell with a loud crack and rolled off into the spring. For long moments, the three men held their breath, waiting for the beast to rise up and attack them. But nothing happened, the massive insect didn't stir.

"Ok. It's not going to wake up, or it's already dead. Bath time." Osolin had drawn her sword, and now she set it down on the flat ridge beside her pack.

"The jungle has driven her mad," Brakkar muttered.

"If you're afraid, you timid Khemerians can scrub each other there in the shallows. But I'm having a bath." They gaped at her until she began to strip off her clothes, and then Sandros and Gregary hurriedly turned away. Brakkar had no such shame, and he stared at her hungrily until she picked up her sword. She aimed its point at his crotch and then raised her chin at him, eyes blazing. With a leering grin, the big priest held up two palms and turned away, though she felt his eyes on her the second she turned to walk to the spring. She wheeled at him, sword at the ready.

"Go ahead and look, you swine," she hissed, and his eyes were wide now. He'd seen the wicked scars of the lash on her back. He did not grin anymore as he cast his eyes at his feet. Satisfied, she turned and waded to the big spring, steeling herself to climb upon the shell of the sleeping giant.

The three men watched her, not daring to breathe as she climbed onto the slick hull of the centipede. She stepped gingerly, ready for the beast to rise and try to buck her off, but it was still as stone, its features obscured beneath the thick husk. Standing on its back, she peered down at the monster. The thing's eyes were milky and still, its antennae had curled into two tight spirals. Its legs were a bright ruby red and its body a dark coppery color.

Satisfied the thing would not wake to attack her, Osolin looked down into the spring, remembering the horrid beast Ahel and Yamel had pulled from the docks. She saw only perfectly clear water. Within the spring, there were rippling veins of minerals, mostly white and pink, but a few bands of a deep cobalt blue. She'd shown no fear to the others, but here she felt a stirring in her stomach for a moment, staring down into the darkness. Anything could be down there.

At last, the stink of quilg was stronger than fear, and she dipped a foot in carefully, finding the water almost too hot to bear, but not quite. Slowly, she lowered herself in, leaving the sword wedged in the suture between two of the centipede's tergites.

Ahhhhhhhhh!

How long had it been since she'd bathed? Well before they made Ten, and much had transpired since then. The water rose past her thighs, up above her waist, and she had to inch in to get used to the heat. At last, she sank until she was sitting on the ledge, the water just below her chin. Sublime!

She sat there, feeling as though she'd melted, not caring if she did. The endless noise of the Kalparcimex seemed very far away now, the death that had loomed at arm's length for days distant and unimportant. She closed her eyes and drifted, unburdened as the air itself.

"Are you well?" a voice asked, and she heard Sandros up on the centipede, but she did not open her eyes.

"Never better." She pointed her toes and rolled her head.

"You've been in here for a while, just wanted to make sure you were OK."

"I'm never leaving." She was nearly serious. "Come in here and get clean, it's wonderful. Tell those idiots to get in too, I don't want to be smelling that awful caterpillar on them for the rest of the trip.

"Uh… ah… I brought you this."

She opened her eyes to see Sandros, clearly flustered, trying to hand her something and look away at the same time. In his hand, a thumb-sized purple-white sliver.

"Soap!" she cried out, and then looked at the centipede, half-afraid she'd woken it, but it did not stir.

"Where the hell did you get soap? And don't be stupid, look at me. It's nothing you haven't seen before."

"I uh… can't really remember. I was very drunk."

"There wasn't much to remember."

With that, he scuttled away, and she lathered up, unable to believe her luck. Of course the shants had soap. Wonders never ceased.

Three nude men crested the centipede and she noticed Brakkar was not so bold when the tables were turned. The priest quickly slipped into the water well away from her, wincing at the heat. Gregary selected a spot some five paces away on the other side and lowered himself in slowly. Sandros seemed to have gotten over his embarrassment and hopped in nearer to her. It was clear the heat bothered him not a whit.

For a long time, the four of them luxuriated in the scalding spring, the mists swirling around them, passing around the bar of soap, each doing their best to scrub the quilg's stink off themselves. Sandros even ducked beneath the surface and swam down into the center of the spring, looking about, then emerged at the center, drawing a great breath of air.

"Don't do that," he said, warning in his tone. "It's a lot hotter out at the center. I think it would cook a regular person."

"How much heat could you bear? How do you do that?"

"More than this spring can offer. Part of my art. No mortal flame can harm me."

"He's crap against boars, though," Gregary grinned.

"Oh stars, not that story," Sandros groaned, exasperated.

"You see, this one time…"

"Here, I'll save you the trouble. We were hunting a man who'd killed a local shepherd's herd and his young son with poison. Poor man, youngest of the Kalahees, a good family on the north slope. We heard a noise in a bush. Thinking it was the poisoner, I went after it. No, it was a boar, and I shat my pants and we had to scramble up a tree and stay there all morning while the biggest boar you've ever seen circled below us and kept trying to knock the tree over. Hilarious."

"What happened to the poisoner?" asked Osolin.

"The boar wandered away at last, and we caught the killer's trail, found him rolling about on the ground in a glade, naked as a jay. He was a madman, a traveling knife sharpener from Khemeria named Rez Whanch. He didn't fight, surrendered at once, though without a thread of shame for what he'd done. The madman claimed the stars had black faces, just like the moon, and the other side of the stars told him to do it. We'd thought he meant to kill the herd and not the boy, but it was the other way around, he was convinced the boy was destined to usher in the end of times. A zealot..." Sandros tilted his head in Brakkar's direction, and the big priest scowled but had no retort.

"So he poisoned the pool the boy watered his herd at every morning. Seven years old, the Kalahee boy, wanted to usher nothing more than his sheep into the pen each night. We brought the madman to the Kalahees and they flensed him and then boiled him alive in a cauldron of lye. They hung him from a rope and lowered him in, an inch at a time. That's that story."

"It's less funny when you tell it," Gregary complained, wincing inside at the memory of that awful cauldron. The stench... until he'd smelled burning quilg, it had been the worst stink he'd ever encountered in his life.

"Well I tire of having you forever telling people I shit myself and not explaining the rest. Can we have a different tale, for the love of the right side of the stars."

"The black faces of the stars the poisoner spoke of... it is a common heresy among the Void Cult. How they love to profane all that is dear with their lies. They're worse than the Wyrth," Brakkar rumbled.

"No," Osolin said bitterly, thinking of the Set'Assul. "No one

104

is worse than the Wyrth."

The other three men looked on expectantly, but Osolin was silent, peering into the bubbling water.

"You know our stories…" Gregary trailed.

"You don't have to tell the tale," Sandros shot in. "If you don't want to."

She let out a deep breath and shook her head. She wasn't ready, but it was like as not she wouldn't see the end of the day in this wretched jungle. If she didn't tell the story now, it might die with her.

"Alright. You, scribe, remember this well. Write it down if I fall."

Sandros nodded and she began her tale.

16

What know you three of the lake? What do you know of crime, of desperation, of poverty?

Nothing.

I was born in Infractus. Vile Infractus, where Mere the Black brought the river, then stole it right back. A place of dust and thirst, where only fools go and the hopeless remain. My mother was a tavern whore and a thief, as her mother was a thief, as everyone in that wretched place was a thief. There wasn't enough for anyone, you had to steal or starve. My first memory was a half-eaten apple, a caravan guard set it down at the edge of the table so he could use both hands to argue. I swooped on it like a gull and ran. Before he made the door I was around the corner, and before he made the corner I was on the roof. I watched the man stalk around with his knife, furious, shouting at people on the street. I was certain he would find me and kill me. But another man took umbrage to him waving his knife about and they got into it. The one I stole from died in the street, over half an apple. I can still remember the way it tasted, like it was exploding in my mouth. I even ate the stem. I might have been three or four.

My mother never even scolded me. The knifeman's death was just a thing that happened, the way things were. She had her hands full with the others. I had two brothers, two sisters, and another on the way by that point. The woman laid like a hen, regular as clockwork. She raised us like a crop, gave us no more than what we needed to stay alive, skinny and bound in sackcloth, black as Amechee from the dirt.

She beat us and she was cold to us, but we never starved. We never had to drink yellowwater or sell ourselves for a drink like some children did. She sold me, of course, the moment I had value to anyone. I never expected different from her.

I hated her since I was old enough to speak, for the beatings, for the hunger and the squalor, but as I grew older I came to understand. We were in hell, and she was doing what she could. There was no angle she didn't play, no swindle she didn't try, no one with coin she refused. She must be dead by now, the stars only know how many of her children made it, or how far flung across the lake they are.

The ones who bought me were from Fang, a caravan of oily Ibexians, their beards braided into single knots, capped with lacquered insignias, and their hair slicked with perfume. They marched me across the Curse tethered to a camel, and I had to walk or be dragged, but at least they fed me. Ten years old and I marched across the whole of the Curse, stepping around camel shit all the way. The caravan brought me to Fang and sold me to the Scorpions of Aran, for the brothels thought me too coarse and gangly to make their money back from me.

The Scorpions are a thieves guild, you have nothing like them in the north. Perhaps it's the heat, or the bad water, perhaps it's just the way people are, but in Ibexia, there are no thin prefects. They're all bent, they take money from merchants for protection from thieves then they turn around and take money from thieves for protection from themselves. Then they go sailing in the Lie and idle the day away fishing. The king's men are even worse, their hands are always out, their eyes always hungry.

In this jungle, you can see how a rotten tree can hold an endless host of pests. A rotten city is the same. Fang is a place where every crime has its niche. Whole gangs of thieves exist, banding together for protection, to buy a measure of indifference for their whole group. In some neighborhoods they are more powerful than the crown, and the prefects pay them for protection. Some of them have been around since the fall of the Dog Star. Mere himself is said to have founded the Scorpions and they fought hand in hand to bring down the God King.

Those were good times for me. I was born to take, and the Scorpions were happy with what they'd bought. Orphans from Infractus are highly prized, for we've already learned all the hardest lessons. All the ones who've been caught are already dead.

I learned all the cons. I was a burglar, a cutpurse, a con-artist, a wall-walker, and a smuggler. In the north, all these words are insults, but in Ibexia it is different. It's accepted there—a successful thief is even admired for bravery and cunning. Up here, you just cut off their hands and throw them in a cell, and if they live, they can do nothing but beg. Idiocy.

I had much success and learned a great deal. As I came of age, I saw the other girls who had come up with me one by one drift into working the soft trade. How much easier it is to lie on your back than to climb across a rickety tile roof and pry a window open in the dead of the night! They became dancers in smoke-houses, prostitutes, concubines, a few even fucked their way into wealth, becoming second or third wives for merchants.

But the trade was not for me. I was never beautiful, no one ever called me pretty. The best I ever got was "solid." Ha! Well I'd rather be solid than some empty-headed whore. I'd rather be solid than have my looks fade and wind up in the street without a trade, selling myself to rum-bums for coppers. So I kept on stealing. I was as good a thief as any in the Scorpions. Soon I had a place in all the big plays, ship capers where we'd creep alongside in the dead of night in blacked canoes, vault jobs where we'd tunnel under the homes of moneychangers, kidnappings, little wars with the other guilds. If I'd wanted to, I could have stayed in that life.

But I saw too that there were few old thieves. The smart ones got out and had the younglings take the risk and lived off them. I had a close scrape, another guild tipped off the temple we meant to rob and we walked into an ambush. I got this scar there, and this one. I had another when I was nearly killed by a poisoned spike concealed in a drawer, it was a hair's width from piercing my glove and ending me. I wasn't afraid, mind you, but I was aware. Sooner or later I would run out of luck.

I had always been fascinated by the docks. I drank in bars with sailors and listened to their far-flung tales and lies. There were smugglers who'd flown from salt pirates, Terhaljatani slavers, Khazan press gangs, and Khemerian taxmen, sneaking through their secret ways on the broken coast. There were gray-eyed men who told of the deep lake, and none of their stories agreed. There were men of all shapes, all hues, from every corner of the lake, and they all had a story.

They told stories of standing at the great gates of Grimbalgon, of peering into the pit of Yarlsbeth, of praying at the cathedral of the One True Star. They claimed they'd fought sea serpents and dragons, battled with witches and shape-shifters. I spent a small fortune buying drinks for sotted old crows, dreaming of far-away lands.

When at last I decided to go, my guildmates barely tried to get me to stay, they could all see I'd caught the wanderlust. I was sixteen years old when I convinced a trader to take me on, and I learned as much in six months on that ship as I had in six years before it. I learned how to fight. When the pirates came it didn't matter if you were a deck hand or the captain, you fought. I learned how to rig and sail, learned how to row and fish. I got strong. And I learned that men are dogs, and it doesn't matter if you're merely solid, at sea or in their cups, they'll do anything for a bit of gash.

Anywhere a ship can take you, I've gone there. I went from ship to ship, from company to company. Sometimes I fought pirates, sometimes I was the pirate. I looted, I plundered, I fought, I fucked, I was alive. I never thought I could lose.

So you can guess, when I lost, I lost big. It was meant to be a swift run up the coast from Khemeria, delivering a prisoner to the Yarlee. Just a little boat, for no one was supposed to know about it, we didn't even know who the prisoner was. But the Wyrth did. I was the one who sighted their longboat behind us, three hundred oars bearing down on us, and we were but twelve and the prisoner.

Our so-called captain was for surrendering right away but he was a fool, the Wyrth never show mercy. I cried out that we should run for the shoals and flee where the longboat could not follow. All of us had our hearts in our mouths as we slid over the first reef. There was a terrible grinding but we made it over the reef and into a long channel where the longboat couldn't hope to catch us before nightfall.

We couldn't believe our luck, and shouldn't have. There was a tremendous lurch that sent us all flying to the deck, and then laughter. One of the rowers had dropped the anchor, the chain caught on a reef and tore the back out of our little sloop. He freed the prisoner in the confusion and the two of them leapt free and started swimming back for the longboat, cackling like fiends at their betrayal. Our ship went down swiftly, and I and the other men had no choice but to start swimming up the channel, hoping to find a way up the cliffs before the sharks got to us.

Then a sail appeared upstream, and we saw we'd never had a hope at all. A Wyrth pinnace, her rail lined with crossbowmen, she sailed swiftly past us and collected the prisoner and the traitor on the shoals. The boat turned back around and came for us, and we knew we were doomed. The prisoner took a crossbow and the ship circled around and around us as he shot the crew of my ship, one by one, until only I was left. When my turn came, I didn't scream or plead as the others had. I understood there would be no mercy for me and I wanted to die as strong and free as I had lived. But he never shot me, instead they lassoed me and dragged me aboard, just moments before the sharks would have had me.

Soon I found why they'd saved me. It was nothing I hadn't faced before, remember I was a child of Infractus, after all. I knew how to survive. It turned out the Khemerians hadn't a clue who they'd captured, he was no mere pirate but Rhez'ranokh, a war prince of Urth'Wyrth, commander of an entire legion. They'd sent just ten men, one woman, and a traitor to guard him, the fools.

I had to… prove my value to them as a slave. I had to learn Wyrth from sailors, the foul language even fouler on their cracked and leering lips. I was brought to Urth'Wyrth and sold at auction, had to hear the jeers of the crowd as I was paraded naked in chains before a stadium full of the filthy Wyrth. Thank the stars the one who bought me was an old fool!

Not six weeks later, I was more his master than he was mine, and I escaped, stowing away in the hold of a Tck'Hurr galleon. But they found me out too soon, just a day's sail from Urth'Wyrth, and it was worth their time to turn around and claim the bounty. Many of the scars you see on my back came from that. My old master accepted me back, thinking me cowed by the lashes. He didn't even give me a second notch. His foolish leniency would save me later.

A year I spent biding my time until I found the next opening when a friend of the master came to visit. He was a caravan leader who thought to steal me away on a trip north, and pimp me to the hunters of the Malskernoor. I escaped from his caravan that very night, and I would have been free if the fool hadn't gone back to Wyrth and told the legion everything. They sent out their hunters and their dogs. For three days I eluded them, but in the end I could not hope to get free. I hate dogs.

The idiot caravan master expected me to go back with him, but I revealed his own crime to the hunters and they clapped him in chains right along with me. The would-be pimp became a slave himself. The old man was heartbroken at the double betrayal of his slave and his friend, and the second notch came, along with more scars. The sad old man sold me for next to nothing to the worst master he could find, Garakatoc, a man of notorious cruelty.

With the sailors, with the old man, I could merely play the role of slave, hiding away my true self. But Garakatoc could see through the sham. All of his slaves had two notches, he got them cheap and then he broke them as no one had ever broken them. He set on me as I have never been set on, he starved me, he kept me awake for days, he hung me upside down and beat every inch of me. I swear he was no man at all, but a demon, feeding off pain and misery like a swollen tick. You cannot imagine the depths of his depravity.

Vilest of the vile, Garakatoc, and I broke like all the others. The strength I'd thought I had? A sham, for it was my own foolishness that had landed me in the claws of Garakatoc. I had never been free, I was born a slave in Infractus, I would die a slave in Urth'Wyrth whenever Garakatoc willed. There was no escape. A year of this misery might have been a century, and every day I thought of ending it all, of climbing the volcano to cast myself in.

That's the only charity in Wyrth, you know. Anyone, be they servant or slave, can give themselves to Urth'Wyrth and no one can stop them once they set foot on the black path. But by then I hadn't even the courage to leave the house, though the door was unlocked and unguarded.

I was lost. I became another of Garakatoc's shades. My eyes seldom left the floor, I drifted though his keep cringing from the sound of his voice. The only thing separating me from the others was I never desired to please him the way they did, like dogs licking at his toes. I only feigned that, and if Garakatoc could tell, he cared not, knowing that I was broken enough. I told myself that on the day I found myself like the others, wanting to please Garakatoc, that was the day I would give myself to the volcano.

I thought I'd lost everything, that the terror and torture had taken it all. But then he bought a new slave, a girl no older than I'd been when my mother sold me, yet still somehow she had two notches like the rest of us. She even looked like me, though she was from Fang, not Infractus. Her father had put her up as a stake in a game of dice and lost her. Garakatoc thought to use me as a tool to break her, he showed me to her and told her that this is what she would become. Another cringing dog. When I saw the horror in her eyes, something in me awoke for the first time in a year.

Anger.

I was thin and weak, and Garakatoc had been a legionnaire, he was double my size. Yet still I flew at him. He laughed and batted me away like a gnat, tossed me into a desk. When the desk broke beneath me, I knew I would die for what I'd done. In the shambles, I saw a little knife, the blade no longer than my middle finger. I grabbed the knife and faced him, and again Garakatoc laughed. I moved toward him holding the point far from my body as if I'd never fought with a knife before, and he moved at me eagerly, thinking to disarm me. Garakatoc didn't know my story, we were all just shit to him. He had no clue I knew how to fight.

I was ready for his move. I caught him off balance and I was upon him, stabbing and stabbing and stabbing. He got his hands around my throat, but all his strength was not enough to stop me. I can still remember the look in his eyes before I cut them out.

I escaped Urth'Wyrth that very hour, stopping only to wash that devil's blood off and to grab a few supplies. I offered to take the girl with me but she refused, for there is no doom so terrible as a slave who kills their master in Urth'Wyrth. I told her the legionnaires would kill her anyway but she was too afraid, so I left her and the others to their fate. I wish I could believe that they saw the light and fled, but they were all shades. Surely they all paid the price for my act. If I were stronger I should have given them a kind death then and there, but instead I ran.

I spent sixth months hiding and stealing, trying to remember what it was like to be human, struggling to survive in the wilderness. There was nowhere for me to go, no one I could trust. When they caught me in Millmauth, I was nearly feral. I fought like a cornered rat. You know the tale of what happened next. The time in the dungeon was actually good for me, if you can believe it. I had time to stop and think, to come to terms with what I'd suffered, with what I'd become.

"That is my life," Osolin finished, looking at the faces of the three men. They were all deeply shaken by the tale.

"If you ever do assemble your army to attack the Wyrth, come and find me. I'll be the first through the breach," she swore, clenching her hand into a fist.

Brakkar looked like he wanted to speak, but he could not find the words.

For a while they sat there, steaming in silence, and then there was a tremendous creak as the great centipede shifted in its shell. The four scrambled over the edge and ran away naked as fast as they could.

"Where are you going?"

Sandros actually leapt a foot into the air. Ink stepped out from behind a tree as the other three raised their weapons—mace, shortsword, and longsword. They had walked a long way from the Saltbeef Springs.

"Some welcome." Ink snuffled at the air and took a few steps back from them.

"Those talking flies have been after us all morning, they keep diving at us. Thought you were one of them."

"Lieflies. They just want you to talk so they can steal your words and use them in their mating songs. They don't actually understand."

"One kept swooping down and screaming that we were all doomed. Another kept crying out 'BLOOD! BLOOD! BLOOD!'" Sandros grimaced.

"Rangers. How they love to jest. You can get a liefly to repeat anything," Ink said. She sounded annoyed. "Where are you four going? You were supposed to wait for me."

"We tried. Some awful caterpillar got caught in one of our traps and burned. We had to get away, and we've been wandering since. We found a spring to wash up in, but the memory remains."

"Oh my... swallow the stars... I wondered what the hell that smell could be. You burned a quilg. I can't even imagine. It's been a rough go for you four, hasn't it? I wish I brought better news."

They looked at her and steeled themselves, unsure how much more they could take. Things kept going from bad to worse.

"Xan has driven all the bashyskyla but one into the inner Kalpa. The one that remained he killed so that we could not take it from the jungle."

"All of them?" Gregary could not look more miserable.

"All. I have looked everywhere, they are gone. The one he killed was a monster. Double the size of the biggest I'd ever heard of. He really hates you."

Gregary drove his sword into the earth and stood with both fists balled.

"That miserable faceless cunt opposes us at every turn. We've done nothing to him, we went to him for aid and he pissed on us, pissed on our quest. All for what, because our uncle didn't uproot his whole fucking kingdom to suit some bugshit crazy ranger? Gods, what I wouldn't give for a piece of him! I'd tear him in half!" Gregary was shouting now, and from up in the canopy, his words came buzzing back at them, humming and disjointed. Each fly had picked a different part of his diatribe to mimic.

Faceless cunt! Faceless cunt! Bugshit crazy! Fucking kingdom! Faceless cunt!

The fly that picked up *faceless cunt* flew down and zipped around them singing it, rolling through the air in delight. In a moment, Osolin had her crossbow unslung and sent a bolt after it, but it darted upward, spiraling around and around, and the bolt plonked uselessly into a tree in the distance. With a sigh, she began to reload.

"They'll keep that up forever," Ink said, watching the liefly's zig-zagging flight. "And they steal from each other, too, so you might come back twenty years from now and hear your younger self shouting at you from the mouth of that one's great-great-great-grandchild."

"Trust me, I will never return to this place, even if I live to be a hundred. So we've lost, is that it? To go deeper into this hell is certain doom, and nothing says the ranger won't follow us even then. We might as well go home." Gregary's shoulders slumped as he spoke.

"Home is back that way, by the way," Ink pointed, and each of them swore beneath their breath, not wanting to give the flies more to parrot. They had been walking in the wrong direction.

"There is another way. I can go back to Joymont with you and slay every tink."

The four looked at her incredulously. They'd lost a hundred men trying. Yet none of them were about to tell the black mage what she could not do.

"What's the catch? You could have offered the same back in Ten," Sandros asked.

"I want something from you first."

No one spoke, and the air was heavy with dread. Each was imagining some awful thing the black mage might want, a pledge of eternal servitude, a finger, or their firstborn sons.

"I want Xan dead."

All four of them stared at her with various expressions of surprise.

"We want the same thing, but..." Sandros began.

"But what? Help me slay him and I will save your little kingdom."

"Why?"

"Because I want him gone. What more do you need? We can start right now."

"Shouldn't we just wait for him in town and ambush him there? You keep talking him up as some lord of the jungle. Bedding she-mantises and the like."

"A joke. He's just a man. No one is invincible."

"I'll do it," Osolin said, and the other three looked at her, surprised. Ever since the stirges, it seemed her eyes were always upon the black mage. Keenly they remembered Ink's words, "You owe me your life."

"Well," Gregary said, looking at her curiously. "I won't. I haven't come out into the middle of nowhere to try and murder a man just because you want him dead. Especially not that one."

"Gods, what I wouldn't give for a piece of him! I'd tear him in half!" Ink spoke, but it was with Gregory's voice, exactly as he'd said it before. Gregory held a hand over his mouth as if she'd stolen his tongue, then his face reddened.

"They were just words, it was just a thing to say while I was angry," he said, looking away from the mage.

"I am more than just words."

"No," Gregory said. "I will not kill a man just to suit you, or just because he's angered me. We aren't assassins. Why should I trust you'll even make good on that promise? You could just as easily kill us to hide your crime."

"So. You would trade away your kingdom for the life of a faceless cunt who swindled you. What about you, scribe? Or you, bloodpriest?"

Sandros only shook his head, as if he didn't trust his tongue. Brakkar crossed his arms and jutted his lip, his stance was clear.

"Surely one of you has some balls."

The face behind the black veil stared at Osolin, and for a moment it seemed she would step toward Ink and abandon them, but instead, she stepped back to her companions.

"I must go with my friends." Her voice was barely more than a whisper. The others watched her, here was a side of Osolin they had never seen. She looked as if he might cry.

"Fine. Find your own way back. I'm done with you." Gone was the mirth, the playfulness. Ink spoke without emotion, as if addressing an empty room, then she turned and vanished into the trees.

"Oh fuck," Sandros said.

Ink had abandoned them in the Kalparcimex.

The leaves of the banner tree were strands of brilliant red, a hand's breadth wide and a hundred feet long, dangling down from the tree's wide black branches to skirt the jungle floor. Thin as paper, they billowed and fluttered in the rising wind, twisting and weaving in graceful tangles. Nothing grew in the shadow of the banner tree, and the ground around it was piled deep with insect husks dyed a deep crimson. Sandros stood as far from it as possible, at the clearing's edge with Brakkar and Gregary.

The banner tree moved of its own accord, the flowing leaves drifted in ways the wind alone could not account for. They danced along, one moment they hung almost still, softly billowing outward, and the next they would ripple and twist, spinning in great hoops, flicking the air like a dancer's ribbon. The motion was wild, but the hints of a pattern there caught his eyes, and he watched the tree for a long time, waiting for Osolin.

When the banner leaves grew too tangled, they melted together into a single strand and then split again, the new strands freed, glistening bloody with sap. Even standing twenty paces away, he could smell the unusual scent in the wake of a split, peaches and sweet rot. Small winged insects swarmed the newly reformed leaves, sucking greedily, and many were caught there. He watched them die in droves. The tree sucked them dry and then shed their empty husks, tinged red from its poison.

118

The storm was growing fiercer by the moment, but they could not find their way. Three times, Sandros had tried a charm to sense the way back to Ten, and each time the cantrip had led him to the trunk of one of the enormous selas trees, giants that caught the lightning and cast pillars of light up at the sky. Sorcery was drawn to them, and when the scribe dared to glimpse into the demiplane, he gasped at the enormous energies they contained. They were like rivers of power, wicking from the skies into the earth. Beneath his feet he could see the pulsing roots, twisting down a hundred fathoms below. How small he was!

High above him, there was a ruckus in the canopy, branches snapping and steel clanging against chitin. He squinted upward but could see nothing through the leaves. A moment later, a boulder-sized beetle hit the ground not ten feet away from him, hard enough that the impact hurt the soles of his feet. The beetle's legs flailed outward and it tried to right itself, but these were death throes, and soon it was still. A yellow faceted eye had been pierced and black ichor leaked from the puncture.

The dead beetle had two sets of mandibles. Short and thick, they looked like they could chew through solid rock. Along its underside there were rows of translucent green sacs with nipple-like discs, and Sandros could only guess at their purpose. The beetle's whole underside was glistening with sap.

Brakkar and Gregary were edging away from the base of the tree and Sandros thought that wasn't a bad idea at all. A few moments after they'd cleared out, a man-sized spider tumbled from the branches above and hit the earth. All the legs along one side had been severed by what looked like a single cut.

With half its legs missing and its carapace shattered by the fall, the spider still began to drag itself away. Haltingly, it lurched into the banner tree's clearing. Sandros held his breath, and in a moment a red leaf drifted down onto the broken spider, wound around it, and began to twist. As it did, bloody sap beaded from around the leaf, and then another strand found it and another and another. Soon the spider was nearly mummified, and in a few minutes the leaves withdrew, leaving nothing but a ruby husk.

Sandros was agog. What if they'd just blundered into the clearing? That could be them, drained and stained in the husk mound. Had the spider known it was done for? Did it just intentionally move into the banner tree's embrace? The questions weighed heavy on Sandros, but Brakkar and Gregary were just staring up at the canopy.

"Woman's handy with that sword," Gregary said, clicking his tongue at the two vanquished insects.

"Handier than a lot of men I've seen. If only I could open her eyes to the truth of the Red Giant. How powerful she could become!" Brakkar squinted up at the leaves, as if he could will it to be so. The priest's gaze had grown fiercer since the sorceress abandoned them, his muttered prayers to the Bloodstar had grown heated and nearly constant. As their confidence drooped and death loomed all around them, Brakkar only grew more confident, more present. Madness was not without its advantages.

"I hope your Giant sees us out of this place," Gregary said solemnly. "I wonder if we should have taken Ink's deal."

"No, it was right. The man deserves a beating, not a beheading. He told us true the witch would leave us, he warned us of all this. Perhaps he is right about the tinks as well."

"Still, one man for a kingdom."

"Bah, what good is a kingdom built on injustice? What worth a land cursed in the sight of the gods? Who will prosper where murder is spent as a coin? Look to the Wyrth to see the end of that, whole districts of rich men cowering behind their legionnaires and their high walls, waiting for the day their sins come due. For murder begets murder, and at last all must come to account. And so they shall. When the Red Giant comes, they shall be weighed in the balance and found wanting." The priest's voice was sure.

"She would have betrayed us. I am certain," Sandros said. "If she needed us to fight the ranger, it was as meat in the jaws of some trap, nothing more."

"Everything has betrayed us, the swindling ranger, that crooked Varagoi, the sorceress… but it matters not. Even if the very ground at our feet should try to swallow us, even if the air should turn to poison and the sky crack open and rain fire, the Giant shall never abandon me. And if I die in his service, I shall burn on in the after, while the unbelievers are snuffed."

In his zeal, Brakkar's hands clenched the air, his eyes darted around the brush, hungry for a threat. Gregary and Sandros glanced at each other.

"You are a warrior, you have been blooded, you have dealt death. You need only believe," Brakkar offered, but Gregary only shook his head.

"I cannot pretend to a faith I don't have. It is easy for you to believe, for you say he revealed himself to you. I have seen no sign. Look here at Sandros, I have seen him wield greater power than any servant of any star. Should I worship my brother?"

"His sorcery is but a pact with demons, and when it comes due he will be their plaything for all time. The service of the Star has no such shackles."

"That's absolute dogshit. Look at my hands. Do you see any fingers given over to demons?" Sandros held up his hands. The right still bore the sorceress's stain. "Only fools take such bargains, Yarlee imbeciles who think themselves immortal. My power is my own, not on lease from any god or demon. If your Giant is truly powerful, let him show himself, let him appear before us this instant and save us from this wicked jungle. Let him save Joymont."

"Fool! You cannot conjure a god with demands! They are ineffable, unknowable!"

"Ineffectual." Sandros could not stop himself.

Brakkar stared at Sandros, and the scribe did not shrink. For a moment, there was violence on the wind.

"What are you dolts on about?" Osolin asked, breaking the moment. She'd climbed down the tree and crept up as they squabbled.

"Just foolishness. What have you learned?" Gregary shot Osolin a thankful look. The last thing they needed was infighting.

"I learned not to wake up those fucking beetles. The thing was burrowed halfway into the tree, I thought it was just a bole in the trunk. When I tried to climb it, it attacked. The spider I took unawares, I wasn't about to wait to see if it was friendly."

"What of the way?"

"Look in any direction you want, it all looks the same. Those lightning trees are lit up in every direction, and the canopy is as flat as a table as far as I can see. The mountains are hidden in the storm. I can't even tell whether the land slopes up or down. From above or below, the place is a labyrinth."

"Nothing that looks like shelter?"

"No treetop inns, no enchanted castles. Just wind and insects as big as pigs on the wing."

"And you have no spells to find the way?" Gregary asked his brother.

"It's like I said, the lightning trees…"

"Which way does the Bloodstar say to go?" Gregary asked, nodding toward Brakkar. The priest was still stiff with anger.

"We can't just let—" Sandros began, but Gregary held up a hand and silenced him.

"You had your chance to lead us, but your magic doesn't work. Osolin tried to scout and got nothing. I can't even tell which way leads back to the shell. I say it is time we give Brakkar a chance."

"It's no different than flipping a coin to decide!"

"I was going to suggest that next. Only I haven't got a coin," Osolin said. "And I'm not trusting chance around this one again. Look where he led us." She glared at Sandros, and he tried to keep his face calm.

"What do you mean?"

"Do I have to say it? We could have been in the Tck'Hurr sun, eating pomegranates, fucking master fencers. Instead, a crooked cantrip led us here. Don't think I didn't notice."

"Pah." Sandros looked around for support but there was none for him. The storm overhead was growing fiercer by the minute, the scent of rain to come rose above the banner tree's perfume.

"We *all* noticed. It doesn't matter. Brakkar, guide us," Gregary said, relieved to have an answer.

"A drop of blood in my palm from each of you."

They looked suspicious, Sandros most of all, but at last, each of them pricked their fingers and squeezed a drop of blood into Brakkar's giant palm. He curved his middle finger inward, and of its own accord, blood welled around the rim of his fingernail and dripped into the pool. He stretched his palm out, the bead of blood quivering there.

"GIANT! LEAD ME TO BATTLE! SHOW US THE PATH!" Thunder roared overhead as Brakkar lifted his head to scream at the sky. The blood was spreading, the four drops had welled up until his hand was drenched in blood, and he held his hand up with his fingers outstretched, blood flowing down his arm. At last, he pointed the dripping hand to his right.

With a gasp, they saw that his eyes too were full of blood. It ran down his face in trails of crimson. His skin had become ghostly pale, and he stood there like a statue, so that they wondered if he might collapse. At last, he lowered his hand and scrubbed at his eyes with his unbloodied hand.

"That way," Brakkar said, his voice distant and haunted.

Thunder cracked overhead and the rain began. There was no preamble—in an instant, they were drenched. In the direction Brakkar pointed, a selas tree began to glow, raising its light to the storm.

19

"Xanadros!"

Her angry cry rose above the insect pandemonium, and for a moment the whole jungle was still, heeding the roar of the great sorceress. Slowly, the chittering, clicking, and singing began again, all the louder for the momentary lapse. The endless din of the Kalparcimex could not be denied.

Overhead, a great storm was brewing, not just another momentary downpour but a true squall. Up in the heavens, great plateaus of ebony and jade smoke wheeled and crashed together, advance guard of the shipbreaker blowing in from the lake. Tonight, it promised, the stars would shout and the skies would cry. In the west, the mountains were hissing up great pillars of black ash and cinders, announcing their intent to join the fracas.

Already the mountains rumbled with impatience, and beneath her feet she could feel the tree shake with the tremors. There could be no finer night for the final battle between two great powers. She would destroy the impertinent ranger as volcanoes erupted and skies exploded. The squall would carry his death cry to every corner of the Arc.

"Xanadros!" Ink shouted, and again the jungle was still. In the east, three pillars of light touched, one, two, three. In a few heartbeats, the air shuddered with thunder. She stood on the highest limb of a selas tree that had been killed by black strangle. Every inch of the selas had been braided with the parasitic vine, grown so thick you could not see the original tree anymore, just its shape beneath the weave. The strangle was in full flower, the trees beneath it dusted thickly with its pollen like deadly black snow. Soon enough, the vine would overtake them too.

From here, she could see it all, the cones of other uncorrupted selas trees breaking through the swaying expanse of green treetops. The ones that had caught a lightning bolt glowed with weird blue light, drinking in the power. Each gust of wind sent a wave of leaves rippling across the whole canopy. The storm was rushing in from the east, already poised over the Roanoa Caldera. The town would be in a frenzy of battening shutters and securing things that might blow away. Nod's Hole would be jam-packed with those looking to ride out the storm in a pleasant haze. For a while, she thought of all that lovely dark heat going to waste and longed to be back. The storm began to sling fat, cold drops of rain that pelted against her exposed skin hard enough to sting.

To the north, a huge cloud of war ants was swarming, a humming frenzy of yard-long fliers trying to get in all the mating they could before the storm. Many queens would be made this night. At the edges of the great mass were flashes of silver here and there, the stingers of blackwing wasps diving at ants that were coupled and defenseless. Then, suddenly, a great green flash and a peal of squealing and buzzing. The boiling mass of fliers and wasps had drifted too close to a wink's nest and now they were falling from the sky in droves, twisting in halos of green chemical fire. It was enough to call off the dance. The swarm dispersed in a great confusion of angry chittering and mournful chirps, and the wasps fled for all they were worth as the ants chased after them, screaming for revenge.

To the west, the trees sloped downward into the first ring valley of the inner Kalpa, where the ranger was probably hiding. A realm of swift death, where he thought she would not follow. What did he know of what she dared? What did he know of her?

My name.

He should not have it, no one should have any part of her. Hadn't she sunk deep enough into the black, vanished into the night so dark that no one could follow? Yet here it was, from the man's ruined lips came *Insolade*, carrying with it the girl who was long gone and could not return. Pain that was a hole in the nothing she'd become. *Insolade.*

The sky collapsed on her, walls of water crashed down, and the choked selas bent wildly with the wind. Only sorcery kept her from being flung off into the canopy. With will alone she steadied the treetop, and threw back her cowl and veil, letting the rain beat down on her bare face.

"XANADROS!" she screamed, piercing some hard core within her and letting the anger roar out in a great flood of twisting black cracks that shot through the sky, as if the clouds overhead had shattered. The thunderstorm rankled at the disturbance, and her hair rose as the lightning began to build around them, a great bolt to smite the woman who dared spit against the storm's fury. Yet she screamed on, and the scream swallowed the lightning before it ever was, the energy drained away into the Void, stillborn. There was a great mute place where the thunder should have been.

"What?"

The ranger's voice jolted her out of her howl. In an instant she was bringing up two different wards, a force skein and an eidolon, expecting a blade or an arrow, but a gloved hand simply waved at her dismissively. Xan emerged from the stranglevine wound around the selas' trunk. As she watched, a million threads of twisted black unwove from the glittering shells of his cloak and melted away like spider web. She hadn't noticed that the trunk was too thick there, hadn't had any idea he was there. The magic of the beetleshell cloak was powerful indeed.

"How?" she asked, wondering how in the hell he'd found her here. Xan had been there the whole time. He'd seen the whole outpouring, he was looking at her face. She knew her veil was down but her hand shot up stupidly to check it anyway.

"I always come here. It's the best place to watch the storm. Strangle keeps the selas from drawing the lightning. Usually." He'd anchored himself to the strangle vine with his right hand. He had no sorcery to keep him in place, and the winds were wild and powerful. It took great strength to cling there, but he paid the gale no mind, staring at her from behind his mask as if there were nothing else in the world.

She could have died of shame, but no color came to her cheeks, for they were black as the vine that strangled the tree. The rest of her face was no different, her eyes, her teeth, her hair, everything was pure black.

This was her face, the curse she bore. Now he had seen her, now he had something else of hers that no one should have.

"So that's what's beneath the veil. Do you mind?" She was too stunned to respond as he pointed to his own, then peeled it off.

It was like cresting a hill, expecting a city below, but finding instead a smoking ruin.

She gasped, wondering how he could have lived through such an injury. Every inch was whorled and scored with scars, save his eyes. It took her a moment to realize the lenses of his mask must have saved him from being blinded. His eyes were weird, too green, too bright. Something had happened to him in the inner Kalparcimex.

"You and I, Ink, you and I..." Lightning crashed down on another selas, close enough that they both winced, and then a column of blue light rose from the cone. All over the jungle there were pillars of selas light, holding up the storm.

"We're never going to make it on our looks."

Part of her wanted to grin, even here, even now. Another part of her pitied the grotesque mask the ranger wore beneath his other one. Neither part could be allowed, he had her name. He could not live. Still, she wove a quiet around them with three fingers, and bent the wind so they could speak without shouting.

"Where did you get it? Who told you my name?"

"Ah, well, you know. The things I know.... they aren't free."

"There are no banks in hell, Xan. I'm going to kill you, so you might as well just tell me."

"Oh, are you?" The unaffected way he said it infuriated her, he'd simply disregarded her threat. Disregarded her. The ranger was good at making people angry.

"Yes, I've almost worked up the nerve."

"Well then, I should deal quickly, I imagine it won't take you long. I will tell you where I learned your name if you go find those idiots you dragged down into my Kalpa and bring them back to Ten."

"After you die."

"Sure."

"Why do you even care?"

"My spirit will rest easier if I know there aren't a bunch of dolts loose in my jungle, stumbling and bumbling. There are things slumbering here that I don't want woken."

"Deal," she said, slipping off a glove, and thrusting out a black hand. If she could mark him...

"Forgive me if I don't shake. I've a cold," Xan said, sniffing theatrically at the air. It was hard to tell when she rolled her eyes, only the little muscles of her face gave it away. Still he clung to the tree with his right hand, not trusting the sorcerous calm.

"On with it, then."

"It's nothing special. Two drunks in Reth'Wyrth, trying to re-member the name of that thief, the one who was always robbing magicians. You know, she stole so many scrolls they started to call her Ink?"

"Oh, bullshit. When do you ever leave your beloved jungle long enough to travel to Reth'Wyrth."

"There's more to ranging than collecting bugs and swindling idiots. They used to have a real problem in Reth with the Void Cult. People vanishing, the mark of the Devourer showing up in all kinds of uncomfortable places. The cultists were actually going to build a temple and worship the Blackstar openly. And of course, that's a big problem for the ones that worship Urth'Wyrth. They have some stupid prophecy that says the end times begin when the temple of the Void rises."

"Used to have... what do they have now?"

"A red queen in black robes."

"Oh stars..." She looked at Xan, trying to read that catastrophe of a face. It was so terrible that she could barely believe it, even against the Void, even in Wyrth. A red queen, in a city... It made the plot to drive a bashyskyla into Joymont seem tame.

"Ah, but that's another story. As for yours, one old souse, missing every finger on his left hand but the pinky and thumb, he thinks it's Kayana, but the other thinks he's wrong and I agree. Just doesn't fit right on you and besides, how do you get from one to the other? Kayana doesn't just turn into Ink. So they started rattling off all the names that started with 'I' they could. Ita. Ivy. Imari. Iris. Indigo..."

"Stop moving," she ordered. Xan's hand was sweeping through the air as he talked, as if he were conjuring every name, but always the motion drew it closer to the dagger on his belt. For a moment they were both still, eyes locked on each other, but he refused to engage her stare, he blinked slowly and deliberately.

"Of course, just an itch. You wouldn't believe how I sweat in this thing. Anyhow, they got as far as 'Irene,' can you imagine that? You, an Irene? Then the one missing fingers just stops cold and says it..."

"Insolade," he finished, and in an instant his hand darted at her, just as the name tugged at her heart. At her, not at the eidolon that stood in the place where she'd been. She needed just one word to end him but she only got out half of it before his gloved hand lifted her up by the throat and pinned her against the strangled trunk. Instinctively, she tore at his glove, trying to peel his hand free, but it was like a piece of iron.

"Listen to me, little girl." Her spell was broken, the wind roared around them, but there was nothing else in the world but that growl. He was squeezing the life right out of her. Panic ran through her legs and arms in jagged little waves but she could do nothing.

"This isn't a game. I am not a sorcerer. I can't do a fucking thing with your name, and I'm not about to tell anyone else. We aren't enemies. I don't give a shit what you do or who you do it to, as long as it's not here. So this is the last time we do this, understand? Go get those fools out of my jungle, and don't return. Next time I won't be nice."

Her eyes had rolled back, and she was starting to go limp when he loosened his grip, but he didn't let go, for she would have tumbled off the branch and fallen into the canopy below. He held her by the collar of her cloak and that was all that kept her up.

"Don't..." she whispered, rolling her head slowly back up. Her voice was just a pained hiss, the rest was blown away by the wind. He stared at her, into those black eyes that gave nothing back.

"Don't stop."

It startled him so much that he nearly let go. A tiny thing, only the hint of a grin at the corner of her mouth, and he gaped as she faded through his fingers and into nothingness, a low moan seeming to come from every direction at once, echoing in his ears.

The storm raged on, and he hung onto the stranglevine, looking at the place where she'd been and blinking away rain. The palm of his glove had turned pitch black.

They thought they had known rain, but it was nothing. This was rain, this was standing beneath a waterfall, this was drowning on their feet, buckling under the deluge that could drown the world. They were staggering blind, wincing at the lightning, shrinking from the never-ending thunder. It was true misery. Even the insects seemed upset. Though the four were completely vulnerable, nothing was hungry enough to try for them in the storm. Everything they drew near scuttled away.

"DO SOMETHING!" Osolin shouted through the din and the storm. They were caught in the open and there was nowhere to take shelter. They would gladly take the stink of the quilg just to be back under the great shell, but it was far behind them now and no one knew the way back any more than they knew the way forward. The path beneath their feet sloshed with water that was calf-deep and rising.

What shall I do, burn the storm away? Sandros thought, but there was no use saying it, no use trying to speak in this madness. Always they thought he could magic away their troubles, as if they walked with Merriweather the Master instead of Sandros the Scribe. Was the great one ever so wet and weary? Had he ever felt so helpless?

"MARCH ON! THE RED GIANT BECKONS!" Brakkar roared, but then thunder drowned him out. The rain had washed the blood from his hand and face. It was increasingly clear to Sandros that they were following a lunatic's delusion straight to their doom.

It felt as if his red robe were a sheet of lead, dragging him down into the froth of water below. The flood was at his knees. If it kept up like this, they would be swimming before long. He was so cold, so tired and miserable, he just wanted to fall backward into the water, to lie down and let the flood rise over him. In his fantasy, when the black water receded, there would be nothing left, no bones, no scraps, there would never have been a Sandros at all.

As if she had slipped into his daydream, Osolin took a step and then vanished beneath the water.

The mage stood there, too stunned, too beaten to cry out. Gregary screamed something but a roar drowned him out. A wall of churning water and debris was thundering toward them.

They'd walked right into a river. Osolin's head broke the surface downstream, choking and sputtering. Her gear was dragging her down, and the others had no time to try and save her, for the flood was upon them. They were all scrambling for trees at once, but when the water hit, only Sandros had managed to climb high enough. Brakkar slipped as he tried to shimmy up another tree and was swept into the rush of muddy water. Sandros looked down to see Gregary trying to shout something to him, but he could not hear it, he could only see the hopeless look on his brother's face. He was wearing armor.

"No..." Sandros cried, his voice swallowed by the rushing water. If only he had a spell for this, something to lift Gregary up or transport him through the demiplane to safety. But he had no power over such things.

At once, he was back in the tower of the Scourer, crying tears of frustration as he tried to work a simple magic, freezing a cup of water. For hours and hours he'd tried, speaking the words, but the cup would not listen and the water within defied him. It was always this way, the fire came so easily and everything else was simply not there. Finally, he'd burned the cup into slag, then the table it sat on. Sandros howled with rage, and the water that would not freeze vaporized. The fire poured from him unchecked, lashing every inch of the practice chamber, until the stones themselves began to burn, and still he felt he had more, felt he could burn until the world was gone. The Scourer had lashed him half to death for that one. That tin cup would haunt his dreams forever.

All I do is burn, said a bitter voice in him as Gregary tried to cling onto a tree trunk while the floodwater tore at him, almost chest deep.

Something to help him, anything!

Gregary was clinging to a vine with one hand, and he had a dagger in the other. He was hacking at the straps of his armor, trying to cut himself free. It was a hopeless gesture. He could get the breastplate off, but there was still the mail shirt beneath it, the thigh plates, the bracers, the sword belt...

Gregary finally got through the leather strap and shucked off the breastplate and his pack, and then a tree limb swept into him and he went down with it. The vine wrenched away from the tree and Gregary clung to the taut cord with all his strength as the rushing flood tried to carry him off. Sandros dared to hope Gregary could pull himself back to the tree, but the vine broke and Gregary was swept away, tangled in the limb.

They were all gone, all swallowed by the great wash of water. Still the cold rain poured down on it all, and the tears of Sandros the Scribe fell with it. He wept, clinging to a tree that might be uprooted and swept into the flood any moment. Without thinking, his hands were stripping off his robe, the heavy thing would only drag him down.

He was midway through his leap into the rushing floodwater when a thought crossed his mind, *What the fuck am I doing?*

He crashed into the flood and was dragged under at once, his nose filling with muddy water. Sandros had forgotten to take off his boots, and he had to kick them off and thrash his way to the surface. Gasping for air, he started to paddle downstream, hoping he could make it to Gregary somehow, help him before he drowned.

Now we'll both die, fool. He fought his way through the dark water, against the wild current forever trying to drag him below, and the world became a close place. The darkness of the canopy and the storm seemed just overhead, the cold black water all around him and the rain forever striving to fill in the gap between the two.

The rain went on all night.

"So. This is the secret lair of the mighty Xanadros."

How many years had it been since something had truly surprised him as he slept? Enough that he'd forgotten what it was like, the sudden unwelcome clench in his chest, the muscles in his neck hard as iron, his mouth stupidly wide with nothing to say. She'd woken him and he couldn't move. At first he thought it was sleep-weakness, but it was more, his wrists and ankles were bound. He lay on his sleeping mat covered only with a blanket. His suit and mask hung drying on their hooks.

"My guards...do they live?"

"Recipitors can't eat what isn't there. They're fine. It's so noble of you to think of your pets first, Xan."

Oh, but they had tried, the beasts had clawed around the upper chamber like mad, somehow sensing her passage through the demiplane. They were the largest recipitors she'd ever seen, their hulls glossy and clean, free of the husk barnacle parasites that usually riddled them in the wild.

Recipitors were quadrupeds, built like armored hounds. They had three tongues, two forked manipulators and one long sticky tongue they could fire out to capture winged prey. They hunted in packs, clever as wolves. They were known for their ferocity and their insatiable appetites, they would eat trees, grass, insects, men, even stones.

In their strange triangular eyes, she'd seen the glint of intelligence. Again and again, they had trilled an alarm, but the notes fell dead within her dampening field. They had butted their horned heads against the false wall that concealed the entrance to Xan's cavern, but this, too, her magic denied. The stone wall was too strong for the things to batter their way through, but only barely.

"Whatever happens here, don't hurt them. They're spawning soon."

"Everything here is. You're breeding them. The recipitors, the juggerwurms, the spellspiders, I can't count them all. This whole temple full of your handiwork. I've seen your egg chambers, your nurseries. How can one man do all this? How can you feed all of these things?"

As the storm raged above, she'd flitted through the black temple Xan had claimed for his own, seeking answers. She had drifted through the shadows in the temple complex above, wondering who had crafted such a place. Beneath the overgrowth, it was all obsidian, massive slabs of volcanic glass, and there were no joints, no hard angles. Wherever two pieces met, some force had fused them together smoothly, the welds a shade darker than the obsidian itself. The temple was built in a spiral, rising up a hill, and she beheld it curiously.

This place was not the work of men.

The egg chambers were spires shaped like teardrops, their vine-wrapped points rising as tall as selas trees, and she counted thirteen spires, all forged of the same black glass. Exploring one, she was immediately homesick for Nod's Hole, for they were dark places, full of the same unnatural warmth. She wondered if they, too, had been built over hot springs. She could not ponder long, however, for the recipitors swiftly found her and drove her back into the demiplane. Finally, she'd given up poking about and made for Xan's hiding place.

Bound to the floor, Xan was silently considering his options, but there were none.

"The recipitor packs hunt for us."

"You have other packs?"

"Two others. One is hunting now, the other rests. Shifts."

"How, in all the stars that have ever been, did you tame recipitors?"

"They aren't tame. They're partners. We cooperate."

"What of the temple? Who built this place?"

"Ancient, I haven't a clue who built it. I could converse easier if I weren't ensorcelled to the floor."

"I'm sure you could," Ink said. She left him bound to the floor and began to walk around the cavern, rifling through his things.

Xan's bedchamber was enormous, a cavern deep within the earth, with vaulted ceilings nearly thirty feet high. There were stalactites and stalagmites throughout, the air cool and wet. It was cold enough that she saw no insects, and after days in the Kalpa, it was strange to see surfaces that didn't ripple with tiny crawling things.

Ink heard the sound of running water; at the far end of the chamber was a deep, wide pool fed by a spring. A stream flowed from it into a passage too low to crawl through. The room was lit greenish-white by firefly orbs that were pleasantly aged, just bright enough to read by. The bare orbs hung from nets tied to stalagmites high in the air. Apparently, Xan never bothered to cover them.

There was little personal here. A workbench with some tools, cluttered with insect parts and scraps of leather, and on a rack beside it hung a mostly-completed spare jungle suit missing just the gloves and mask. A pair of boots were half-finished on the bench. Near the workbench was a flat rock with a pile of money and gems left lying on it, out in the open. He'd clearly never expected anyone to come here. There was a chest not far from his bed, sealed against the water, but when she opened it she found only books, and not even interesting ones. They were breeding records and observations of the Kalparcimex, all written by Xanadros for Xanadros.

There were no keepsakes, no letters, no locks of hair tied with ribbons, nothing that told her anything about him. Missing were the vast hoard of gold, the piled skulls of other rangers, the harem of stolen children... the legends were all pigshit. He was silent as she looked through his things, and it bothered her. Ink tore a page at random out of one of the books and crumpled it up, but he didn't protest. Frowning, she flipped the ball of paper at him. It bounced off his forehead and drew no more response than a blink.

"So difficult," she sighed.

The real wealth of the room was on the shelves. Long banks of them ran along the far side of the room, a glass library whose volumes were all jars, meticulously labeled and organized. More jars than she'd seen in any apothecary's, thousands of different things, carefully preserved. There were whole insects and parts of insects, secretions and distillations, a hundred different kinds of eggs, a thousand things she could never have guessed at if they hadn't all been clearly labeled. An incredible fortune. Varagoi would sell his whole family for the contents of a single shelf. And there were many, many shelves.

"Such wealth, and you live out here all alone with your bugs. How lonely you must be."

A snort.

"It must feel strange, to be here, in your fortress..." She walked slowly over to him.

"Surrounded by your faithful guardians..." His eyes were on her as she stood over him, but he said nothing.

"Completely helpless."

With her boot she kicked the blanket off him. He lay nude on his sleeping mat, unmasked and exposed. The veiled hood moved as Ink looked him up and down, surveying the expanses of lean flesh forged by endless ranging. Only his face was ruined, his neck and collarbones like a mantle of scar around his neck. The rest of his skin was like any other man's. She lingered on the strong hands that had choked her, on the wide shoulders, the long slash of a scar on his side, then her eyes widened when they fell between his legs.

"All that going to waste. The whores in Ten don't know what they're missing." Perhaps it was just because he lacked any sort of body hair, but he seemed better equipped than most.

He did not respond, wasn't even looking at her. His mind was somewhere far away, and she kicked him in the side, right on that long scar, but he did not even flinch. She planted a boot at the center of his chest and stepped down, slowly increasing the pressure until she thought his ribs might snap.

"Hey. Pay attention to me. Don't you want to know how I found your little bug farm? Which of your minions betrayed you?"

"The gloves you marked. I should have thrown them away after you blackened them. They're just hard to make, and I didn't have spares."

She frowned again. She'd hoped to taunt him more, hoped there would be more pain in his voice, more weakness to exploit. He seemed mad at himself, instead of her. She had played out this exchange in her mind many times, but she hadn't expected him to be this way, to give her nothing. She took her foot off his chest.

"What a bore you are, Xanadros. I should just start emptying those jars onto you, one by one."

"The blue crystal one marked 'bashyskyla' is the fastest. Third shelf, on the left."

"What if I don't want fast?"

"Then the year ticks hurt the worst for the longest. More than ten would probably kill me outright though."

"Year ticks? Like a common criminal. How ordinary. No, not quite right."

Ink stepped over him, one foot on either side, and sat on his chest like a schoolyard bully, with her knees on his shoulders.

"The legendary ranger, all mine. I can do anything I want to you, Xan"

"Then do it," he said.

What did she expect from him, fear? Begging? He was sure there was no pain in the world greater than that he'd already known, no indignity a faceless man could not bear. Already, the ghosts were rising up, specters of grand agonies, months spent wasting with debilitating insect maladies, whole days spent awaiting the torturer's knock at his cell door, and the big one, the pain so large it eclipsed the word and became a new thing entirely. When it hurt so bad there was nothing else in the world but the screaming insistence that it had to stop and the terrible wish that it could go on forever. What could she do that could compare to—

Insolade bent down over his face and kissed him through her silken veil. The softness of it shocked him, the sheer fabric backed by the warmth of her lips, and his eyes shot open with surprise. Some long-forgotten instinct made his own lips move through the confusion, pressing back against the veil. When she felt the movement, Ink pulled back and drew her veil. Her face of polished jet was carved into a wicked grin, drinking in his bewilderment, and a gloved hand stroked the ruined skin of his cheek.

"You're so stupid, Xan."

Again she'd taken him by surprise.

Her hand ran down his face, along his jawbone, down his neck, barely touching him at all. She climbed off his shoulders and ran gloved fingertips down his chest. Two fingers walked down the long scar on his side like a path, and then her hand was at his thigh, slowly twisting in toward his groin.

He shuddered. How long had it been? So long ago the memory was just wind and fog, and despite his resolve to give her nothing, he tensed against the bonds. But it was futile, his efforts did nothing but deepen Ink's grin.

"Oh yes... struggle."

The hand at his thigh slid down until she had him by the balls. With her other hand, she stroked along the length of his cock, and swiftly it came to life.

"Oh my."

139

He threw all his strength against her now, straining against the sorcerous binding as hard as he could, but it was for nothing. The hand that cupped his balls gave them a sharp, painful squeeze.

"When you strain like that, I can feel you twitch," she said, and she gripped his shaft tightly, running her gloved fist up and down.

It had been a long time. He forced his mind away, but when his eyes went dull, she slapped him as hard as she could, leaving a pink glove print on his cheek.

"Right here. This is happening."

She went back to stroking him, her eyes locked on his face, those black pools sucking in every quiver, every minute expression. Again, he fought back, pulling at the stone until he felt he could wrench the whole earth up with him, and again she squeezed him. Unconsciously, the point of her black tongue slipped between her lips and ran across them.

"I like it when you fight." Her voice was just a breathy whisper, and the hand that wasn't locked onto his cock roamed across her chest and cupped a breast through her robe, seemingly of its own mind. When she noticed, she looked down at her hand for a moment, as if to chastise it, but then she bit down on the fingertip of her glove and drew it off with her teeth, never letting him go. Swiftly, the bared hand slipped under the hem of her robe and writhed between her legs.

"Oh!"

Her scent was in the air, and he took on a new fullness, hard as the stone under their feet. All his resistance was slipping away, he could not believe it.

I was tortured. They did everything to break me and I held.

But the man who bore that pain was not here. There was an animal in his skin, more in control with every thundering heartbeat. The scent, gods, the scent. Every breath dragged him down deeper into it, until the sides of his face were on fire, until there was nothing but that pulsing *want*. The nearness of death made it even worse.

140

Both of her hands were working like mad, her breath just one swift gasp after another. She had really meant to draw this out, to make it last for hours, but it was just so intense, so much more than she had expected. The sound of his sharp, halting breaths, the way his eyes rolled up beneath tightly-clenched lids, made her cheeks burn.

She let go, and he did not cry out, but his eyes opened wide, and the look on his face shouted *Why did you stop?* Grinning, she slowly disrobed, taking off everything until she wore just the one glove. If he were resisting, he should have shut his eyes, or stared past her, but he did neither. His eyes roamed over her body hungrily as she let down her hair, taking in the small pointed breasts, the skinny legs, coming to rest on the notch between her legs which she kept shaved smooth. If she weren't cursed, she would never have caught men's eyes, but she had his. Right now, she was the only thing in the world to him, and she was soaking with it, on fire with the power.

She leaned down next to his ear, her lips just hairs away from touching him, so he could feel her hot breath.

"I want you," she whispered, low and insistent. "You're so difficult. I've wanted you for a long time. If it weren't for the curse I would slip you inside of me. I would take every inch of you." As she said it, she ran her gloved hand slowly up from the base of his cock, twisting up around his head, and at last he cried out and she let him go. He was close, so close that it seemed a breeze could set him off, and she brought her face close to him and blew, wondering if she could do just that. He squirmed and thrust up toward her. She drew back just in time, grinning.

"Careful now, you don't want to get blackened... Or do you?" She ran her covered hand down his chest, along his stomach, down his thigh, everywhere but where he wanted it to be.

"I won't mark you unless you ask me to." She had a hand between her legs, and she slipped a finger in and out of herself with small wet noises. Xan's eyes rolled back and his whole body trembled. She could see the conflict raging as she played with herself, his body betraying him with every twitch, and she moaned with pleasure, the *control* tightening in her muscles, singing in her temples.

141

"Please…" he said at last.

Ink took off her glove.

He was only a man, after all, beneath that mask. But what a man! She hooked a fingertip at his navel and painted a line down, watching his skin darken beneath her touch until it was as black as her own. For a moment she lingered at the beginning of his manhood and smirked, thinking of drawing a spiral around his shaft and then just leaving him like that. But she could not deny her desire any more than he could. She ran her fingers along him, watching transfixed as his pale velvety skin turned to black.

He was watching himself be marked, watching the taint that would never lift sink into his flesh, but there was no horror in his eyes, only fire.

I could release him and he would take me, he would pin me down and just have me, I could do nothing…

Just the thought made her hand tighten, and his whole body quivered. Against her bare skin, it seemed like the pulse traveled through his cock to her hand, running up her arm to tremble in her neck. He was so hot, so soft, so *alive*. She wanted it all, and every instant she waited hurt. But still she grinned, because it hurt him worse.

"Shut your eyes," she ordered, and he stared back for a moment, resistance beginning to rekindle. Xanadros was not a man who took orders from anyone. She let go of him and looked into those rebellious eyes, needing only the lift of her chin to say it.

If you don't, I stop.

He shut them, and then suddenly he was surrounded by a soft wet warmth. He screwed his eyes tight and arced his head back against the sleeping mat with a gasp so loud it echoed back at them from the chamber's heights. He writhed, he shook, he tried everything to keep his eyes closed, but at last he had to open them, and he looked up to see her eyes staring back at him, her mouth wrapped around the head of his cock. Never breaking his gaze, she slid her mouth down, taking more of him and drawing back, leaving darkness where her lips had been. With each bob she took more, and the black stain moved down his shaft like the tide lapping at the shore.

142

Finally, he felt a tightness. She was trying but she could take no more of him, and she drew back, defeated, leaving him glistening like jet, her brows knitted in frustration.

"...So much," she whispered, and she could see she'd gotten no better than half of him. Her hand ran between her legs uncertainly, wondering just how much she could bear. She was soaking, and finally she could wait no longer and straddled him, her thighs painting his sides black as they touched. She hovered over him, feeling the heat rising from him like a stone in the sun.

Slowly, so slowly, she lowered herself to touch him, her lips against him in the faintest kiss, and he moaned. She did it again, and then again, pressing harder, then began to grind herself against him, and then she was moaning too. It had never been like this, she had never been so aroused. She kept teasing him, and it seemed like at any instant he would enter her, but always, she drew back at the last instant. Poised there, she stopped, looking down at him, her hands leaving prints on his shoulders.

"Please," he said. There was no guile left in him, no fear, only desire.

She smiled and took him into her hand, then began to lower herself onto him. They both closed their eyes, and there was no more light, no more anything but this, the feeling of being slowly enveloped, of being filled, and they were so close together and yet leagues apart. Slowly, so slowly, she slid down, and it hurt but she couldn't stop, and at last she paused, with tears in her eyes. For a long time she stayed there, her head thrown back, reverberating with the intensity of the feeling. She wanted to move, but she couldn't. She lay down on top of him, her chest against his, her breasts pressing against him, and sought his mouth desperately. They kissed with a frantic abandon, and the slightest movement shot through them both, and they gasped, this thing happening greater than either of them.

All over his body, there were swaths of black. Everywhere she'd touched him, the flesh had darkened. His face was half-masked by her fingers stroking his cheek, his mouth blackened, his tongue and teeth painted by hers.

"*I need... I need... I need...*" She was almost babbling and neither of them could hear the words. She slid upward until they both cried out from loss, and slowly she slipped back down. Her legs were shaking so hard she could barely stay up, she needed his hands to hold her but they were locked in place. Again she rose and fell, and she knew she could not take much more, knew she would die if it stopped. Again, again, again, and then on the seventh stroke she slid all the way onto him, and they cried out in unison and came. The lights were gone and she felt a scream rippling through her whole body, felt herself breaking into pieces and spreading out, no more her, no more anything but the heat and the dark, the pulsing inside of her. She let go completely.

When her senses returned, she was weeping against his shoulder, and his arms were wrapped around her. She'd lost her spell, he was freed, she was totally vulnerable. He could crush her to death now, squeeze the life out of her while he was still inside her.

I don't care if he kills me. Nothing matters.

But it was only an embrace, his hands running through her hair, then softly along her back. They forgot how vulnerable they were and sleep caught them.

144

The rain drove on, but the Kalpa never stilled. All through the wild storm, trills rose above the downpour, voices cried out against the night.

In the wake of lightning the triple crack of two hookfingers rang out, the creatures rapping their three forelegs against the trunk of a sawleafed gobon tree as they hunted. The five-legged solifugids looked like pale severed hands scuttling up and down tree trunks in search of prey. Along with the thunder rolled the booming growl of the banneret toads they sought, calling out warnings to the others. A pair of hookfingers could beat one of the armored toads if one hand distracted it while the other caught it from behind. But in single combat, a toad would snap a finger-like limb off a hookfinger in one quick bite and leave it crippled, dying from the toad's withering poison.

So the hands and the toads stalked each other all through the night, their calls ringing through the high crooked branches and glittering golden leaves of the gobon tree. As the night wore on, several more hookfingers joined the pair and they massed for an assault on the nest. At their approach, the leader of the toads inflated his vocal sac and split the night with a thunderous call to arms. The bannerets sprang from the nooks of the gobon to form a defensive ring around the trunk and drive back the invading hands, each joining the battle cry in a deafening chorus of croaks.

While their little war raged, opportunistic lieflies flew screaming down to steal eggs, darting through a gauntlet of venomous
tongues from the defending banneret females. The lieflies swift
enough to make it out with an egg were easy prey for silverjacket
herringmoths concealed beneath higher branches. A sudden flash
of bioluminescence reflected against silvery wings was the only
tell. Before the lieflies could recover, the herringmoths swooped
down to knock the stunned flies from the sky and devour them
and their stolen eggs.

A liefly which had escaped the gauntlet of tongues and the
deadly flash of the herringmoths sang with jubilation as it shot
through the sheltered flight path beneath a sheaf of sawtoothed
leaves, only to blunder into the rain-beaded strand of a spell-
spider's web. Again and again it cried out, tangled in the strands,
but the spider was upon it swiftly. Two powerful chelicerae silenced the fly and then the spider's spinnerets set to work. The
stolen egg slipped from its lifeless claws and crashed into a fungal
bed below, igniting a minor war between a troop of hatchethead
ants that sought to steal it from the three ambrosia beetles that
nested beneath the bed.

Overhead the battle raged as the thunder roared. The swarm
of lieflies had thinned considerably but still they dove into the
gauntlet. It did not matter how many perished, there were always
more flies, and they were always willing to try their luck. A banneret egg would convince nearly any female to mate with a male
swift and clever enough to steal it.

All night the racket went on, escalating as the storm began to
subside. The sounds of the gobon tree's inhabitants vied with the
rising noise of the adderalm that grew beside it, where a clutch of
multipedes had joined a humming and clattering mating ball, and
a host of creeching stirges set upon a dying bark slug. In the black
morleyelm opposite, four dawnpipers joined in a clarion call to
the morning as the first rays broke through the canopy, their
devil-horned heads swaying and their chitinous beaks thrumming
in an alien harmony.

From any angle there was some drama unfolding. All over the jungle, cries rose above the pandemonium to join the dawnpipers, voices without number calling out to the new day as the storm broke and the sun rose over the Kalparcimex.

As the first rays shone through the canopy, a single powerful song stilled the others. Sweeter than any flute, deeper and richer than any toad's cry, it shattered the great din, and for an instant there was only the sound of flight as the insects fled the predator's song.

Morning found Brakkar treed, far down the river.

His shield and pack were gone. He'd lost his boots, his friends, all his supplies. Everything but his mace, looped at his belt. It had nearly dragged him below, but he would not cut it loose. The mace was all he had left.

The mace and his faith. It was enough.

He'd managed to swim long enough to latch onto a clump of debris, a jumble of branches and leaves tangled up in the spindly limbs of a boar-sized dead spider. The spider's body was buoyant and he'd been swept along in the flood for what seemed like forever until he'd managed to climb onto it and grab ahold of a branch. He'd crawled his way up the limb until it was thick enough to support his weight and pulled himself up onto it, leaving his arachnid raft behind.

On the tree's trunk, there was a pear-shaped silvery bulge as big as a man's torso. It moved at his approach, the six legs that had been bored into the tree unfolding, and the thing's head dislodged from the tree, revealing a proboscis as long and sharp as a fencing dagger. Some kind of tree louse, perhaps meaning to defend its host.

He would never know. With a flick of his wrist, he twisted the mace from the loop at his belt and smashed the creature's head. It splatted against the tree and he drew back the mace, ready to hit it again if it lived, but there was no need. The parasite plunged into the floodwater below with its legs twitching wildly and green-yellow sap poured from the wound in the tree where it had fed.

It was just a small thing, but the relief was immense. For days, he'd been in this miserable jungle, beset by fighting dwarves and sorceresses and masked men, endlessly frustrated. Listening to the squawking and wheeling of the others, watching the demise of their stupid plans, doing nothing. The simple act of killing something released him from all of it. His mace dripped with the insect's sticky ichor and everything seemed clearer, simpler.

He was alone, in the heart of the deadliest jungle in the Arc. Surely he would die, and there was nothing left to do but to go out fighting, to flood the jungle with offerings to the Bloodstar. He reached into his pocket and drew out Ink's charm, scowling at the sorcerous thing.

He had dedicated his heart to the Bloodstar, he needed no protection but the Red Giant's blessing. He flung the opal into the river, and at once he felt better, cleaner, without its taint upon him. He began climbing from tree to tree, making for the flood's edge, for solid ground to make his stand.

"I want to paint you."

They were the first words she said to him after they woke. She hadn't needed words for what had come before. Xan had awakened to find her straddling his face, brushing her sex against him, and for a moment he had been too confused to understand what was happening. When she grabbed the back of his head and pulled him against her, he pieced it together. He could taste himself, mingled with her, but he didn't care. He set to it with a restrained, maddening skill that had her shrieking until the whole chamber echoed with her cries.

When it was done, he took her from behind savagely, with her face pressed against the mat. It seemed that he could go on forever, he had something to prove after the swiftness of their first time. When it was over, she felt like she'd been shattered and never wanted to be put back together. She lay there, full of him, and for a long time she made no move but to breathe, slowly and luxuriously, as tremors ran through her.

"I haven't canvas," he said. He was at his desk, recopying the page she'd torn out. The whole book had been cut apart. He meant to rebind the entire thing, rather than just stick the replacement page in. It said much about him.

When she looked up at him from the mat, he looked down at the page, then to the book, then to her, and his expression said *NEVER AGAIN*.

"I'm sorry, I get carried away. Sometimes. All the time. But no, not a picture of you, but you. I want to touch every inch of you."

"That wasn't enough?" He set down the pen and capped the ink bottle. She watched his muscles ripple as he rose. Much of his front was black, but around his sides she could see the white skin, and one of his calves was nearly untouched. With a note of panic she saw that he was almost half ready again.

"Oh stars... more than enough. I've never been taken so, I'm not sure I can walk." She'd meant to jest, but it came out earnestly, for it was the truth. Never this way. Never so good. She would be sore for a week. Still, she got up and moved gingerly toward him.

"You look half piebald, is the thing." She indicated the calf, the triangle of untouched skin beneath his left arm. "And piebald is no way for a man to look, even if he is part stallion." She brushed her fingers along his length and he was ready again. She took him in both hands and twisted them in opposite directions until he groaned. She sank to a kneel and began to flick her tongue against his slit while she twisted, and his knees nearly gave out.

"Stand there and shut your eyes," she ordered. She saw a flash of rebellion in his look, but he shut his eyes.

"Every inch of you..." she murmured, kissing her way down his leg to his calf, running her lips over him until the pale flesh was gone, then she was kissing his feet, flicking her tongue between his toes, along the soles of his feet. She ran her fingertips across his face, across his eyelids, watching the darkness spread. She kissed behind his ears, up the back of his neck, ran her fingers all across his back, behind his knees... slowly possessing every inch of skin, until he was black nearly all over. Always, she returned to his cock, keeping him fully aroused, until he was dripping with anticipation.

"Put your hands on the desk."

Hesitation, as he wondered what she was planning, and she could see the words of some dire warning about tampering with his work beginning to form, but he dismissed them and set his hands on the desk's surface. She spread his legs apart and began to work her tongue at the last place on him that wasn't black, stroking his cock fiercely as she tongued his asshole.

He tensed in alarm, even cried out, but she would not be denied, and she felt him begin to loosen, felt his shaft twitch and his balls clench as she licked him. He came swiftly and suddenly, thrumming wonderfully in her hands. She kept stroking, pointing him down away from his desk so she didn't ruin more of his papers. She was surprised he had anything left at all, much less such a volume.

"Now you are all mine," she said, and again, though she'd meant it as a jest, it came out serious. There was a coldness in his brilliant green eyes. They looked out at her from the newly pitch-black face that said otherwise, and she felt a cold twist in her stomach that he was done with her now, that he would thank her for the fuck and send her on her way.

Fury threatened to rise and swallow the whole chamber. She had opened herself to him, had given herself to him freely... if he turned her away... *I would kill him, I would annihilate everything.*

"Let's take a bath," he said, and his eyes lost their coldness, but she did not forget.

"I'll fix you something to eat after," he added, almost gently.

The fare was simple, krei eggs and conemeal cakes. Xan cooked without a fire, mixing two liquids together in a tray and then resting the pan on top. There was no smoke, yet the eggs sizzled and the cakes crackled, then he dusted the whole dish with purple pepper powder until it was spicy enough for an Ibexian. He had the knack of cooking. The krei eggs were cooked through without the shells hardening, and the cakes were crisp and salty. They were both ravenous, they sat at a small worktable Xan had cleared and devoured the meal without a word.

"We had a deal. Rubes out of my jungle. Yet they remain," Xan broke the silence as Ink finished the last cake, black beads of sweat at her temples. The spice was punishing, but so satisfying she never complained.

"I thought that was just flirting."

"No, I want them gone, preferably alive. They may be idiots, but they can do tremendous damage, especially if they blunder into the inner. I suffer the gatherers because they are careful, they leave no ripples as they pass through my Kalpa. But these idiots you've brought... they know nothing, and their ignorance can do great harm. Especially that mage. There's something strange about him."

"Can't you get rid of them?"

"Surely. But alive? No. They don't trust me. They'd fight. And lose."

"What do you care if they live or die? They're just rubes."

"Why speak with you of morality? You'd never understand. I might as well try to teach you shame, or restraint."

"I know plenty about restraint," Ink said with a superior grin, and his blood burned at the memory. "Strange to hear talk of morals from a man assembling an army of man-eating insects. Or were you just going to start a zoo here at the fringe of the inner?"

"An army? Ha! Is that what you think this is? And what would I do with such an army, little one?"

"Take your revenge, of course. Raze Ten to ashes, then march on Joymont, Bashas, Rildemont, conquer the whole region and forge a new western kingdom, then an empire. Break Wyrth, smash Yarlsbeth, then descend on the south with an unstoppable horde of bugs and rule the whole Lake."

Ink was still grinning, caught up in the fantasy. She was wrapped in one of Xan's blankets that had once been blue. All over his cavern there were little black footprints. Even the water of his spring where they'd bathed had a faint tint. The woman left her mark.

"My revenge? What did Ten ever do to me?"

"Someone did spread that rumor you had crotch mites."

"So I should wipe them out, for some whore's whispering that only fools believe? The same people who think I kill all the other would-be rangers and steal children out of their beds at night. Hopeless dolts. A town should die for their idiocy? And then the rest of the Lake, why do they deserve to be conquered?"

"They're weak."

He looked at her across the table, calculating what was jest and what was real, what was her and what was shadow.

"Weak, strong, I care not. Rule is impermanent, fools clamoring to stand atop a haystack, always surprised when someone pulls them down by the ankles. Kingdoms fade. Empires crumble. None of it matters. What I do here will last."

"And what is that, Xanadros?" She was brushing her foot against his calf, the blanket wrapped around her head like a hood, her long hair spilling from under it. Already the hunger was beginning to kindle again. "What is this all for? Where did this temple come from? Why are you breeding these beasts?"

"I will tell you..." he said, reaching under the table to part the blanket and run his fingertips lightly along the inside of her thigh until she shivered.

"Once you do what we agreed." He drew his hand back as she moved herself toward him, and her mouth opened in outrage.

"This first. Don't tease me," Ink demanded, her lips slightly parted.

"I thought you weren't sure you could walk?"

"I don't need to walk. I need to fuck."

"After," he said, and he turned and took the plates from the table. As he walked to the stream to wash them, Ink watched, eyeing him hungrily. She sighed with frustration, then stood to look for her robe.

At last the light came, the lance of morning piercing her heavy lids and casting her into confusion. It hurt to breathe, and she could not see. Her slitted eyes brought only a bleary muddle of green-tinged light. She was damp and cold and when she tried to rub her eyes, she found she hadn't the strength. She was propped up against something, a tree or a stone, she couldn't tell.

What happened? Where was she? She had never been hungover like this before. She could remember black rushing water and nothing else. Every time she tried to focus, that horrible buzzing distracted her.

Osolin blinked rapidly and everything rushed back to her with horrible speed, the flood, the quilg, the stirges. She was lost in the insect jungle. She fought to rise, to do anything, but she could do no more than feebly move her fingers while the drone of wings grew louder all around her.

Were they stirges? Had she lost the black mage's charm? Finally, she blinked the silt from her eyes and began to focus. There was blinding light all around her, she was caught in a wide swathe of sunlight that pierced the canopy where a tree had been uprooted and carried downriver. She lay on a floodplain surrounded with scraggly plants drowning in muck, and hundreds of insects were mired in it: beetles as big as hogs, mantises as big as horses. Clouds of winged insects wheeled above the still ones. A few others were not quite dead; they twitched their legs on their backs, unable to right themselves, or they hobbled on broken appendages or beat their ruined wings uselessly.

Am I broken too?

She could wiggle her toes, she could clench her fingers. She was weak, not lamed. If she could gather her strength, find food, perhaps...

The drone of wings came back, all the louder, and she saw its source, a sleek black flyer. It was a wasp as big as she was, its hull an oily black banded with thin rings of brilliant crimson. The wasp's eyes were a glittering vermillion, broken into a million tiny lenses. It hovered over one of the still-moving insects, a boar-sized beetle stuck on its back, then landed atop it and in one swift movement jabbed a stinger as long as a broadsword into its underbelly. The beetle beat at the wasp with its legs, but it was weak and could not dislodge the predator. Osolin couldn't see why it was bothering to kill this beetle when there was a dead one just like it only a few paces away, and she wondered foolishly if it was an act of mercy. But then she saw the thing's thorax quiver, saw a bulge ripple down the length of the stinger, and it all became clear. It was laying eggs.

After the act, it vibrated there for a moment before withdrawing its ovipositor and lifting back into the air. It settled onto the next living insect, a blue mantis with all the legs on one side broken. The mantis swiped with a scything claw, but could not connect with the nimble wasp. Soon the ovipositor was buried in its back, and the wasp was humming with satisfaction as the mantis gave a weird clicking scream.

Oh god no.

It meant to plant its young in everything that lived. Methodically, it lifted from insect to insect, hovering over them, and then came the spike, the wail of anguish, and that awful buzzing. Panic raced through her, thundering and alive, but it could find no purchase on her legs and arms. Using all her will, she managed to draw the dagger at her belt, but it tumbled from her numb fingers and slipped into the muck. Her crossbow was gone, sunk beneath the flood. Again and again she tried to stand, tried to flee, but the wasp drew nearer, until it was plunging its stinger into the giant larva just a stone's throw away. She would be next.

154

At once, she stopped her efforts and gave a last, theatrical sigh and froze in place, not breathing, willing her very heart to be still.

Prayers now, coming in a confused jumble. *Please don't have more eggs, please think I'm dead, PLEASE.* The names of the stars began to run through her mind, one after the other, and she begged each in turn as the thing lifted once more into the air. She tried, tried to stare straight ahead, not to let her eyes catch the crimson bands, or follow along the deadly glistening length of its stinger. Her chest burned with emptiness, and then she felt the wind of its wings.

The awful thing was hovering over her. She was staring at herself, a million reflections of her frozen face glimmering in the wasp's compound eyes. It wasn't fooled. In an instant she would be impaled.

NO! Osolin screamed inside.

"No."

The wasp pivoted in mid-air toward the sound, and Osolin gasped, hungrily drawing air. The black mage stood at her side, holding an ebon hand up at the wasp.

"She's mine. Go away."

The wasp's mandibles chittered angrily, the buzz of its wings grew louder, and Osolin found her eyes locked on the monstrous stinger, leveled at Ink like a rapier. So swift it was only a blur, the wasp darted at the mage, but Ink simply melted. The wasp had flown into her shadow. As if it were made of tar, the wasp was caught fast, beating its wings in a fury.

"I warned you," Ink said, and then Osolin saw darkness boiling from the wound in the larva, the wasp's egg carried out of it on a tendril of shadow. All over the clearing, the eggs were drawing out of the wounded insects and returning until a dozen of them hung poised around the wasp, borne on lines of jet black force. The wasp was struggling wildly now, thrashing its head, but there was no escape.

With a flick of her fingers, Ink formed the shadow lines into needles and drove the wasp's eggs back into it. In an instant it was penetrated in twelve places at once, through the back, in its underside, and one needle planted an egg in the thing's eye. The wasp gave an awful cry of pain, spasming from the wounds, and then from behind Ink's veil, Osolin could hear that same awful orgasm-hum the wasp made after laying, perfectly mimicked.

Ink slew the wasp with its own young and then taunted it with its voice.

The shadows melted away and the wasp fell into the muck, dead. Ink turned to Osolin, her movement light, as if the awful act had no weight at all for her.

"That's twice you're mine," Ink said, and Osolin tried to speak, but it came out as an incoherent wail and then she burst into tears. The black mage simply stood there until Osolin was through weeping, staring down at her from behind the veil.

"I will save you from this place. But if I do, then you belong to me, mine to do with as I please. I am your master." Osolin could not see the mage's face, but she could hear the grin in her voice, picture the predator's smile.

Osolin lay there, blinking, her relief quickly turning to terror. She was caught in the black mage's trap.

She thought of the wretched low-caste slave women of Wyrth who were led through the streets in chains with their breasts bared, collared like dogs. Their eyes never left their feet, and they were always silent, for if they uttered a single word their tongues would be cut out. She thought of the rice-men of Fang, four to a yoke, their backs just ugly masses of scar, young men whose faces were so withered by the endless sun that they looked like grandfathers. Most of all she thought of Garakatoc, wicked Garakatoc, who'd shattered her and left her an animal thing, skulking through the woods, haunted by him every day, long after she'd cut out his eyes and killed him.

And theirs was only bondage of the body. To be enslaved by a mage... it was one of those classic misfortunes that always became disasters in the tales.

She could use me in some ungodly experiment. Barter my soul to a demon. Who knows what she wants from me?

But the alternative was death. And Ink was a woman, at least. Though her mind shrieked against it, Osolin would pay any price to live.

"...Yes," she managed to say at last, her voice just a weak hiss.

"Perfect," Ink said, drawing back her veil. Osolin looked at the pure black face in horror.

"This will be *fun*."

"What are you doing?"

Sandros did not reply, and in the darkness, the glow caught his eyes and painted his face a fiendish red. Gregary's eyes flashed with alarm, but he dared not speak again, instead watching the slow fire Sandros held in his hands. Embers moved through the darkness, slowly devouring the stick he held, and the air was filled with the smell of smoldering wood, a much-needed reprieve from the stink of scorched flesh. The cave, or more rightly, the hole they were hiding in, wasn't even tall enough to stand up in. They'd crawled in on their hands and knees.

One by one, flaming circles burned along the stick's length and then Gregary figured it out.

"A flute. Stranded in the middle of the Kalparcimex, and this one carves himself a flute."

"Might as well go out with a song," his brother said, blowing through the end of the flute and sending a puff of smoke curling out. The flute still glowed a deep red in his hands, but he lifted it to his lips as if it were stone cold and sounded a few notes. His fingers danced across the holes and never singed. Gregary was used to it. When they traveled to places where their names weren't known, Sandros would often wow the rubes by snuffing torches with his bare hands. Or he would claim the hearth was full of money and then reach into the coals to produce a golden coin.

Gregary smiled, remembering how once a Sun Priest had claimed it was all a glamour and demanded the coin, to show it all false. How the man had howled when Sandros handed him the red-hot gold! For a while it had looked like it might come to blood, but everyone hates a Truestar fool, and the man was simply laughed out of the tavern. Gregary would give everything he had to get back there. It would be no great sacrifice now. He had nothing.

Sandros played a few scales and frowned, then at last he shrugged.

"It's no Yarlee silver, that's for sure. But it'll do." He began to play, trying to get a feel for the flute. Slow mournful notes filled the cave, and Gregary thought he could almost hear the smoke in its tone, a breathy, wavering sound. For a while he listened, entranced by the closeness of the air, by the swirling song, and then just as Sandros was beginning to play a soft section, Gregary's stomach rumbled louder than the flute, breaking the spell.

"Sorry," he said. Sandros lowered the pipe so swiftly Gregary thought he might get cracked over the head with it, but the mage just sighed.

"Not your fault. I just thought I might forget about all this for a moment." He pointed with the flute to the stone walls that surrounded them, to the pile of melted chitin and scorched meat that had been the cave's former owner. They'd been half-dead with fatigue when Sandros had dragged them down here, and when the insect began to rattle at them, Sandros had opted not to negotiate. They had no idea what it was, only that, mercifully, it wasn't another quilg. Some kind of crawling borer, it had gnawed this cavity out of solid rock. The walls bore the marks of its teeth.

"Gods, I wish one of us had kept our packs," Gregary said. His pack and armor were gone, as was his sword. He'd managed to keep his boots. Sandros had saved him, swimming to the limb and helping him out of the armor. If he hadn't, Gregary surely would have gone under once his strength was gone. They hadn't spoken of the act, as if neither of them quite believed it had really happened. They had nothing now but their lives.

158

"I should never have listened to that idiot priest. I should have made my own decision," Gregary admitted at last, and Sandros gave a slow, thoughtful nod.

"How do you like our chances of finding something to eat?" Gregary asked when Sandros did not reply.

"There's plenty to eat. A veritable feast hanging from every branch. But what is potable and what is poison? I haven't a clue."

"I suppose we'll find out when we get desperate enough," Gregary said, and at once he knew he'd said the wrong thing. The silence was heavy as lead.

It was Sandros that broke it.

"I... can offer us a clean end. If it comes to that. Pure flame, no time to feel."

Gregary shook his head swiftly, not wanting to even consider it. "We're not dead yet. We can maybe find the others, make our way out of this. We've spent long enough resting, we should get moving."

Even in darkness of the cave, he could look into Sandros' eyes and see there was no hope left in him.

"Could you play something before we go? I'll see if I can keep a lid on my stomach."

Sandros hesitated for a moment, but then he lifted the flute and began to play. The song rang back at them from the walls of the borer's cave, slow and sweet.

24

"*AAAAAAAAAAAAH!*"

Xanadros looked up from his desk as the screaming woman unfolded from a swirl of darkness. A moment later, Ink slipped from the Void without a sound. Osolin screamed on and on, wailing as if she were being boiled in oil. Xan was on his feet, headed for his medicine shelf, but Ink waved him away.

"Oh stop it. I do that all the time, it's nothing. A dozen times a day. You'll simply have to get used to it."

The words gave Osolin no comfort, she only screamed louder, which neither Xan nor Ink had thought possible.

"What's this all about? Why is she here?" Xan demanded, roaring above the caterwauling.

Immediately, the wailing stopped, and they both knew at once why he usually spoke so softly. Xan's raised voice was a commanding rasp that could halt a tavern brawl or bring a battle to a standstill. All flint and nails and broken glass, it set shoulders hunching and spines shivering like fingernails on slate.

Ink winced, and Osolin shrank back from him on her hands and knees, trying to disappear. Xan's bright green eyes were upon her, looking out from a face as black as Ink's. She wanted to flee, but there was nowhere to go.

"Found this one washed up on a riverbank, about two seconds away from being lanced by a redring. Figured she wasn't ready to be a mother. She's weak, needs food and rest."

"Why all the screaming?"

"She's a baby about traversing the Void."

"You *KILLED* me! Dragged me across the plains of death for centuries! I saw the most horrible things—" Osolin was pale and her red eyes were wide.

"Please don't be melodramatic. It's just a little jaunt through the shadow. You let your imagination run away with you. There will be many more, trust me."

"I'll never go back! I'd rather die!"

"Would you?" Ink asked. She'd drawn her veil, and she smiled with a row of jet black teeth. Osolin's mouth shut.

"Why would you bring her here?" Xanadros asked. He seemed as relieved as the two women not to have to shout.

"It's part of my plan."

"Has she seen..."

"No. And it doesn't matter anyway. She belongs to me now."

"Oh gods above. Fucking magicians, forever enslaving and ensorcelling. All you care about is power over others," Xan said bitterly.

For a moment, Ink stood there with her eyes wide, looking like he'd run her through. But the expression fell from her face, leaving only a blank and soulless landscape of black.

"It's only a means to an end," she said, cold and distant.

"And what is that end?"

"I thought I might come out here to land a rich husband, settle down and raise a litter of cursed children. Set up a quaint little cottage in the Kalparcimex and grow old together." Ink's voice dripped with venomous sarcasm.

"And you need to ensorcel this woman for that."

"I'm not good at cooking and cleaning."

"Is there a real reason or is this all just a joke to you?"

"I honestly thought I would help these dolts save their ratshit little town and maybe see some sights along the way. I'd never even seen a bashyskyla before. How could I know which legends were true and which weren't?"

"If you want to go save Joymont, go and save Joymont. Then do it again in two years, when more tinks come, then two years after that. Then whenever a larse decides to wander in and flatten half of their town looking for a place to nest, or a wink burns down the other half trying to hunt the larse… if you want to spend the rest of your life trying to turn the tide, you can go there and plow the sea. I told them what was coming and they spat on me for it."

"So there's nothing to be done?"

"You want to do something good? Really? Go to Joymont and scare them all away. Rain darkness and curses on them, drive them to the sea. Sell them to the Wyrth wholesale if you have to. I promise you it will be kinder by far than what awaits them."

Osolin's eyes gleamed with anger at the remark but neither of them paid her any mind.

"And I thought I was the cold-hearted one."

The ranger and the mage glared at each other while Osolin looked unhappily between the two, wondering what the hell she'd gotten into.

The first sting had come before the black mage's bane hit the water, a fiery jolt in his shoulder. He'd shrugged it off, thinking the pain was a small price to pay to be free of the sorcerous taint. Before he was on dry land, something else had bitten him in the knee, on the back of his heel, and he felt a twinge on his ear. When he raised a hand to his head, he pulled off a tick as big as a copper coin. His spine squirmed with revulsion and he flicked the thing onto the ground and smashed it with his mace, but when he pulled the mace back, the thing was crawling out of the dent he'd made in the wet earth, making for his bare foot. He stepped hastily over it, then stifled a cry as something bit him directly on top of the first bite on his shoulder.

Brakkar called out to the Bloodstar to shield him from the accursed pests, looking up to the endless green of the canopy overhead, but the god was silent. Nothing came but more stings.

With every step he took, something new bit him. He slapped and slapped, but there were always more. When something stung him on the eyelid, his left eye began to swell shut. Another got him on the knuckle of his ring finger. Its poison was pure burning agony. He shrieked, feeling as if his hand had been struck by lightning.

Why had he thrown the bane into the river? If he'd simply set it down, he could go back and find it, he could save himself. He'd thought the Red Giant would approve, would armor him in its place, but his cries went unanswered. The final confrontation he'd envisioned, standing atop a pile of vanquished beasts, roaring his defiance... it was a childish dream. Instead, he would be devoured on his feet, brought low by ten thousand tiny stings. As he stumbled forward and batted at himself with his hands, his frantic movements drew more and more insects until he was swarmed so thickly he could barely see the ground in front of him.

His next step sunk calf-deep into mud, and for a moment, he feared that he would sink into quicksand, then he felt a frantic, animal desire to do just that, to burrow under the muck, anything to get away from the pain. Yowling from another of the lightning stings, he leapt into the mud, rolling in it like a swine to try and evade the swarm.

For a moment, the cool, wet mud was the greatest balm in the world, and he wallowed until it coated him from head to toe. Beneath the coating, the stings itched on, some too fiercely to ignore. As he scratched, insects dove at the flesh his fingers exposed. Carefully, he slathered more mud on, swiping a hand over his eyes constantly to keep the biters out. Now he knew why the ranger dressed as he did, why Xan had scoffed at them when they entered the jungle unprotected.

Beneath his armor of muck, his skin crawled and burned, and he twitched with every step he took, fighting the urge to rip and tear at his flesh. But it worked. Some insects still found chinks to sting him, but not enough to kill him outright. He staggered forward without direction, step after agonizing step.

Again and again he called out to the Bloodstar for guidance, but there was no answer.

The terror of the shadow plane faded as quickly as a dream, the details melted to nothing, and only a vague formless dread remained. Perhaps the things she'd seen really had been phantoms, hallucinations brought on by stress or fatigue. The gods knew she'd suffered enough of both.

Xan and Ink were fighting.

Like a child caught between two quarreling parents, Osolin shrank within herself, hugging her knees with her back against a pillar of stone. They'd moved away from her and stood on the other side of the cavern whispering at each other, trying to stay out of earshot. Over the endless burbling of the spring and the dripping of water, she could catch only little bits of their argument. Yet she could hear their tones, if not their words, and their postures said much.

Xanadros was angry.

He stood straight, staring down at Ink, and the back of his head never moved. His tone was calm but demanding, and it said *This is the way things will be.* Ink's posture was all excuses, she would turn her face from him, or cast her eyes at the floor. Once or twice, Osolin could hear anger in Ink's murmurs, see her hands grab at the sides of her robe and ball into fists, but the ranger was unaffected as a statue. How strange it was to see her without the upper hand, almost cowed!

Why does she let him talk to her like that? Osolin wondered. She'd seen firsthand the black mage's power, surely she could end the ranger with a word. She wondered if the ranger could be Ink's father, surely he scolded her like it. And both had that coal black skin, perhaps they were Amechee.

"Only the mage matters. He's the one who can do real damage..."

As Xan spoke, Ink looked past him for a moment and caught Osolin watching them. The hangdog expression dropped off her face as if a curtain had fallen, and the blank stare of those pure black eyes unnerved her. Osolin could not look away quickly enough.

She only pretends to be shamed... what is she playing at?

Osolin looked around the chamber, taking in the firefly globes, the shelves, the spring, the stairs that were too far away to run for it. On the floor, she could see the little black footprints the black mage had left everywhere. There were tracks all around the chamber, leading to the spring and then back, circling the desk... and at once Osolin knew Ink had not been here long at all, for the tracks would be trails, the floor would have lines of black instead of individual prints. It made sense. This was too much a man's lair, and a solitary man at that. The cavern was cold, the furniture was all artless and utilitarian, the bed was just a pallet on the floor and...

She saw the black handprints on the floor around the pallet, the blankets stained with swaths of black.

Oh. They're fucking.

They hadn't acted like lovers on the boat over. But now that she knew to look for it, it was unmistakable. They weren't squabbling, they were smoldering. Ink's demure act, Xan's stern tone, it was all just a prelude to more screwing. She was half-worried they would go at it right in front of her.

But their voices raised, and perhaps it truly was an argument after all.

"You can't just leave her here alone, she'll try to escape and die."

"Nonsense, she is bound to me. She'll do *anything* I say."

The emphasis made Osolin's eyes flash with alarm, but Ink ignored her.

"I'll go and take care of them. I didn't want to do it this way," Xanadros said wearily. If Ink had been making an offer, he had refused it unequivocally.

Ink said nothing as the ranger stalked over to the workbench and cast off his robe, wearing nothing underneath. His whole body was jet black. Osolin could not help but raise her eyebrows at the sight.

Did she do that to him? Osolin thought of the stain on Sandros' hand that had never faded. An evil so profound her skin could not contain it.

Her eyes lingered on Xanadros as he dressed in his jungle suit, wondering, until Ink caught her looking. Instantly she cast her eyes down at the floor, her cheeks burning. When she dared to look up again, he was slinging his bow over his shoulder and making for the stairs.

He means to kill them, she realized.

"Don't!" she cried, and both of them turned toward her. "Don't kill them. Please."

"I don't want to. But they're fools, and fools don't listen. I warned you all this would happen."

She had no strength to fight him, she could only stare hopelessly.

With those words, he disappeared up the stairs, and the quiet he left behind grew more and more unbearable. Silently, Ink drifted across the room and then loomed over her. If she were standing, Osolin would be almost a head taller than the mage. She got the sense the Ink enjoyed being above her, that there was a secret grin behind those black eyes.

"You don't speak anymore unless spoken to," Ink said flatly.

Go fuck yourself. She'd meant to say it, meant to shout it right in that black face, but the words would not come. Desperately, she tried to speak, tried to scream, but her tongue would not obey.

"Much better. Now let's get you a bath. You're filthy."

Ink walked toward the spring, and Osolin tried everything she could to resist, gritting her teeth, balling her fists, but she found herself rising anyway. She locked her legs, trying to keep herself from moving toward the stream, and nearly toppled. It hurt, hurt badly to try to resist the order. The longer she tried, the worse it was, until she would have screamed in agony if her mouth were her own. It felt like she was being ripped apart, like her bones were trying to walk ahead without the rest of her, tearing their way out of her flesh.

"Now."

With one word, all pretense at resistance was gone, and her body hastened to comply with Ink's demand. The pain disappeared completely, its absence an icy wonderful bliss that made her shudder. Stupidly, she hoped Ink didn't notice, but of course, the mage's eyes were on her, a tiny knowing grin at the corner of her mouth.

Oh gods, what have I done...

"Undress and get in. And start doing what I want without being told, it's tiresome to order you about."

Osolin was caked with muck, and silt seemed to have worked its way everywhere. Still, she hesitated. She did not want to disrobe in front of the mage, did not want to be ordered about like a child.

"...Release me..." she said in one exhalation that cost her everything. Immediately she doubled over as if she'd been punched in the gut. She sank onto her knees, tears squeezing from her eyes, and began to sob silently.

"This isn't me hurting you. You do it to yourself." Ink sat in front of her, cross-legged, and fixed Osolin with her all-black gaze.

"Do you want to know a secret? The ones who resist hardest are the ones who submit completely in the end. Their defiance is a sham, they long to be ruled. Isn't that funny?"

Again Osolin tried to protest, but she could not even squeak out a sound. Pain washed over her, so bright and blinding it drowned out everything else. For a moment, in that discordant space, she thought she saw an exit, a place that hurt so badly she could not return from it, but it was only a glimpse, and it vanished as the world rushed back in. She had slumped face-first onto the stone floor, her eyes staring half-focused at a black footprint, her whole body quivering as if everything had cramped up at once.

"A strong will. But utterly misplaced."

She had to let go, she had nothing left to fight this with. Gloved hands were on her, tugging her shirt off, stripping off her leggings, and she lay limp and naked on the floor, the memory of pain reverberating through her body.

"Get in or I will throw you in," Ink ordered. "I'm not in the mood for play."

Osolin could only crawl to the edge of the spring, and then she slumped into it, gladly taking the shock of cold water over the pain of resistance. There was a moment of panic when she sank and felt nothing under her, a memory of the rushing black water, and she kicked her legs furiously to get to the surface and gulped air.

"Now wash." Ink nodded toward a wedge of soap that rested at the lip of the spring.

The mage's eyes never left Osolin as she worked the grit from her scalp and behind her ears, beneath her arms. When she went to replace the soap, Ink shook her head.

"Everywhere."

Osolin's cheeks burned, and she looked away as she swiftly washed between her legs, returning the soap only when Ink nodded her approval. When the mage grinned, something in Osolin snapped, and she ducked her head under the water and began to swim down toward the dark mouth of the spring. Furiously, she kicked her way down, feeling the pressure building on her ears and nose, thinking only that if she got far enough away, she would be beyond the reach of Ink's magic. In the instant of decision, a clean death by drowning had seemed far better than life as a slave. It was a long, long way down.

But as she got deeper and felt the air in her lungs shrinking away to nothing, she knew in a panicked instant that she was wrong. Nothing was worse than the darkness closing in all around her, and she'd gone very deep indeed. Looking up, she could just barely see the light of the cave above, and the frenzied strength that had carried her down was gone. Twisting around, she kicked for the surface, but it seemed to get no closer.

I can't make it! Though she was still fighting toward the surface, it seemed like it was farther and farther away. Hopelessly, she wondered if Ink would dive in to save her. Everything was fading away, and she could not feel anymore to know if her legs were still kicking.

The darkness had nearly swallowed her when her head broke free, and she choked and nearly drowned trying to suck in air. Ink only watched as she dragged herself out of the spring. Osolin expected to see a mocking grin on the black mage's face, but there was nothing there, no emotion at all.

"Anytime you want. Only your life belongs to me. Your death is your own."

She left Osolin there, naked and cold on the stone floor, and went to scrounge something to eat.

25

The words rolled on the back of Sandros' tongue. Words that would blossom into petals of radiant light, words that would sear and scorch. He held them in his mind with great effort. If he let them slip into meaninglessness, or succumb to semantic satiation for even a second, they would lose all power. If he let the weirdness surrounding them capture his attention totally, the spell he was holding ready would vanish.

Jing-jing!

It happened so fast. Two eyes shot open and the air whistled with the talons scything at them. The words Sandros had nursed so carefully were loosed, snapping out of his mouth and popping in the air like burning wood. Red flowers bloomed before the hroradrora's wide eyes, and the fireball caught it mid-pounce, blasting it backward. It landed on its back, its face black and withered, the rest of its body still trying to ape the fireball, turning a thousand shades of white, orange, and red. As it died, the colors slowly drained away.

"Cover me," Sandros said, the words falling from his mouth like lead, and Gregary nodded, raising the point of his makeshift spear. A pitiful thing, really, a branch with a point scraped into it with a rock and hardened by fire. Both knew the spear was useless, sure to snap in two long before it even dented the armor of these insects, but neither brother mentioned it.

Gregary needed to hold something, needed to feel like he could at least try to fight back. If a pointy stick gave Gregary confidence, Sandros wasn't going to spoil it for him. The red mage was on his knees, trying to gather his strength. Their many encounters since leaving the borer's hole had all ended in immolation. But calling the flames took its toll. Noon was long gone, and they needed shelter, needed water and food. They'd found nothing but more ambushes, more beasts trying to devour them. Slowly, Sandros began to rise.

Jing-jing! Jing-jing! Jing-jing!

"No..."

When Gregary heard Sandros whisper the word instead of a spell, he knew it was over. He hadn't had time to recover, there would be no fire to save them this time. With a howl of pure frustration, Gregary thrust the spear toward the ringing, all his strength behind it. He felt it drive home and the spear wrenched backward, dragging him with it.

He hit the ground and felt it shake under him, and he wondered if this was Sandros calling the pure flame, if the earth would open up to swallow them. Then he saw movement at his side and heard a hissing in the air, saw a flash of light. Somehow, Sandros had found the fire.

Gregary scrambled to his feet. His spear had snapped in half, and he held the end of it, looking around for something to club. Sandros had fallen to his hands and knees, the smoldering corpse of a hroradrora nearby. Looking down, Gregary saw that he'd speared the other through the eye somehow, it lay on the ground, going through the final display that had become so familiar.

There had been three rings, he was sure of it, and there was an acrid smell in the air. As he turned, looking for threats, he saw it. A giant insect, so huge they must have passed right by it, thinking it was a hill. Its sides were covered in moss and vines, colonies of mushrooms and countless scuttling insects, but as it moved they could see each great segment shift. They saw the horned head, three ruby red eyes gazing back at them. Sandros and Gregary froze as the thing lumbered toward them, the ground leaping beneath their feet with every step.

The third hroradrora was fizzing and melting five paces from them, taken by a gout of acid.

"How do you... Fire..." The words began as a buzzing dirge and then resolved into words with a twang like the string of a guitar. On the sides of the thing's head they could see gill-like ridges fluttering. They could do nothing but gape at the behemoth.

"Hard talk... long time..." it said, just ten paces away from them, the voice so loud they could feel it rattling in their teeth. "Long time. Strange words." The sounds were becoming more and more intelligible, the beast was shaking the dust off its ability to talk. There was something oddly familiar about its voice, but the way it spoke, just a word at a time, made it impossible to pin down.

"How? How fire?"

"Magic," Sandros said. It was just one word, but still his voice broke halfway through it, his whole body trembling. At his side, the stick had slipped from Gregary's hand, and the warrior was mouthing little senseless prayers to the Sword of the Stars.

"Tell me. Teach me." It lowered its volume after seeing them cringe with every word. It was still thunderously loud, but not so bad that their heads were in danger of splitting open.

"It uh... it isn't easy. It takes a long time."

"Have forever," rumbled the bashyskyla.

It had seemed so easy when Xanadros had done it, a little of this jar, a little of that, and then abracadabra, perfect eggs. When Ink tried to do the same, a column of fire she could feel but not see roared up from the tray. If she hadn't been leaning back, she would have been engulfed. Desperately, she tried to add more of the other liquid to balance it out, but that only made things worse. She had to flee as the tray spat globs of invisible flame around the cave to crackle on the floor. For a long time, the reaction hissed and spat, and both of their mouths made Os of stunned disbelief as the floating pan warped, folding in half like a clam before it melted into slag. When the fire finally burned down, it was clear nothing would ever be cooked in that pan again.

"Stars piss on saints, he'll be furious," Ink said. For a moment, there was genuine fear in her voice, and Osolin wondered how much of the ranger's ire she would share. But then Ink seemed to shrug it all off.

"I wonder if he'll whip me," she mused, and the fear was gone, a sly grin taking its place. "Let's see if he's got anything that doesn't need cooking."

It took some rummaging, but she put together bittersweet black jam on dried traveling biscuits and some jerky that was so salty and spicy they both had to stop mid-meal and rush to the spring for water. Tears of pain sprang up in Osolin's eyes, but she was so famished that she ate it all, then let her head roll back with her mouth open, as if she could breathe out the heat in a gout of fire. She was wrapped in a blanket—after washing her clothes in the stream, she'd left them on rocks to dry.

"Gods, how can he eat that? If I didn't know better, I'd say his tongue were made of tin." The sorceress winked, inviting confidence, but Osolin just stared back angrily, holding her plate between two hands. If only it were pottery instead of tin, she could fling it, maybe catch the mage off guard.

"It doesn't have to be this way," Ink said, moving toward her. "I protected you. I saved you." Her voice was warm, but Osolin knew better than to trust her. She'd seen the mage's masks, seen her cast them away without a thought.

Osolin moved to speak, and then the memory of the pain stilled her tongue. Ink nodded, bidding her to continue.

"I... I fought so hard to be free. I escaped, I cut a man's eyes out for presuming to be my master. Don't do this to me. I don't want to be a slave," Osolin said, struggling to keep her voice even. It was hard, with the tears from the spice in her eyes, with the black mage an arm's length away.

"You do," Ink said. "This is what you wanted. This is who you are. I wouldn't have taken you if not."

How deep those words cut!

"That isn't true. That's not me," Osolin protested. She had traveled the whole breadth of the Lake, risen from the slums of Infractus. Her mind filled with the images of men she'd stood up to, men who had underestimated her and died for it. Lovers who could not hold her down, used and discarded. Wounds she had taken, battles she had fought, all of it shouting to the world who she was, a woman who could not be mastered. Nobody's slave. But the sorceress looked at her as if she were nothing at all.

"I'll show you. Get on your knees," Ink ordered. Something in the way she said it had Osolin moving toward the ground before she even realized it.

She checked the impulse, and then the pain came, wrenching and terrible. She was rooted to the spot, the hurt rolling up her body in waves, crashing against her until she thought she would shatter. She cried out, senseless and wild, until there was nothing left in her but pain, and then Ink snapped her fingers and it was gone. Her eyes shut tightly, Osolin gasped with relief.

"Again. Get on your knees."

Without even thinking, she fell onto her knees before the pain could reach her, and found herself looking up in confusion. The stone was cold and hard against her bare knees. There was a little voice at the back of her mind urging defiance, calling for her to rise and strike the mage. Behind it was the fear, fear of that awful pain, but they were both just quiet whispers. Foremost was the hope that she had done it right, that she had knelt quickly enough to please Ink, a warm and welling feeling.

"Wasn't that easier?"

It was. Osolin was revulsed by her desire to please, and the backlash was swift, hating this place, hating the mage, but most of all hating herself. Hating that part of her. She wanted to tear herself apart, to rip herself in half to get it out. But when her arms rose to rend her cheeks, they instead circled the black mage's legs. For an instant, both women were confused, but then she buried her face in Ink's robes and sobbed. It broke something in her, to cling to Ink, to weep into her skirts like a child, and everything else began to drain through the crack.

Ink stroked Osolin's hair with her gloved hand, cradling her head and waiting for it to pass. When it was over, Osolin was hollow, and when Ink took her by the hand and led her over to the sleeping pallet, she simply followed. The mage laid her down on the pallet and there were flashes of fear, urges to run, but they seemed distant, they belonged to some other person. She rolled onto her side, not to defy, but simply because she could not face what she thought was to come. Surely there was some depravity to follow.

Ink simply climbed onto the pallet behind her, then drew close and embraced her. For a long time, Osolin lay still, her heart thundering against Ink's glove, and she tried not to respond, to be perfectly stiff.

"Now we can begin. The hard part is over," Ink whispered, holding her tighter.

The woman had enslaved her, but she was still warm, still a body holding her, and Osolin was a long, long way from home. By tiny degrees, she began to succumb to the fatigue and torment, and at last, sleep found her, curled in the arms of her captor.

It didn't take long to place the strange familiarity in the words of Yither the bashyskyla. It was Xan's voice, each word pronounced exactly as he'd said it. Beads of the ranger's voice, strung one after the other by a beast a hundred times his size. It was odd, but everything here was. The alien jungle had long ago exhausted their appreciation for novelty.

"The spiders, they have magic. But it is not magic for me, I can not make... bind... net..." When Yither said "magic," the word was in Sandros' voice. Perhaps Xan had never said the word. Yither had stalled out. When it did not have a word, the bashyskyla clicked three times.

"Webs?" Gregary offered. He had gotten over his initial terror faster than Sandros. That was one thing he was good at, conquering fear.

"Webs." It used Gregary's voice for the new word. "Their magic is in their webs. Webs I cannot make. But your magic is in words. Words I have."

"But it isn't just saying the words. It's the understanding behind them, the conviction... It's..." Sandros struggled to complete the thought. "My master once called magery 'speaking falsehood so convincingly that reality itself is fooled.' If it were simply repeating words, everyone could do it."

The great insect's head turned slightly to the right.

"Smaller words," it ordered, and for a moment, Sandros was at a loss for how to make his point.

"Here. Try this."

Sandros spoke a word of power, and a single spark rose in the air, spiraling upward into the green canopy above.

"Now you."

Yither repeated the word exactly, and no spark came.

"You try, Gregary."

Gregary tried as well, his pronunciation so poor that Sandros winced, half-expecting the Scourer to pop out from nowhere and beat them black and blue for profaning the arcane tongue. Would he never be free of the old man's ghost?

"So you see? I can teach, but I do not know if you can learn. It is not enough to speak, one must know." Sandros had to check himself twice, trying to speak more simply.

"There is no sense in your words." The bashyskyla's rumble was louder now, and its head moved slightly from side to side. For a single awful instant, Sandros and Gregary were both certain they were about to die.

Instead, Yither thundered forward and began to eat the hroradrora. Each corpse was gone in two bites, the bashyskyla's teeth crunching through their shells with a crack like a falling tree, gobbling them while smoke hissed from the ridges on either side of its head. The display did nothing to calm the brothers' nerves. The bashyskyla turned back to Sandros and fixed him with its unblinking triangle of ruby eyes.

"It took me years and years to learn, and it seemed the same to me at first, all nonsense. It will take time. But I will try."

"Should not be so long. Bashyskyla are greater than men."

Looking up at the massive insect, Sandros and Gregary could only nod their heads.

26

This way...

He'd been bitten by an armored serpent, or a plated eel, it swam away too quickly for him to tell. But the poison remained, simmering in his blood, boiling in his brain. He'd called for the Giant, tried to purge the venom, but miracles were in short supply, it seemed. He did not die, but the world spun with every step, trees in the distance shrank and fled as he stumbled forward, and those at his sides loomed impossibly high, with shadows of things that could not be dancing in the spaces between them.

... This way...

It was not a voice, just a feeling. He knew not if it was the Star or mere hallucination, but he plodded toward it anyway, for he had nowhere else to go. Under the thick ceiling of leaves, he could not even tell where the sun was, and he dared not climb high enough to find out. All he could do was strike a tree with the mace every so often, a mark to keep himself from moving in circles. Was this how it ended? Ground down to nothing by poison and fatigue?

...here here here...

He heard wood cracking and feet scuttling ahead and drifted forward, carried along on a stream of drugged lightheadedness.

Ahead, a four-legged beast was chewing through a stump, splinters flying as it took great gnashing bites, whipping its head from side to side and flinging hunks of wood in every direction. As it did, tongues darted out of its mouth to snatch grubs and larvae dislodged by its frantic attack, so fast it became it a patter, fap-fap-fap-fap.

...no no no...

The call was coming from that stump. Somehow, the beast devouring it had to be stopped. It was the size of a large boar, its shell riddled with barnacles sprouting green waving stalks. As Brakkar approached the recipitor from behind, the stalks shrank back into their holes. The wild recipitor paid him no mind, completely absorbed in its feast. He looked blearily at the beast, surely he had no strength to fight it. But the voice he heard, it must be the Star. For Tyrias he could be strong.

...help!...

Brakkar's head cleared as he lifted the mace and drew close to the beast, then he brought it down on the thing with a great thump of steel on chitin, expecting it to collapse under the weight of the blow.

Instead, the strike was turned away by the thick armor and the beast ignored him completely, still gorging itself on the stump. The insistence gnawing at Brakkar grew stronger, it had to be stopped!

His head ringing with alarm, Brakkar took the mace in both hands and delivered a downward strike with everything he had, aiming for the same place. This time it landed true, and there was a loud crack as the plate crunched under the blow. The beast shrieked and twisted to kick Brakkar with its back leg. The kick drove the breath out of him and sent him stumbling backward. The wild recipitor was as strong as an ox. It wheeled at him, abandoning the stump, but then its front leg gave out and it sprawled on the ground with a horrible whine.

Brakkar hadn't grinned like this since... since the spring? Since the ball beetles? Whenever it had been, he was grinning now, though his head was swimming from the poison and the gut kick, though he wobbled a little as he stood. His foe had ignored him, underestimated him, and now it was crippled. Now it would die.

The recipitor thought otherwise, and as he advanced to finish it off, it shifted its weight to the other three legs and pounced. But the shift gave away its spring and Brakkar was ready. He swung the mace in both hands, and again, he gave it all he had, splitting the air with a furious roar. This was the way to die, in glorious battle.

The beast had just opened its mouth in mid-air to bite when the barbed mace blasted into the side of its head and obliterated it. The recipitor's armored head shattered like a clay jug, bits of shell and brain sprayed across the clearing. It was probably dead before it hit the ground, but Brakkar made sure, raining down blows until the recipitor's legs stopped twitching and its head was little more than bloody paste.

Triumph sang in his veins like fire and his head began to clear. He looked down at the shattered corpse, wondering if he could eat it. He felt he could devour the whole world, crunch it between his teeth, and spit fire at the gods.

...here here here...

From the stump, the call resumed. The one he'd saved. The exhilaration drained away as he moved forward, and he found that the strength he'd felt was only a cruel illusion. He made it only a few steps before he slumped to his knees and retched, with nothing to give. The mace tumbled into the dirt. Why wouldn't the Red Giant heal him? He'd fought to the last, vanquished foes, cast away the sorcerer's taint. He'd done everything right.

Doubt twisted in him. The star had no power here, no power anywhere. It was a fraud, just like the firemountain. It seemed like the trees around him were closing in, like they would topple at any moment and crush him. The same gravity was pulling him toward the ground, toward the carpet of moss and leaves that would swallow him gladly, carry him down to darkness.

...come come come...

"My faith... I will not break!" Brakkar hissed, his tongue heavy in his mouth. "Sanguis!"

Slowly, he put one hand in front of the other, shuffling his knees forward, crawling toward the stump. At last he made it there and found only a broken tree, scored by the teeth of the recipitor. The surviving grubs and insects had burrowed deeper, leaving only pinholes.

Dumbly, he stared down, wondering what the hell it was all about. Was it all just a phantasm? A final idiot whim? Would he die peering into a stump?

A crack formed at the heartwood of the stump and blood began to well from it. He gasped. Surely this was his sign! As he stared, transfixed, he saw insect legs rise from the crack, prying it apart.

With incredible delicate slowness, it emerged, and he could not tear his eyes away. One by one, it unfolded its legs, and began to clean the blood from itself. As it dried, it looked like nothing so much as a living ruby: colored a deep, translucent red, the lines of its body perfectly edged like facets.

Brakkar was not one for art, scenery did not move him, and women were just something to fuck and discard. But he was spellbound by the sight before him. His pulse pounded in his ears, and the death awaiting him seemed to matter less now that he had seen this. He barely breathed for fear of spoiling this moment.

...want...

She was looking at him with all of her many eyes, and the feeling plunged into him, his mouth hanging open in shock. She wanted something, something from him, and he felt a surging desire to give it to her, a thrill at being selected, acknowledged by this beauty. His hand trembled as he moved it toward the stump, setting it down at the edge, not trusting himself to draw too close to her. He felt as if he might die the instant she touched him, and he didn't care. She crawled toward him, every step taking an eternity, and when she touched his fingertip with her foreleg, his mind exploded with joy.

Each step she took, climbing up his finger to his hand, was a point of pure pleasure rippling through his entire body. As she climbed up his arm, he wondered how much he could take. His heart was ringing in his chest like a bell, his bones thrummed, and his flesh seemed as if it might spread out into this perfect feeling and melt away.

When she made her way to the back of his neck and began to burrow into him, he cried in ecstasy, all his senses flooding, his ears deafened by a pure, perfect note, his eyes flooded with brilliant light, every color at once. His spirit sang, even as the world vanished. He was the one. He had been *chosen*.

Two songs ran through the Kalparcimex, one chasing after the other, and a great multitude of heads cocked at the sound, trying to place the strange music—was it predator or prey? A few juvenile daggerflies sought to find out, the whine of their wings zipped toward the source of the song. Then they saw the bashy-skyla and turned their bladed tails and fled.

Sandros sat on the lip of one half of a broken eggshell that was big enough to hold a full-grown ox. It was full of rainwater, moss, and a whole village of crayfish grappling and scuttling beneath the clear water. The shell itself was nearly half a foot thick, and Sandros shuddered to think of the babe that could break its way through that to be born. He was playing, his fingers dancing across the blackened holes of his scorched flute so quickly they were just a blur. As the song went on, it grew more and more complex until at last he had to shut his eyes. He needed every bit of his concentration for this. Sweat ran down his temples in rivulets.

The song was the Third Flute of the Terhaljatani Anthem, a fiendishly difficult piece. The Mad Prince himself had penned the anthem as a jape to confound his musicians, baffle his foes, and vex the leaders of other cities. It was five times longer than any other kingdom's anthem, and a dozen times more complex, requiring nearly two hundred musicians to perform the full composition.

The tale went that when his bandmaster protested the arrangement for violin, claiming it was impossible to play, the Prince seized the violin and bow right out of his hands and performed the entire piece, note for note, and then for the finale, smashed the violin against the bandmaster's skull, leaving him witless until the end of his days.

The whole anthem had not been heard since the fall of Terhaljatan. Superstition said that if the entire song was performed, the Mad Prince would be there at the finale. But there was little danger of this, as no city of the lake had an orchestra even half that large. Instead, the anthem lived on in its individual parts. They were given as assignments to humble overconfident students, played by rivals in musical duels, and used as show-ending pieces to wow yokels.

For Sandros, it served another purpose, something that was hopefully so complex the bashyskyla could not mimic it. He'd tried a dozen things to teach Yither the difference between mimicry and actually forming words, without success. At first, the bashyskyla had kept up easily, whistling the tune right back at him, flicking its mandibles in what Sandros thought might be contempt. If it weren't for the flute at his lips, Sandros would have smiled, for he knew what was to come.

Now the piece truly began.

As the minutes passed, the bashyskyla slowly trailed off, for the tempo went faster and faster until the notes came in an avalanche, a barrage of sound that left the mind reeling and the soul muddled. Only one song played now. The bashyskyla could not hope to keep up with this. The song ended with three clear notes ringing into the canopy, and Sandros lowered the flute and wiped the sweat from his brow.

"I cannot hold it. There is too much," the bashyskyla said. Sandros was breathing too heavily to respond at first.

"That is only the first part. There are seven," he said, still slightly out of breath. "I can play them all, but I'm too hungry and weak right now."

"Why do you show me this thing? To mock me?"

"No... to show you the limits of the way you speak. This is only a song. If you miss a note, or cannot hold the whole thing in your mind at once, it only spoils the song. A spell can destroy everything around you, it can kill you."

"Nothing kills bashyskyla."

"Untrue," a third voice said, and Xanadros unraveled from the brush, the threads of distortion twisting their way back into his beetleshell cloak. Gregary picked up his club, and Sandros readied a spell, but the bashyskyla seemed unconcerned.

"Xanadros. I hear you felled Wiyitrup at last. Long we suffered him, you have our thanks."

"I did it because he threatened the order, not because you don't like him."

"I care not for the cause, only that he is dead, and good riddance. May we never know a tyrant like him again. Why did you not tell me this one was a magician? I would not have gone to the inner if I had known, I would have sought him out."

"That's why I didn't tell you, Yither. I remember when you captured Redfish Robbis and tried to have him teach you alchemy. Or that gatherer from Yind who used to be a painter, it didn't end well for that one either, did it?"

"He angered me with his impertinence. Redfish Robbis was a fool. He died of a..." Yither clicked three times.

"A velveteen slitherine. You're talking better, by the way."

"I have been talking with these two all day. Your language is simple, barely more advanced than lieflies. Sandros is a far better teacher than you."

"I can believe it. He doesn't know the danger. Hasn't got a fucking inkling what he's doing." Xan stared at Sandros, expecting him to wither, but Sandros was too tired, he'd fought too long to care.

"Scribe. Your thief is alive, but Ink has ensorcelled her and claimed her as a slave. I think she will free her when she tires of her, but who knows with that one?"

184

"Better than death, I suppose." Sandros sighed, he'd given everything to the song. "We can't fight the black mage, she would destroy us utterly."

"She isn't the only one," Xan said, nodding at the bashyskyla.

"Yither has agreed to come to Joymont with us to destroy the tinks," Gregary said, oblivious to the threat, actually cheerful. "Have you got any food?"

"Oh gods."

Xanadros put a palm to his forehead, and rubbed his scalp through the mask, shaking his head from side to side.

"Yes, with Wiyitrup gone, I am free at last to leave the Kalpa. This one will teach me his magic, and I shall happily eat his tinks. Then I shall finally see the Lake you have told me of, the great cities, the fine castles. All will benefit."

"Wait… it was Wiyitrup keeping you bottled all this time?"

"Wiyitrup was the alpha of the outer. We could only go east to the limit of his territory, and he is slow to nest, slow to abandon his old nests, still keeping the choicest mates for himself. There are many like me who were impatient, many who would go further but the tyrant cared nothing for what others desired. Wiyitrup would suffer no intruders. Two died trying to pass, and since then none have tried. It is a great thing you have done for us."

Xan stood there with a hand against his brow as if he'd been struck. Slowly he shook his head from side to side.

"Sandros, may I speak with you privately?"

"No, I would prefer to live," Sandros said, edging sideways so there was a clear line between the bashyskyla and Xan.

"Have I told you anything false? Did I not warn you that Ink would dump you, that the jungle would ruin you? Remember how I said the plot to bring a bashyskyla out of the Kalpa was the greatest folly?"

"And yet here we have a bashyskyla ready to come and save Joymont. We've made a deal. It is done."

For a time, Xan was silent behind the mask, determining the best approach.

"How much money have you got?"

"None."

"Ten cows a day in meat. Or better. That's what he eats, and if he doesn't get it, he'll start eating people. We're prey to him. How are you going to get ten cows a day all the way back to Joymont with no money?"

"We'll have to steal them, I suppose. It's for a good cause."

"Good enough to slay a dozen men on the way to Joymont? Because those ranchers won't give up their cattle without a fight. They're hard men who know how to live near the Kalpa. Then there's their families to think about. I guess they'll starve too. But that's just fine, because you don't know them. They're not under your king's banner."

The brothers looked ashen-faced. Of course they hadn't considered the logistics. How could they?

"What is a cow?" Yither asked, indicating it was a question by spreading his mandibles.

"Big four-legged idiot grazers. The size of a hleiner."

"Ten hleiner isn't nearly enough. For a whole day?"

"Hleiner are all armor and thorns. Cows are just meat."

"I shall have to eat one and see."

Xan raised his chin at Sandros. *You see?*

"Yither, what will you do in Joymont once you eat all their tinks?"

"Nest, of course. It will be well past time. Their realm is far. A few circles perhaps. Then I shall move, I wish to see all of the Lake."

"A circle means about fifteen years. Do you see what you're doing? Do you know how bashyskyla nest? They dig—"

"Xanadros. Do not anger me," Yither interrupted, and its voice grew louder. "This is not your concern. Long you have overstepped your bounds, thinking the masters do not notice. Do not think that because we have suffered you, we cannot remove you."

The bashyskyla used all three men's voices for the threat, selecting words from each. Gregary and Sandros exchanged a worried look, the beast just learned so damn quickly. The lenses of the ranger's mask were pointed straight at the bashyskyla's neck. As if sensing his stare, Yither brought its head up to defend its vulnerable spot. Xan nodded, seeing his threat delivered.

"Still the same Xanadros, forever you meddle. But I am not Wiyitrup. You cannot just kill me to speed your mad quest. Kill one mad old tyrant, and no one cares. But a second? Then you are a threat. Then the others will rise. Have you forgotten what happened to you in the inner?" Yither asked, and though there was no way to hear fear in the patchwork voice, it seemed the delivery was just a bit too fast.

"I can never forget," Xan said, his voice flat, crushed by the memory.

"This is a lie. You will forget when you die, everything will be gone. It will not be long, your whole life is but a glimmer to me, a flicker in the space between two meals. I will remember a long, long time. And the great ones, they will remember forever. Always remember the ant that dared to rear up and challenge them, and the consequences that could not be otherwise."

Xanadros did not reply, only stared at the bashyskyla, while the two brothers stared at him, trying to make sense of it all.

"Now we are done," Yither rumbled. As they spoke, its head had sunk low, into the normal position. It noticed and snapped back up to protect itself. "I have not forgotten the kindness you showed me before, I will not kill you now. But if I see you again, you will die."

Xan turned his attention to the two brothers.

"Last chance to listen. This one will destroy your whole realm. Not just your crops. There will be nothing left. It will start a new Kalpa in the ashes of your kingdom."

"A fanciful lie. I have made a bargain with these two, magic for tinks. That is all. A good thing, too, for if they had no use to me, I would simply eat them."

Sandros and Gregary grew pale, and at once they knew they had no choice in the matter. They had thrown in with Yither, and he would not let them recant.

"You fools. You great, stupid fucking fools. You have no idea what you've done."

"Well, it's done. So unless you have anything to eat, good-bye," Gregary said, looking weary and defeated.

Xan spent a moment just standing there, his fury kept in check only by the three ruby red eyes that never left him.

"Here," Xan drew something from an inner pocket of his cloak and winged it at Gregary. It was jerky, wrapped in a little packet of waxed paper. Gregary sniffed at it suspiciously, but the hunger in his eyes burned as brightly as a torch.

"Enjoy your folly," Xan said, melting into the shadows as Sandros and Gregary divvied up the jerky and began to devour it, cramming their whole portions into their mouths at once.

He was long gone by the time the moans of pain and cries for water began.

It was the first time in days she'd woken up warm and clean. The arms wrapped around her, the body pressed against her back, the thighs tucked under hers, all radiated an intense, wonderful heat. Ink had drawn the splotchy blanket over them, and beneath that she still wore her robe and veil, so warm she should have glowed. In another place, it might have been too much, but in the cold damp of Xan's cave, it was perfect. It was a battle to even think about moving, but she thought this might be her chance at last.

With all the care she could muster, she slowly slipped Ink's velvet glove from her chest, and against all reason, she found she missed it.

She enslaved me. She hurt me, dragged me through hell, Osolin reminded herself, but the thoughts felt forced and thin. It would be so much easier to stay here, to bask in that warmth just a little longer... but the safety she felt in the black mage's arms was an illusion.

She slipped out of the mage's grasp, into the cold air, and made for her clothes. Her dagger was gone but there was the shiv, a three-inch metal spike hidden in her belt. The air was cold enough that she began to shiver. It took a while to work the shiv free without making a sound.

Stupid, there are knives on the workbench, I could just take one, she thought, but she remembered the invisible fire that had melted the tray. She would touch nothing here unless there was no other choice.

189

The shiv was familiar, it felt good in her hand. Too long she'd been powerless, but this steel changed that. Without a sound, she toed her way back to the pallet, taking care to avoid the mage's black footprints. Who knew what sorcery lay in them? Already, the fear was twisting hard at her insides. If Ink woke, if she missed and didn't kill the mage on her first strike... she tried not to imagine the horrors that awaited her.

Kill her quickly, don't think about it. It would not be the first time she had taken someone in their sleep, it was easy. She stood over the mage with the shiv, giving her body the order again and again to bend down and kill.

"Osolin," the mage said, and the voice pierced her like a crossbow bolt. It was a death sentence, she was awake, she *knew*.

"Drop that thing and come back to bed. It's cold without you," Ink said, not lifting her head, her back to Osolin.

The shiv clattered to the ground. Osolin stood there, struck dumb. The sorceress was not afraid, was not surprised. Osolin moved to obey as swiftly as she could, and the rush that came from obedience was tempered by terror. *I tried to kill her. She should destroy me.*

But instead, Ink wrapped her arms around Osolin again and squeezed, as if she'd come back with a drink of water instead of an assassin's blade. Ink murmured something and there was a strange, lifting sensation, as if something that had been tightly wound around Osolin had suddenly snapped. She felt so light for a moment she was nearly flying, and then it passed.

"No more, little one," Ink said sleepily, and words of protest formed but never left Osolin's mouth. "The hard part is over. I'm sorry I had to be so cruel to you. Sometimes you have to break things to put them back together true."

They clung together in the dimmed glow of the firefly globes. Ink had done something to the firefly globes, stolen their light until they were like distant candles in a fog. Everything else seemed far, far away from them, as if they rode through the black lake entwined on the sleeping mat. Osolin laid there in the gloom, her stomach churning with confusion.

"Isn't this better?" Ink asked, snuggling closer to her, surrounding her in unreasonable warmth. She could only nod. She had a sudden intense fear that Ink was about to strangle her. The mage moved closer till her veil pressed against Osolin's hair, then her lips nuzzled at her neck through the veil. The hand beneath Osolin was cupping her breast, and the fingertips of Ink's velvet glove stroked against her stomach. Osolin made a confused sound that was almost a bleat, and the mage laughed.

"Much better." Ink's voice was husky, her mouth against Osolin's ear. She could feel hot breath through the veil. Ink's fingertips traced down Osolin's side, so light they were barely there, and Osolin shuddered. She hadn't expected this, wasn't one of those women... The glove came to rest just above her bush, and she shook her head from side to side, mouthing no but unwilling to speak, her whole body tensed so hard it hurt.

"Oh, never before? Worry not, I won't do anything you don't want me to. But I could have sworn..."

The hand slipped through her hair, brushing down between her legs, and she cried out, though it barely touched her. Then Ink held up her glove, the fingertip glistening.

"Mmmhmm," she murmured, and Osolin felt as if her cheeks had burst into flame. She shut her eyes and shook with embarrassment, wishing she could shrink into nothingness.

"Don't run from it. This is what you are," Ink said, her voice soft and low.

"No..." Osolin breathed, and she winced, expecting the pain, but it didn't come.

"When you're ready," Ink whispered, and then she held her tightly, setting aside her advances. They were silent for a long time before sleep found them.

...hungry...

He could not tell if he was hungry or if she was. It was strange to have feelings that weren't his. He'd woken from... he hadn't words for what he'd felt, they would only cheapen it. The glory of battle, the thrill of victory, the women he'd lain with, they were diluted experiences, weak and worthless by comparison. Only this was true.

Now her feelings were laid atop his own, adding to them, not replacing. He'd felt her marvel as she began to see through his eyes, and he was stunned by the new sharpness, the vast splay of colors and depth he could perceive. Her own eyes were buried beneath his flesh. He'd brought a hand to the back of his neck, wanting to touch her, but she was already in him, the wound where she'd entered scabbing over. Then she began to hear as he did, and again he felt her thrill, for he was tuned to hear a different world. His heart surged with joy, as if he were watching his firstborn child learn to see and hear, and tears beaded in his eyes.

He did not know how long he'd been unconscious, but the poison was gone, and more than that, the countless lingering bites and stings that had plagued him since he'd cast away the mage's charm were no more. She had changed him somehow. There was a warmth in his blood, a sense that she was reaching out to every part of him, entwining with his insides.

...hungry...

His eyes fell on the corpse of the recipitor. Already, a host of opportunistic insects were devouring it, but as he moved toward the body, they began to flee. Astonished, he watched the frenzied migration: centipedes scuttled, fliers swarmed away, and crawlers were all but galloping at his approach.

What has she done to me, that they all fear me—us?

...eat...

He looked down at the dead recipitor, and not even the hunger of days could make it seem like something he would ever eat. Yet he felt her urging, and memories swirled from nothing, a mother whose face he could not remember, forcing him to eat something, telling him it would make him strong, the threat of the wooden spoon forever looming. For an instant, he was back

192

at that place, was that small again. She wanted him to eat the legs, the meat in them was good. He cracked them open with his mace and began to eat the pulpy sweet flesh within.

The act of eating awakened a beast within him. It was like eating an enormous crab, and he found he could not get enough. He'd eaten nearly the entire leg before he slowed, though he was still hungry. There was an aftertaste building, a pain spreading through his gut that told him he'd been poisoned again. Then the embers in his veins rekindled, and he reclined to lie flat on his back with his hands over his belly. For a long time he laid there just digesting, a war going on in his guts. He wondered if he would die.

When the feeling passed, he was surprised to find that not only did he feel fine, but he was hungry again, and he set to cracking open and eating another leg. This time, the poison barely slowed him. When he was through, he marveled: he'd eaten more than he ever had in his life and still he hungered. Where was it all going? So much was different, so much was in flux, that he would have been terrified if not for her constant reassuring presence.

She's changing me, he thought, and this was good. He needed to be changed.

After the ranger left them, Sandros hadn't quite believed it, thought it must just be more manipulation from Xan. Yither wouldn't *really* eat ten whole cows a day, would it? Surely it would forage or make do somehow. They began to march and he put it out of his mind, and the going was easy as the brothers followed in the wake of destruction left by the bashyskyla.

Yither was moving faster now, so they had to walk quickly to keep up. Again and again it tasted the air, darting out a long purple-black tongue that was forked into three points. As if it were gripping the scent, the forks of Yither's tongue curled into spirals and then unfurled, and then its pace increased. The brothers shot each other worried looks, but dared not ask the monster to slow.

Ahead there was a clearing with an enormous termite funnel, a huge tapered spire of daub that rose fifty feet high, reaching into the lower canopy. Workers the size of dogs spiraled up the tube, bloated with water and food, or carrying bits of mud or pulverized wood in their jaws. More issued from the top, some climbing out into the trees, others scuttling down the shaft. Sandros and Gregory froze, afraid the termite army would notice them and attack. Then the bashyskyla gave three joyous clicks and charged.

Surrounding the workers were the warriors, as big as wolves, heavily armored with massive hooking mandibles. Seeing the bashyskyla bearing down on them, they began to form a wall of points, but Yither would not be denied, and it blasted through their line and slammed into the funnel at full force. The impact was loud enough that Sandros and Gregory flinched. Yither wheeled around in retreat, but as the warriors pried uselessly at its heavy armor, it turned back and charged again. This time, a great crack formed in the funnel.

It turned and ran back for a third pass as the warriors piled themselves onto the crack, trying to defend it with their bodies, but Yither was a juggernaut they could not stop. It slammed into the funnel and the wall buckled and then the funnel collapsed. Workers at the top flailed their legs and howled chittering screams as the tower toppled, sending huge pillars of dust into the canopy. Sandros and Gregory looked on, without a clue why Yither had attacked the structure.

The remaining warriors were attacking Yither in the great cloud of dust, and workers were swarming out of rubble and surrounding the bashyskyla. They were so thick that the brothers feared the great insect would be brought low, but then they saw its head moving, snapping up workers and devouring them in two bites.

More and more spire mites boiled out of the earth until the whole hive was attacking Yither, and it simply continued to eat. The termites brought up their acid spitters and their royal guard, but the bashyskyla devoured them too. The streams of caustic acid simply beaded and rolled off its armor. Yither answered in kind, expertly spitting at the thick-armored royal guard and dissolving their heads, one after the other.

It gorged itself on termites, and the brothers soon saw that it preferred the workers, gobbling them in droves. Eventually, it had its fill, and it rolled over and over on its back, flattening the soldiers and workers still trying in vain to defend their broken funnel, until the ground was carpeted with husks and ichor.

Yither returned to them with the slow, deliberate steps of the truly sated.

"Delicious," Yither said as they looked at it, awestruck. Termite blood was trickling down its sides. "I believe they are poison to your kind, how sad. I could eat them forever."

"Why did you knock down their tower?" Gregary asked. He could scarcely believe Yither had done it. The termite funnel had been better than thirty feet wide at its base. In his mind, he saw the gates of Castle Joymont, huge oak logs banded with iron. They would be nothing before this living battering ram.

"The workers will not all come out until the tower falls, for that dooms the hive. They seek revenge, but find only teeth. Stupid creatures. Still, it is a waste. Usually I would dig down to eat the queen, they are the most delicious of all. I would spend days to reach her, and then her poison... I would be caught in visions for many days afterward. Wonderful visions. But there isn't time. Too bad, too bad, they are a rare treat. The spire mites take great pains to build far from where bashyskyla roam, you can see why."

"Xanadros is right. We will have a devil of a time finding food for you. Many will suffer."

"I would have left the Kalpa anyway, once Wiyitrup died. All of this is fixed, the future is bound like flies in a web. Your kind are formed to suffer, it is the lot of prey to suffer predators. Theirs to flee, ours to follow and to feast."

Yither seemed glib, and there was a slight waver to its step. Sandros was sure the termites had done something to it. It had eaten so many that the mage had begun to wonder if there was some sort of dimensional rift in the monster's gut.

"He says you will shatter our realm."

195

"Xanadros is mad. He will say anything, do anything, none of it has meaning or sense. Your kind cannot stand the Kalpa for long, it is too strange, too alien to you. The other rangers cannot last a cycle before they die, or slink away, never to return. The jungle breaks them. Xanadros has been here for seven cycles, how could he not be mad?"

Sandros nodded carefully.

"What keeps Xan from killing us? You have your armor, but one arrow will end either of us if he ambushes us."

"I would slay him the instant he did," Yither rumbled. They'd seen the bashyskyla's accuracy as it destroyed the termite warriors, they did not doubt it could do the same to Xan.

"He isn't an ordinary man, that's for sure. People say he abducts children, drains them of their blood to stay eternally young," Gregary chimed in.

Despite the pain it brought, the jerky Xan had left had improved his spirits immensely. They had water, too. Sandros had burned a fallen limb into a small pot, and he boiled water for them. Three times he would boil it, hoping to kill whatever parasites or poisons had found their way in as it trickled down the canopy to them. They dared not let it cool. It tasted flat, but they hadn't died yet.

"I know not what evils he does, hidden away on the fringes of the inner. He goes deeper than even bashyskyla go, he deals with dark powers, thinking himself cleverer than they. Of course, he is only their pawn."

"Who are these powers? What do they want?" Sandros asked. The termites had loosened the bashyskyla's forked tongue.

"The great ones. They are old, older than time itself. They live within the innermost, waging an endless war against each other. The gods of your people are but shadows against their power. There are four. The Night Queen, master of the spellspiders. Her great web stretches across an entire valley. The future is written there, for those who can read it. Above flies hated Skylyx, master of the winged ones, lance swift and deadly, slayer of many of my kind. Below in the earth is Wise Arkiend, greatest of the bashyskyla, the true lord of the inner. And in the shadows, the Red

Empress, the Dominatrix. Forever playing the other three off each other, hiding in plain sight."

"And Xan challenged them?"

"He sought to bargain with them. The fool! That is the way of your kind, forever hawing and scheming. He sought me out to learn our language. I taught him what I could in exchange for his own, not knowing what he intended. The hubris, the impudence, it was so great I could never have suspected! The false skin he wears, it was my spittle my spittle he proofed it against. I thought he meant to kill Wiyitrup, and I supplied it readily, never suspecting! If Arkiend ever found out it was I that aided him... Let us say that I will be glad to be far away from the Kalpa."

"What happened? What did he bargain for?" Gregary asked, caught in the tale.

"No one knows but Xan and Arkiend. He sought out the great one, sent the message he wished to parley through Arkiend's generals. When they could not kill him, it caught the wise one's interest, and he agreed to meet. I wish I knew what great idiocy the fool Xanadros mouthed, but it was inevitable that Arkiend would kill him. Once a talking ant loses its novelty, the foot comes swiftly. Arkiend spat in his face and that was that, he left him there to die."

"But he didn't."

"No, the suit saved him, though he paid a heavy price. Somehow, he made it back from the inner to lick his wounds and keep on with his mad schemes. He continues to venture into the inner, though I know he has never gone back to Arkiend. Some say he went instead to the Night Queen, and that she took what he offered. Some say the Red Lady enslaved him, as she has so many others. Maybe even Skylyx, though I think that one would have skewered him without a moment's hesitation, her temper is as swift and terrible as her sting."

Yither shook its head from side to side, an almost human gesture of clearing cobwebs.

"Why do I tell you these things, I wonder. They are not things for you to know. What use to your kind to know of the inner where you will never go? Of a great war that does not concern you? I have overindulged, it is my great flaw, to want too much. The others are happy here, they know what they know and want to know no more. They eat and mate and obey Wiyitrup and Arkiend above, and that is enough. But not for Yither. Why was I born thus?"

Yither stopped, and a sound came from its vents, like a stick run along the vanes of a fence. Ratatatatatat. Ratatatatatat.

Sandros and Gregary looked at each other, eyes wide. Was this how bashyskyla cried? The great beast was a maudlin drunk. At last the three crimson eyes clicked shut, the great horned head slumped against the ground and the beast was silent.

"Finally," Xanadros said, melting out of the trees.

There were strawberries.

How in all the hells and heavens had she gotten strawberries? They were ripe, she could smell their fragrance from the bedroll. And there was crescent bread too, steaming and hot as if it had slid from a baker's tray moments ago. A whole basket full. Osolin rose from the mat, draping the splotchy blanket around her shoulders, feeling the damp air against her bare legs. The scent had hooked her, and she was reeled inexorably toward the food. Her stomach not only rumbled, it cascaded like an avalanche roaring down a mountain.

"Oh my," Ink said, her dark eyebrow raised. "Someone is hungry."

Hunger wasn't half the word for it, she was famished. No emptiness in her belly could convince her tongue that the ranger's living flame disguised as jerky was worth the pain, and the biscuits had barely dented her appetite. Her eyes were wide and never left the basket, her mouth wet in anticipation.

"I've been thinking... about us." Ink selected a berry slowly, considering each one without touching them, and then she delicately plucked one from the bowl by the stem. She wasn't wearing her gloves. The green top blackened, but the fruit remained a brilliant red, and she brought it before her lips and inhaled deeply.

"Anticipation is sweeter than abandon."

She bit in slowly, and Osolin nearly cried out in frustration. Ink savored the look on her face and the sweetness of the fruit in equal measure.

"I don't need a slave. I thought of ordering you about, having you scrub dishes and such, subjugating the mighty warrior woman, but it just isn't for me. Boring." Ink tore apart one of the crescent rolls, releasing a cloud of wonderful steam, and Osolin inhaled deeply, trying to capture as much of it as she could. Never taking her eyes off Osolin, Ink ripped a shred of that flaky, fragrant bread and ate it.

"Mmm... Say what you want about Radia fucking half of Ten, the woman can bake. I don't know how she can afford so much butter, the rolls are practically dripping with it."

Osolin shut her eyes and clenched her fists, trying to get ahold of herself. *It's only bread. Only fruit. You've been hungrier than this. Don't give in.*

"I don't need a bodyguard either. I mean, I'm sure you're very skilled..." she said, but her tone was light, dismissive, and Osolin's heart plunged.

She thought of Rory Morey, shrugging off the best she could throw at him, of Xan disarming her as casually as he'd swat a fly. Before they'd come to this place, she would have been the one casting aside challengers, dispatching foes effortlessly. But she'd barely set foot in the Kalpa before she'd needed Ink to come rescue her. She thought of that black wasp, hovering over her, its eyes alien and merciless, that awful triumphant hum...

"...But ultimately, it would be more me protecting you than the other way around. So I have decided to set you free. Last night I let slip the lay on your heart. You are bound to me no longer. I hope you have learned much during this time."

Shame gave way to shock, suspicion. Would Ink really free her, or was this some trick?

"But... I'll die. If we're still in the Kalpa..." It dawned on her that she had no idea where the cave actually was. They could be under the streets of Aran for all she knew.

"We're still in the Kalpa, in the near-inner. To step outside would be your death. But fear not. I will take you back to Ten, I will give you the money to get home."

An incredible offer. It dawned on her now that she was disappointed. Since she'd been caught, she'd thought of nothing but getting free. But now that it was offered... *when you're ready.*

And now she would never be ready, now she simply wasn't good enough even to be a slave. Ink was casting her away, and she crumpled inside.

"But why?" she asked, trying hard to keep her voice level, her eyes clear.

"Because I like you. I admire your spirit, I think you are strong and beautiful," Ink said, and each word she said was like a bell ringing within Osolin, they spread through her until her fingertips tingled with them. Many men had called her these things, seeking to be inside her, but from Ink... it meant something. All the while, those black eyes were on her, taking in everything.

Ink parted her robe, and then slipped one shoulder free, then the next, baring her breasts.

Smaller than mine. But they were pert and well shaped, her nipples standing in the cold air. Then Ink rose and left the robe behind, and Osolin's eyes traced down her stomach to the smooth cleft between her legs, before her cheeks flushed and she turned her face away. Ink walked over to her, sliding into her field of view, her steps even and sure. Osolin was afraid, wanting to flee, to keep turning away.

I wish I could be like that. She envied that sureness, the fearlessness.

"I want you. But the things I want must be freely given."

Ink was just inches away from her, and Osolin was frozen in her stare. The sorceress had the hint of a grin at the corners of her mouth. The words felt huge, like slabs of granite crashing around Osolin.

Time seemed to slow, and she could feel each heartbeat as a separate ache. She could feel the heat from Ink, smell her... she could remember sleeping with Ink's arms wrapped around her, so warm and safe. Ink bent over the table, almost brushing against her and yet not, and she picked another strawberry from the bowl. She lifted it so that it was nearly touching Osolin's lips. The black eyes were locked on Osolin's, and her mouth watered fiercely from the scent of the berry.

"Give yourself to me, completely." There was a catch in the mage's voice as she said it, a thrill in that black face, and a tremble running through her shoulders.

I'm not that way... I can't do this... It's a trap... Don't give in... I can't... There were a thousand little voices protesting, but they were so small, and when Osolin closed her eyes and bit into the strawberry, it was the sweetest thing that had ever been. When she felt Ink's lips against her own she did not shrink from them. Ink's tongue slid into her mouth, slipping against her own as that sweet taste lingered. The hand at her cheek was so soft, and the other ran through her hair, and she just kept her eyes closed and let go, shuddering as those lips kissed down her neck, along her collarbone, across her breasts... the blanket was gone, stripped from her, but the room had become very hot. A low moan began as the fingertips traced down her sides and along the tops of her thighs, and when her legs parted, it was her own doing, her own choice. Ink's mouth found her and Osolin's eyes shot open, her gasp echoing back at her from the ceiling.

She closed her eyes again and slipped into the sweet darkness.

"We have to go," Xan commanded.

"You'll kill us," Sandros protested.

"If I had been planning to, you were dead the instant Yither's head dropped. One shot, through the throat. Your brother doesn't matter. I'd let the jungle have him."

Gregary gave the ranger a look, but he could not argue. He had no armor, no sword, nothing more than the broken end of a wooden spear. It was pathetic.

"I laid the scent, lured it to that spire. Thank every star in the sky Yither is young and stupid. An elder would not have taken the bait."

"Yither said you are mad, that..."

"I heard what it said. It's the village idiot of the bashyskyla, believes anything a liefly sings. That rot about the inner Kalpa? All pigshit. Yither's never been there, couldn't make it half a mile inside before something ate it. It doesn't know a fucking thing, and neither do you."

"But Joymont..."

Xan pulled off his mask, and their eyes widened at the incredible wreckage of his face. Even with all they'd seen, it was still a shock.

"Time to talk face to face. Man to boy. Joymont is doomed. It was doomed the moment that great fat idiot laid his claim, it'll still be doomed if every one of those tinks dies. It's just time. If it could be saved, I would be there right now, killing tinks by the bushel. But every babe you save now is a family that will die when the Kalpa spreads. You're just multiplying the suffering. Your quest is the greatest idiocy."

The words bit hard. They had no retort. Xan replaced his mask.

"King Joymont... He won't leave. He'll stay and try to fight," Gregary said sadly. Their uncle would never give up his land.

"Then fucking kill him and take charge. That's what you nobles are supposed to do. Otherwise, that great imbecile's stubbornness will kill thousands. And while we're on the topic of stubbornness, either you two are going to leave this drunken slug here and come with me, or I will kill you."

"I'm tired. Tired of threats. Tired of being shoved around," Sandros said, and there was a crackle in his voice as he spoke, a low rumbling beneath his words. Gregary yelped in pain, and began to back away as the air around his brother seethed and roiled.

"You shouldn't have come here. I warned you and you didn't listen. I will take you home, save your miserable hides. But this is it. No more chances." Xan eyed Sandros warily as he spoke.

"Do you remember," Sandros coughed each word in a spray of sparks, "the fire that made you thus?"

His eyes glowed with a wild light, and he looked right through Xan. The whole clearing was sweltering, heat rolling off the mage in waves, wilting leaves, crisping small insects. It was folly to stand there and parley with one so clearly unhinged. Xan should have killed him by now, should have flown at him with his sword and ended it all.

But he could remember. How it had *burned*.

The three of them moved at once, Xan to Sandros and Gregary to Xan, as Sandros lifted a hand and poured a river of roaring flame at the spot where Xan had been. Gregary cried out in pain at the flash, half-blinded. Xan thrust with his sword, but Gregary's club caught him on the crossguard hard enough to knock the sword out of his hands. Xan was on the ground and rolling. Sandros wheeled at him and sent a torrent of flame hissing after him. He tried to lead the ranger and burn him down, but Xan was everywhere, darting and sprinting for his life. He made into the trees, and Sandros pulled back, roared with frustration, and shouted a word of power, giving it the last of his strength.

H!

An arrow came for Sandros, singing through the air as the ball of flame he'd conjured shot toward the trees, doubling in size every ten paces. Exhaustion saved him. Sandros slumped to his knees and the arrow whistled above his head, then suddenly the whole forest was alight. The fireball struck a tree and welled into a massive explosion, painting everything in shades of flame. The blast sent Gregary cartwheeling as he bent to pick up Xan's sword, flinging leaves and moss and dirt in every direction. Overhead, the canopy creaked and groaned with the weight of great trees whose trunks had been blasted into splinters.

Sandros was knocked flat on his back. He lay there with his ears ringing, the world spinning wildly above. Nothing remained but to wait for death.

He had no more power, no more strength. He could only watch the flames rippling and guttering out overhead, thinking of the pure end he could no longer summon. He could smell charred wood and burnt insects as black gusts of smoke swirled around him, and he felt oddly free. Everything was spent.

Now he floated on the river of fate, to drift wherever it carried him, without complaint. Whether the flame or the ranger took him, it was the river's will. He could almost see it, almost feel it through the smoke and haze.

But it was only raining.

The wall of fire hissed and fizzled, and finally guttered out as the drizzle turned to a downpour. Sandros found the strength to turn his head and blinked the water from his eyes, searching the blasted landscape for some sign that Gregary was alive. At first, there was only the rain, the scorched leaves and blackened branches falling to the ground, but then with a soundless cry of relief he saw Gregary. His brother crawled toward the ranger's sword as if nothing else mattered. When it was in his grasp, he rose unsteadily to his feet and looked around, squinting through sheets of rain.

Sandros rose just as unsteadily and the two called out to each other, but neither could hear, the world was just ringing and confusion. Still, Gregary was smiling as he made his way over, using the Xan's sword as a cane. He was a different man with a sword in his hand, grinning like a child at All Stars Festival.

Sandros looked him over, terrified that he'd burned his brother badly, but Gregary had gotten no worse than a bad sunburn. For a while they just stood there, reeling over the destruction Sandros had wrought. Their hearing returned slowly.

"We live," Gregary said with a grin, and he sounded very distant, though he was half-shouting. Sandros could only nod, feeling withered inside. How close had he come to killing his brother? Gregary winced as he gripped his brother's shoulder.

"He must have died," Gregary offered.

As the rain pissed down, Sandros dared to hope that he had killed the masked ranger. But as the brothers plodded through the squelching moss and undergrowth in the twilight, they found only dead insects, their shells scorched and their legs curled up. No men.

"No one could have lived through that," Gregary said, his eyes darting around the trees, as if that would help. Sandros could only nod. Just walking around had him breathing heavily. He needed rest badly. It would be dark soon.

"Yither slept through the whole thing. It must be some wicked drunk, those spire mites."

"Let's leave Yither here. Forget the bargain, forget all of this. We'll go back to Joymont and I'll just burn the tinks out."

"But the crops, the woods... and what do we do when the peasants revolt?"

"I'll burn them out too, if I have to."

Gregary had nothing to say to that. The brothers glanced at the great insect, wondering how the hell it could sleep through such a fight.

Then Sandros noticed the beast's eyes were dark, and it was perfectly still. At the top of its neck, acid blood seeped down from the tink spine bored into its vulnerable spot, hissing in the rain. Xan's arrow had found its mark after all.

The heat, gods, that glorious heat! Brakkar staggered through an inferno, phantasms dancing before his eyes, burning so brightly that the lords of this place turned tail and fled at his approach. She was trying to guide him, trying to calm the fire, but he could not hear her when it raged. Her voice came only in those rare, perfect instants when he was plunged into the cold, and his veins iced over.

Slower... too much... you take too much...

In those frozen moments, he could feel her fear, the panic edging her thoughts, and he resolved to heed her, swore he would do anything to protect her. But then the flames rose and he had to move, had to rise, swimming through the currents of heat, clawing forever forward. There was a warning screech, but he could barely hear it through the howling in his ears, and then he was looking up at a mountain of insect. Somewhere behind the searing, she was crying for him to flee, but he was a creature of the heat now and he brought the mace to bear, bright and flashing, all fear and all thought boiling away.

All around him, legs were crashing down, piercing the earth, but he flowed and billowed around them like smoke, rushing in when the beast thought he should be fleeing. Then he was inside its guard, and the mace smashed again and again at its underside. He howled, trying to vent the fire in his insides before it built too high, before it tore him asunder. He felt the armor cracking under his mace, heard the beast scream back at him, scrambling in circles trying to get away from his assault.

In a moment of cold clarity, he saw that he was beneath the belly of a beetle as big as the one they'd played roke under, saw that it could just drop down and flatten him, and he heard her pleading with him to get away, to save them both. But the heat... it returned, doubly hot for the time it had lost, and he heard only screaming, saw only red.

When it faded away, he found himself feasting on the insect's corpse, distant thunder in his ears that was only the drumming of his pulse. The great beetle was dead and shattered. He was breaking the insect's leg armor apart with his bare hands, tearing out the meat and devouring it by the fistful. Reaching into the gore, he paused. His hands were different.

The burning had left his skin bright red in places, deep crimson in others, but there was no pain. He drew his bloody hands out and touched one hand to the other in amazement. The skin had begun to harden, ridges rising, and lines forming at the joints. He was growing a suit of armor, one he could never take off. For a moment he panicked, but then he looked at the great beast he had defeated, a creature ten times his size.

Why should I ever want to take off my armor? Why ever be vulnerable again?

He could remember the power he'd felt when he first donned the heavy legionnaire's plate, the great weight settling over him. The armor meant he could turn aside blows that would otherwise take an arm or a leg, wade into whole packs of men and emerge blood-soaked and triumphant, his foes nothing but work for the skullman. How he had missed that feeling since he'd struck the collar from his neck. He had thought the Bloodstar's favor armor enough, but the Red Giant had not saved him.

What of the star now? He paused, trying to see if he still felt the god's presence, the finger of the star on him that had once informed his every decision, shaped his every move. Nothing. And she was gone, too. Had the fire burned her out? He felt his guts plummet with loss, brought a hand to the back of his neck, terrified he would find a great hole there.

But she was still there, and as he sought her voice, he realized that she was still with him, she was just angry. She was sulking.

"I don't know..." He spoke the words, but then he felt a fool, for she knew his thoughts, knew everything about him.

"I don't know what happened... the rage took me," he thought. *Vulnerable. Too soon.*

She gave him the image of them as they would be, the whole body clad in armor, his hands formed into wicked talons, crimson and gleaming. Showed him the strength she would give him, the strength to rip and shred, strength to tear the world apart. The strength to rule.

They dreamed this dream together, of vast armies beneath them, waves of men and beasts crashing against walls, then swarming over them, conquering. She wanted an empire, and he would give it to her. He would give her anything.

Eat. Grow stronger.

He nodded, and bent down to eat.

Nightfall came with little warning in this place. The great din reached its crescendo as the infinite insects of the Kalparcimex called out to each other, greetings and goodbyes, lures and warnings. It was something the brothers could never get used to, there were just too many voices, too many songs saturating the air. Yet they had been in the jungle enough nights to know what to expect, the trilling of the triwings at dusk, the chirp of the lune locusts swarming after them, the croaking of the banneret toads and the mating songs of the lieflies. Behind it all, the constant low rumbling of the big-maw worms.

Tonight, it all changed. A song began, so loud it cut through everything, and the whole Kalpa was still, listening. The sudden silence around them struck the brothers like a blow. They halted, turning back toward the source.

It was like no song they'd ever heard before. Long sweeping notes that warbled like a bowed saw and rang like bells pealing, three distinct voices at once, spiraling around and merging into a long harmonious dirge. It was wholly unlike the music of men, yet still they could hear the sadness ringing behind the alien notes.

It was a song of mourning. When it ended, the great din was slow to begin again, as if the insects around them shared their apprehension. No words passed between the brothers. They knew why the bashyskyla sang.

They sought shelter in a borer's cave, this one far deeper than the one where Sandros had crafted the flute. It was empty. Sandros wondered why the borer was gone. Had it mined out whatever it was they ate? Why hadn't anything taken its place? Perhaps borers went somewhere for the night? He had no desire to be woken in the night should it return, but neither did he wish to lay more trapstones. The memory of the quilg still tugged at his guts.

Instead, he had Gregary gather firewood with Xan's sword. It was all wet and green, but it mattered not to the firemage. Soon, Sandros had a mighty bonfire blazing at the entrance to keep the beasts at bay. There was something primal and satisfying about it, one of man's oldest strategies still worked after countless generations.

Gregary turned Xan's sword over and over in his hand. "It's so light. I feel like it will shatter the instant I strike something. But it cuts through trees like a scythe through grass. What do you suppose the blade's made of?" No matter how he held it, it was uncomfortable. Never had he felt so keenly that a sword belonged to someone else.

Sandros shrugged, peering into the fire, where figures swirled and faces emerged for an instant, then changed before they could speak. For some mages, the faces in fires lingered long enough to speak of the future, and there were some among those who could tell when the flames spoke true, and when they hissed fickle lies. But Sandros was no fireseer, as he was no archmage. He was nothing but a scribe. He looked back at the boy who had dared to title himself Sandros the Red and shook his head sadly. What a fool he'd been.

That afternoon, they had reached a desperate place where they had had to take a gamble and eat something. They'd chosen a clutch of white eggs, like hens' eggs in size but glossy and translucent. Sandros had conjured a fire and Gregory had cradled them in the Y of a stick and roasted them one by one. They hadn't dared eat them until they were well and truly charred. The brothers' caution seemed to have paid off. It had been hours since then and they felt fine.

"Sandros." The mage did not reply, just peered into the fire, hypnotized by its endless dance.

"Sandros." Gregary said it more urgently now, and at last his brother looked away from the flames to meet his eyes. He hated to look at his brother's face, for he knew it must reflect his own—filthy, gaunt, with desperation clawing its way past all attempts at suppression.

"I need you with me. I need you to believe we can get out of this."

"We can't—"

Gregary didn't raise his hand, he only thought about it, and an echo of the thought twitched in his shoulder, no more than that. Still, fury blazed in Sandros' eyes. Gregary saw that any hand that struck him would come back as ashes. He tried a different tactic.

"I need you. I can't make it out of here alone. Maybe we can convince Joymont to move. Maybe we can save all those people."

"We couldn't save Osolin. Or Brakkar."

"Osolin lives, at least, if you believe the ranger. And Brakkar has the finger of the Bloodstar on him, he might still live."

"Do you really believe that? This is the Brakkar who'd cure a nosebleed with a fist to the back of your head."

"I wouldn't stake my purse on it. He's probably gone. But until we know differently, what's the harm in hope? We've seen wonders enough."

Sandros was silent now, trying to hold back the bitterness, trying to look through the fool's lens that Gregary saw the world with.

211

"I'll tell you one thing. I think you got that ranger. Wounded him at least."

"Why do you think that?"

"Because there isn't an arrow jutting from either of us. You've seen how he shoots. And the trail we've left... a child could follow it. Every five paces, something is scorched or sliced or trampled. I think you burned him bad, maybe bad enough to kill him."

How did he do it? All evening, Sandros had been thinking of the pure flame, the bright end, with no hope for anything better. Now, a few words and everything was different. Somehow Gregary had sussed out the fear that bit most deeply at Sandros, the spine through the throat that he could not predict, could not defend against. He'd taken the teeth from it. Maybe the ranger truly was dead. Maybe they could make it back to Joymont.

For the first time, Sandros looked at Gregary and saw a leader of men. The simple nature, the stupid optimism, they made men trust, made them hope against all odds. With Sandros to guide him... At once, Sandros knew that if they made it back to Joymont, he would do what had to be done. Remove Joymont and help Gregary rise into his place. Do the things Gregary was too honorable to do, for the good of the realm. He had it within him to do these things, if they could only make it out, if they could only...

"Wish we hadn't left the roke set," Gregary said at last.

"It's shit with two."

"It's something."

Sandros took the flute from his waistband and began to play, trying hard to believe the ranger was dead.

They stirred to the trilling of the recipitors excited at the return of the master. Then they heard the rumble of the stone portal on its rollers. They could not hear his footsteps, could not gauge how long it would take him to get down the spiral stair, and they were loathe to move.

"That didn't take long," Xan said, looking down at them.

He stood over the two black forms entwined in his bed, the lenses of his mask gleaming in the globe light. Just as she had with Xan, Ink had touched every part of Osolin. The thief made a token effort to cover herself with a blanket that was now completely blackened, but there was a slowness to her movement that said she was far past caring. Many doors had been opened, doors that would not close again.

"Longer than you," Ink said, grinning her dark grin.

Xan paused as if to reply, but instead he left them there, moving stiffly toward his shelves. He did not pause to recollect or scan the thousands of jars, he knew exactly where to find the one he wanted.

The women looked at each other, feeling the same pique. They lay there nude, and this oaf was ignoring them completely. At his workbench, Xan began to remove the jungle suit, taking a deep breath before he removed each piece, hissing when at last he took off the mask.

"Are you all right?" Ink asked. Pique had become concern. He smelled of fire, smoke, ash, charred meat. She knew how much pain it took for him to make a sound.

"I'm burned. Badly. I suppose it's hard to tell anymore."

He had the jar open, and he was slathering himself with a thick clear paste swirled with motes of silver and tiny black spheres.

"In a few minutes, I am going to scream a great deal. I may die. I've only done this once before," Xan said grimly. "Which one of you broke my stove?"

"I did."

"Varagoi got me the metal, it wasn't cheap. Replace it. If I live, I mean."

"What happened to you?" Ink asked, concern stealing into her voice.

"The scribe. He's powerful when he's cornered."

"Firemages are all like that. Worthless until doom is upon them, then they go too far. Do they live?"

"I didn't... want to kill them."

"Why not? I thought they threatened the order of your precious jungle."

"I don't like to... kill men. I've tried to save..." Xan trailed off as he clutched the workbench with both hands then screamed like no scream they'd ever heard before.

The scream stung their ears, rang in their teeth, and made their shoulders shiver. It went on and on, as if a lifetime of suffering were compressed into this one outcry. At last he stopped screaming and his whole body shook. He dared not let go of the bench. The salve had hardened into a dull silver shell that began to crack, falling off him in shards and shattering like crystal on the ground.

"Swallow the stars. What can be worth that?" Ink asked, and Xan just stood there, shedding silver, his breath coming in staggered gasps.

"Too burnt. I would have died," he said, grimly certain. Ink could not speak. For a long time Xan just stood there, shaking, taking huge jagged breaths.

"Still might," he said at last, and he made his way to the spring, leaving a trail of silver behind him.

214

He plunged into the water and stayed under a long time. Finally, he surfaced and slowly pulled himself out, then stumbled toward the bed. He never asked them for help. Ink and Osolin looked at each other, neither knowing what to do.

"We need a bigger bed," he said, then he collapsed into it.

A safe place. A warm and wet place...

Her thoughts untangled in him, spreading and soaking in like spilled wine, finding the places no one else went. He was a youth again, clumsily shoving himself into his first, the tower watchman's daughter, eight years older than him and no beauty, but no matter who he'd fucked since, it was her face his mind clawed toward whenever he drew close, her joyous grunts that echoed in his ears forever.

For years, he had teased her just like the other boys had, throwing little stones and calling her names. Then one day he'd walked alone and her eyes had fallen on him, and she'd smiled and told him to come with her. He had followed, and done all the things she bid, and all the while she'd smiled her secret understanding, as if she had the key to the world hidden beneath her skirt. He'd thought her low, but she was above him, had a power he could not resist. How many times had he sworn he would not do that again, only to spring to her like a dog anytime she beckoned?

And then when she was gone, how bitter his disappointment when he found that others did not know her secret. They lay there and made noise or did not, it did not matter. They laughed at him when he withered in apathy, not knowing that it was something missing in them, not him. The fumbling words as he'd tried to explain what he'd wanted to a camp follower, and just as he'd known all along, it couldn't be bought. He'd grown so angry with her half-hearted attempt that he'd kicked her out of his tent, and she'd screamed his desires to the whole camp, so that he had no choice but to kill her. Men acted like they hadn't heard, but of course, everyone knew, everyone snickered when they thought he couldn't hear. Their tongues slowed after his first battle, and they were silenced completely in the second, what a bloodbath...

Dimly he became aware that she was absorbing all of this, taking his memories into her, and he shuddered, a slow flame fanning across his cheeks, shamed that she saw so much, thrilled that she wanted to know, soaring with her complete acceptance.

All that you are. All that you were. All that you will be.

For how long?

The big fear, the shadow behind his joy, forever darting backstage. What if she goes away? He saw himself laid empty on the jungle floor, weeping, with nothing inside of him, like the cast-off hull from a spider's meal. What if she leaves me for another? What if I'm not good enough for her? He would die, he was sure.

What is done cannot be undone.

How long?

Forever.

He stopped there, his heart, their heart, thundering with guileless joy, and for a time he was free of care, free of doubt.

You are the one. You are ready. Find us a place to change.

He hastened to obey, loping through the jungle, hearing a thousand different beasts flee his approach, her words like a drumbeat in his ears.

Safe, warm, wet.

The way he saw, the way he heard, all had changed. Did he see more, hear more, or had she simply taught him to understand more of what he saw and heard? He was attuned now to this place, so that when he scented the shives and tasted its fear, he knew at once what it all meant. What she wanted of him. What must be.

The shives was a mountain of armor that thundered forward on two legs, leaving a warpath of snapped vines and shattered cane. He darted after it, the new strength pumping in his legs, roaring through his arms. At last, the quarry knew there would be no more running and it wheeled to fight, its four clawed arms twisting and clacking in a defensive display, the fluidity of its weaving almost hypnotic, but she was not fooled.

For a moment, looking up at the great beast, he thought as a man, and the certainty of death thrust through him, cold and black. The shives was enormous. Its armored head looked down at him and he saw he was trying to kill a beast as tall as a house with his bare hands.

Plant eater. Prey, she told him, and then he remembered he was not a man anymore, that his hands weren't hands. The red came flooding in, the searing in his blood, and then he was flying at the shives, its pincers too slow to find him. He tore at it with his talons, getting into the joint between its stomach plates and clawing, biting deep. He dipped behind it as it tried to catch him, and ripped at the back of its trunk-like legs, cutting through the thin armor behind its knees like rotten wood.

The shives gave a rumbling cry of panic as its leg collapsed and it toppled onto its side, and then he was upon it, ripping into its anus and tunneling inside while the wounded creature thrashed and bucked, and all around him was blood and gore, in his mouth, in his nose and ears. The man was not there to worry about breathing, to recoil in disgust, there was only the red man, burning inside the beast, feeling it die.

Safe here. We change, she said, and it was all he wanted, to know she was satisfied. The red was draining away to darkness. He curled into a ball, trusting her more than the emptiness in his lungs, more than the weight all around him.

When the change was through, what would be left of him?

The ranger dreamed of death.

Not the death he had known, with fire screaming in every nerve, his insides twisting with panic. Nor the death he had contemplated, cold and grasping, time accumulating on his bones like hoarfrost and breaking him apart slowly over a thousand thaws.

Instead, it was serene, a still pond with no reflection, and then he slowly realized that he was only imagining the pond, giving a face to the emptiness. He saw his life wrapped around the Void like a shell, every instant a thread, the whole of it woven into a great net. Was he meant to contain the Void or to adorn it?

As he wondered, he saw that the perspective was wrong, completely wrong. The emptiness was not within, he was within it. It was all around, in every direction. The entirety of his hollow experience was a marble amidst an ocean of nothing. As he recoiled from the scale, everything continued to shrink, all that he knew, all he could imagine diminished until he saw the whole of the Arc reduced to a grain of sand, and then even that was nothing. The sun vanished into obscurity and more stars twisted into the Void. The vanishing went on and on until his insignificance did not matter anymore.

He came to understand he was in the presence of the Devourer. The Void Star did not speak, did not need to speak. All was made clear through absences. The gods that wheeled and struggled against it were insects, scrambling for the top place on a twig as the flood of darkness rose all around them. He saw that there were infinite planes, layered again and again on each other, and yet all found their zero, all drained away into the same Nil.

It did not tempt him, it was simply there. He could embrace it and be annihilated, it would not embrace him back. It simply did not matter, to do nothing was to be drawn in, slowly, eventually, as all things must be. He was weary. He tried to summon goals, memories, any reason at all to exist, but he could not remember. He could feel himself begin to drift apart.

There was a tiny voice somewhere beyond all of this, calling a name he had forgotten.

"Xanadros!"

He turned toward it, away from scouring emptiness. She was there, somehow she'd followed him to this place. He could see only her silhouette, black against black.

"Xanadros!"

He moved toward her, and it was as if he'd fallen back into himself, donning his body like a worn, familiar cloak. When he opened his eyes, hers were there, staring into his, black and glistening.

"I felt her come. You went too deep. She almost had you."

His skin was burning, searing as if hot coals were pressed against him, but his insides had frozen solid, and he began to shiver violently. The pain outside was nothing compared to the pain within, of having seen too much, having come too close. Ink slipped beneath the blanket and put her arms around him. It was agony to be touched, yet he dared not make a sound. He was certain that she was holding him together, that he would shake himself apart if she let go.

"Xanadros."

"Xanadros."

"Xanadros."

Again and again she repeated his name softly, rocking him back and forth like a child until he stopped shaking.

"Insolade..." The word was cracked and low, so that she grasped more of it from the shape of his lips than his voice.

She was silent, waiting for more, but that was all. Xan slipped into unconsciousness.

Ink sat beside him for a long time, her hand over his chest in case his heart should stop. It beat on, and at last she wrapped the blankets around him and stood, arms crossed against her chest.

"Will he live?" Osolin asked when Ink joined her at the spring.

"He should be dead already. The Blackstar came for him."

Something in her voice made Osolin embrace her. Ink tensed, and angry words began to form but they never emerged. She pressed her face against Osolin's breast and dark tears ran down her bare skin.

"I hate that stupid man," she said at last, and Osolin stroked her hair, worried, yet at the same time pleased to be the strong one.

She does need me after all.

Two long days of blundering through the jungle were behind them, and they'd gotten turned around so many times that Sandros had begun burning numbers and arrows into trees as they walked. They were getting better at avoiding the dangers of this place. Gregary had spotted a nearly-invisible cluster of tree ticks moments before they would have drawn too close. The tree tick clutches were protected by swollen protector drones that burst when foes drew near, spraying everything with acid. A few sharp words from the mage and the whole clutch was nothing but curling legs and cinders.

Sandros had abandoned all restraint with his art. He summoned it when he wanted, as often as he wanted. The Scourer's dire warnings and the countless hours of training to moderate his talent had lost their meaning in this place where death was only a heartbeat away. Better to die by the flame than by the claw. The signs of mage-madness were there, the fiery dreams, the endless hunger, the constant singing in his ears, but he ignored them. Things around him had begun to smolder of their own accord, but it mattered little in this place, where rain was nearly constant and nothing ever had time to dry.

Tonight they slept within the great hollow inside a tree. Before their arrival, it had contained thousands of silverwings, but now there were only burnt wood and blackened husks littering the ground. Outside the hollow, a great bonfire raged. Gregary was keeping watch, both hands on Xan's sword as Sandros slept.

The mage dreamed that he rode atop a great serpent made of flames, burning a path out of the jungle as wide as two wagons side by side. He kept looking back over his shoulder, trying to find Gregary, but the snake would not turn back for his brother, no matter how he dug in his heels…

Then Gregary was there in the firelight, and he was shaking Sandros awake. At first the mage was afraid he'd set something ablaze in his sleep, but then he felt the ground shaking under him. The rumbling was too steady for an earthquake, and it grew stronger and stronger. They could hear branches cracking and trees snapping outside, and finally the thunderous footsteps stopped. Through the bonfire, they saw three red eyes gleaming in the night. Then two more triangles of eyes emerged. Three of the great beasts had gathered outside their cave.

"Men. Come out, Men. We must talk," said a bashyskyla with Xan's voice. "Come out or die."

Sandros stepped through the flames, embers crunching beneath his bare feet, sparks shooting up around him. For an instant the urge to stay, to wrap himself in those flames and leave this world, grew very strong, but Gregary was in the cave behind him. His brother would not make it out of here alone.

221

"Speak," Sandros said, raising his head high to stare at the bashyskyla with feigned pride. As if he had power against them, as if he wore his crimson robe still, instead of his shortclothes.

"Yither is gone," the lead bashyskyla said. It was bigger than the other two, and the other ones were twice Yither's size. It was amazing to see that the bashyskyla they'd thought huge was but a runt. Sandros was grateful for the dark. In the light, the sight of the massive beasts might have scared the wits from him.

"Xanadros. Xanadros. Xanadros," the three chimed, not quite in unison, but all spoke exactly the same way, in Xan's voice.

"Yes. He lured Yither to a spire, tried to turn us against it, and then killed it when we refused. Xanadros is not our friend."

"Nor ours. Not any longer. Yither was... not his to cull." Three times three ruby red eyes glowed with anger in the dark, and Sandros' resolve to live through this encounter wavered, the words of the bright death dancing ever brighter in his mind. He could not shake the image of the ranger's ruined face, the thought of his own melting off his skull.

"Yither was the least of us, but a giant in its way. He will be remembered."

There was something different about this one's voice, and Sandros struggled to place it. It was hard to concentrate in the face of three great bashyskyla. When the nearest spoke, most of the words were Xan's voice, but when it said "giant" it was clearly another man's voice. Who had it spoken with?

"It will be remembered," the other two echoed.

"Yither is the only of your kind I have known, but it struck me as extraordinary. So much desire to learn..." Sandros hoped his flattery of their dead friend was not too transparent.

"Yes."

For a long time they stood there, Sandros growing increasingly uncomfortable, not knowing if he'd said the right thing or given insult somehow. The bashyskyla seemed perfectly content to be silent and still.

"Did Xanadros teach all of you to speak?" Sandros asked at last. It was probably the wrong thing to say, but anything was better than the silence.

"He taught Yither. We have a sharing, once a cycle. What is known to one becomes known to all. Yither brought us the language of men, proud, as if it was some great victory, but the masked one played Yither for a fool. The folly of youth."

Again, silence. Sandros wondered how they might share a whole language. Did they all learn as swiftly as Yither? He had only to look up, to see the massive outlines in the dark, to remember how out of his depth he truly was. Who knew what these beasts were capable of?

"Many years, I have spoken with your kind. The other men of the jungle, they tell me of the ranger's movements. They fear him. He is no friend to his own kind, nor to mine. I have many ears within the Kalpa, I know your tale. You came here seeking an ally. Some fool sent you, and like fools you came. None of you knowing the truth, none of you understanding. You wished to rid yourself of fleas, you walked into the maw," the leader said at last.

"Yes, we were foolish. We have paid a high price for our ignorance."

"Still, you are ignorant. You look to rid your land of tinks, but you do not say, why are the tinks here?"

"Xan says the jungle is spreading, that our land is doomed."

"And who spreads the jungle?"

"I... I do not know. I thought it spread on its own."

"Xanadros. Always Xanadros. He hates men, all men. Men scarred him, tortured him, broke his mind. They banished him to this place. Now, he loves the Kalparcimex though it does not love him back. The Red Empress bids him to spread her domain and like a good drone he does her bidding. He breeds the tinks, spreads them across the lands of men to thin them so he can take his army of insects out to conquer. He brought this pestilence upon you."

Sandros stood there, reeling.

"Long we have sat idle, long we have let him tinker, for his plans were not for us. But now... it was no half-mad tyrant he took, but a child. We shall break this one, shatter his works and scatter them. All will be forgotten."

"You are mighty, and he is but one man. Why come to me?"

"What is death to you, son of man? You have what, ten more cycles upon the Arc? Only if you escape the Kalpa. Wiyitrup was here before your kind existed. Wiyitrup was here before everything you have ever known, would have been here long after all men are extinguished. We are the same. We do not die. Yet Wiyitrup is gone. Yither is gone. A single man, a weak, unarmored fleshling, has done this. And he has an army bent to his will. Against such, even we must be cautious."

"We do not wish to die any more than you do."

"Yet you shall. If we cannot come to an accord, it will be tonight. I have told you that Xanadros plots to wipe your kind from the Arc. Would you flee, knowing this?"

"No."

"Then you shall help us kill him. Use your sorcery to burn him out of his hiding place. Do this and we will take you from the Kalpa. You and your brother will live. Refuse and I shall slay you both. This is the only bargain we will make. We have given enough leeway to your kind." The bashyskyla spoke much in the other voice, only a few of the words were Xan's.

"What is your name?"

"Ristarisk. These are my mates, Matraiene and Jilque."

"RISTARISK! MATRAIENE! JILQUE! The Pact is sealed!" Sandros shouted, and the bonfire roared and rose into a huge pillar of flame behind him.

"The deal is made, I cannot be betrayed. Who breaks a mage's pact dies, sure as the sunrise."

The great bashyskyla's mandibles moved now in apprehension, an expression Sandros recognized from Yither. The three were chattering in their language, and for an instant he was sure he'd gone too far, that they would burn him down in a salvo of acid. But again he saw the fear in Ristarisk's mandibles.

He believes...

"Men and their bent words. I will be glad when you all fade away. Now come, we shall do this thing."

With a wave of his hand, Sandros gathered the bonfire's heat into a fist-sized ball that burned blinding bright, and sent it streaking upwards into the heavens like a comet. He wanted the bashyskyla to think his power was limitless, that it was all as easy as that.

Testing each step with his bare feet, Gregary walked through the dead coals to join his brother. He looked up at the three giants and had no words to offer, nothing but open-mouthed fear. They followed the monsters into the jungle.

32

She could feel it now, was it a change in the air? Shadows dancing at the corners of her eyes? Whatever it was, Osolin could feel the sorceress coming long before she peeled herself from the shadows and appeared in her ring of sigils. Ink had spent hours carving the rings of magic letters into the cavern floor with a little pointed hull hammer she'd nicked from Xan's workbench. It was easier, she'd explained, to carry things when there were rings linking the sides when she walked the shadowlands. The other ring was back in her room at Nod's Hole.

Ink put the rings to use at once after engraving them in the stone floor, vanishing into a whorl of darkness at its center. When she returned, she carried a jar of salve and a round wheel of black-beetle bouillon to make broth. Varagoi taught her the secret of the invisible flame and she shared it with Osolin: the second jar had to be added with painstaking slowness or it would erupt in the unseen conflagration that had nearly taken her eyebrows. Together they managed to get a steady heat going, and then Ink returned to her circle and vanished into the demiplane once more.

Watching her go, Osolin shuddered. Long would she remember the horrid jaunt through the shadow realm. It would fuel her nightmares alongside the glittering eyes of the redring wasp, the cloud of stirges, the grand centipede turning in its husk, the black waters of the caldera, the dying black queen on the docks, Ink herself…

The journey had been long and terrible and at its end, nothing was sure. Was she just a toy to the sorceress, a fancy to be discarded when the novelty was through? Would the ranger wake from his slumber and cast her out into the jungle? Or worse, if he never woke, would Ink destroy everything in her grief?

Osolin held out a hand that was black as the space between the stars. The stain would never leave her. A lifetime of scars were blotted out, dyed with darkness. This was more than notched ears, or an oft-broken nose. She was marked.

In the moment, she'd wanted it, wanted Ink, and afterward… she still burned thinking of it. She had never thought of herself as one of those women, but there was no doubt she was, and Ink had *known*… knew her better than she knew herself. Loved her better than she'd ever been loved. *Give yourself to me completely,* she'd said, and how sweet it had been to surrender to her! But now she wore the curse. Ink might leave but her shadow would remain, within and without. She dwelt on it for a long time, trying to master her feelings.

There was no diversion within Xan's cavern. She looked through the whole wall of jars. For all the wealth they represented, they were, after all, just eggs and bug parts and slime. She climbed the steps and listened at the door, hearing the huffing breath and ringing cries of the recipitors.

The broth bubbled, filling the cave with a heavy aroma, a scent like roasted pine nuts. She lifted the pot from the heat. When it cooled, she looked at the still form of Xan, unconscious on the blackened mat.

"Idiot guild of Ibexian thieves," she murmured, stroking the back of her earlobe and remembering how the ranger had backhanded her when they met. No one would ever notice that tattoo again, darkness had covered it. She resolved to leave him there, to let Ink deal with him when and if she returned.

But there was nothing to do, and the ranger's rest was fitful, he shuddered and made little pained sounds. In spite of herself, she wetted a cloth with cool water from the spring and set it across his ravaged brow, alarmed at the intense heat radiating from him. The cloth seemed to ease his pain some, and at once she felt terribly selfish.

227

The man was near death, and she'd left him there to suffer from pique alone. All he'd done, all his warnings, beneath the haughty gruff tone, he'd been right. They'd had no business coming here. Ink *had* abandoned them, even if she'd saved Osolin after. The others were probably dead. If only they'd listened to him… but they hadn't.

She looked at the jar of salve, wishing Ink had told her what to do, and decided to use it anyway. She twisted off the silver cap and daubed it between two fingers, working it into the swirling scars on his face, and then along his neck, and then she drew back the blanket and rubbed it all over the rest of him, gauging where he was burned worst by the heat he gave off.

Even focused on his injuries, she could not help but be impressed with his physique. There was no doughy castle fat like Gregary or Sandros, no hairy bulk like Brakkar. All of him was hard and lean, as if he'd been chiseled from a block of black marble. Her cheeks grew hot as she smeared the salve on his manhood, though there was no one around to see and he never stirred. When she was through working the salve into his skin, her fingers tingled and buzzed, and she washed them off in the stream, hoping she hadn't somehow poisoned them both.

Afterward she tried to feed him the broth, and it was a messy affair until she got the hang of it. At last she cradled his head in one hand and spooned broth to his mouth with the other. To her surprise, his eyes slid open as she fed him, piercing green, and she froze for a moment, afraid he might rise and attack her. But he only gave her a grateful look, drank a little more broth and then slipped unconscious.

She sat there watching him for some time afterward, looking over the scars, remembering the flash of those eyes. Behind that strange mask and that beetleshell cloak, behind the whispers and the mystery, he was only a man, and she'd seen it. A man who needed her, who would die without her care. Never before had she been in this position, and she felt herself opening, a new feeling blooming. She shook her head and sighed. *Osolin the nurse, what a laugh.*

What a long strange trip it had been.

"Wait… did you use this whole jar?"

Ink had returned through the portal with more supplies and food. Osolin was devouring one of Radia's sourbell biscuits with a pat of fresh butter. The mage had looked on in approval at how Osolin had tended to Xan in her absence, until she found the empty jar.

"I put more on him whenever he starts to whimper. You can tell when it dries out and stops working. It numbed my hand after a while, so I started using one of his gloves from the bench to put it on."

"Gods, do you have any idea what that jar cost? Not that it matters, I suppose. It was meant to last a week. He must be burnt worse than I imagined. The salve helps?"

"Yes. I felt like he was almost gone when I started taking care of him. He's getting stronger now, I can feel it. Please get more. There are two pearls and a ruby hidden in the hem of my shirt if you need more money."

Ink looked at her curiously, surprised at the offer.

"Maybe if the pearls are as big as grapes and ruby is the size of your fist. It's fine, I'm sure Varagoi was only cheating me the first go round. I could take it from him for nothing if I needed to."

Osolin didn't envy Varagoi if it came to that. She had no love for the scheming little merchant who'd sent them on this fool's errand.

"I'm sure Xan won't mind if I withdraw a little from his bank over there." Ink indicated the careless pile of treasure. "I haven't exactly been focused on making money these past few years." Ink settled across the table from Osolin.

"What did you do instead?" Osolin dared to ask.

Ink looked at her curiously, then took a deep breath.

"I built a wall… a neat little shell between me and the world. I lay where it was warm and dark, burrowed in like an oyster, and I lingered. Watching the circus at Nod's Hole. Seeing the world through a veil, handling it through gloves." Ink took off a glove and set it on the table. Where her fingers touched the wood, it blackened.

"How numb I'd become! I'd failed, you see, to lift the curse. Every avenue exhausted. Grand wizards and high priests, alchemists and scholars, all powerless to lift the darkness from me, and I could not be long in a place before some fool decided I was a witch and then… the torches."

Osolin nodded in understanding. She knew what it meant to run.

"I blinded a whole town once. They caught me at my wit's end. I'd just come from Adon the Apparition, a true scribe, not like our little flaming friend. There's perhaps no more learned man on all the Arc. The others sought to twist helping me into their own gain, but not him. He is cursed himself, and he would have helped me if he could have. When he admitted defeat, that was when I knew no one could help me. I'd traveled for years, spent everything, stolen, threatened, cajoled, made enemies all over the lake, and it was all for naught.

"A dozen times I was poisoned by charlatans, racked with unspeakable pain, faced with horrors beyond your imagining. As I lay despairing in the wake of Adon's revelation, villagers gathered around the house with their torches and their cudgels. Whether they meant to simply drive me from their town or burn me at the stake, I did not ask. I took their sight, not for a time as I did to Sandros, but forever."

Osolin could not restrain a look of horror.

"I think about that town often. Xan thinks me amoral, you know. But when I left that place, when I saw the wretches clawing at the dirt and wailing, I had to choose. I could go the route of anger, take out my fury on all the Arc. I could have raised armies and conquered, rallied the Blackstar's Cabal around me. The fools think me an avatar of their empty god. They would have worshipped me. That town could have been where it all began. But you see, we are here. I did not gather an army, I did not raise a black citadel and set out to rule. I fled to the end of the Arc, to a place where there were no torches, where no one cares if a woman in a veil haunts some smokehole."

"So if I am pitch black, know that it is nothing next to what I could be. Leaving behind a village of the blind, stringing those three fools along and abandoning them in the Kalpa, taking you as a slave... they are small things before the enormity of my potential. When you think of sins in terms of cities razed and empires broken, of stealing the sun and blanketing the Arc in ashes... it all seems very small."

Osolin stared across the table at Ink, the food forgotten, barely remembering to breathe.

"So. Now you know what I really am," Ink said quietly, and her eyes never left Osolin's face. It was so hard to read those black eyes. But at last she understood.

She's waiting to see if I push her away.

Osolin reached a hand across the table and set it over Ink's. "I am a thief, a whore, a slave. I was born into bondage—my mother bore me to sell me. I only came out here because there was nowhere else for me to run. Conquer the Arc or let it rot, I don't care. I don't care what you did. I am yours if you want me."

The sorceress's eyes brimmed with tears, and a black droplet struck the table, staining it forever. Osolin rose and embraced her, and their lips met with a sudden, furious urgency. The bed was taken, so they slipped to the ground and made love on the cold stone floor. Afterward they rose with bruised knees and elbows and walked hand in hand to the spring.

"What of him?" Osolin asked, afraid of the answer. It was all so new to her, she could not help but feel that she would be swept aside for Xan if he woke. A tiny, dark voice whispered that she could make sure he never did.

"I have not told him what I've told you... but I think he can tell anyway. He is... he's strong, and true, and strange. In some ways I hate him, and in others I want to be like him."

Osolin felt herself sinking. They could have been her own words for how she felt about Ink. She'd dared to hope he was just a passing lay, but in the sorceress's voice, Osolin could hear she was caught. Ink watched her expression closely.

"It's not one or the other. I will have you both," Ink declared brazenly, reaching out to cup a buttock. In spite of herself, Osolin grinned. The pain lessened.

"Oh! I forgot to mention. Your friends Sir Dunce and Sir Firemage the Bumbling are coming to kill us. With three bashy-skyla."

"What! Are you joking?"

"If only I were. Those fools have gotten themselves well tangled up now. I meant to find them and spirit them back to Ten, a kind of gift to you and Xan. Instead I found them marching upon us, following behind three great ones. They'll be here by dawn."

"What will you do?"

"Destroy them all, of course. I protect what's mine. I didn't spend all this time seducing you both to let some overgrown caterpillars chew up everything. And your friends crossed me when they hurt my ranger. I was too lenient with that scribe." A lioness's intensity slipped into her voice.

"Can you… stars, you're serious. Can they not be spared?"

"Xan tried to spare them," Ink said, her voice suddenly cold.

"Please…" Osolin reached out and set a palm on her shoulder. Ink lifted her own hand to meet it.

"For you, little one, I will try."

232

The dawnpipers sang, even as screaming waves of insects fled before the path of the three great bashyskyla. The ancient beasts rumbled forward in a trident, smashing everything before them. Giant trees were snapped in two by their armored forelegs, boulders were knocked aside, and everything that remained before them was flattened. The two brothers crept forward in their wake, sneaking through the devastation.

At last the party broke free of the Kalpa and into the clearing surrounding the ancient temple. The recipitors had devoured everything along the periphery of the temple for a hundred yards in any direction, so that not even a blade of grass rose taller than a finger. They trilled from the walls, calling out a warning to the intruders. Sandros stepped forward into the clearing as more and more recipitor heads popped up along the wall.

The wall was nearly twenty feet of slick black stone, and the temple was built on a hill, so that at its peak the teardrop towers rose above the canopy, draped with cultivated spirals of vines that hung heavy with fruit.

Sandros and Gregary stared over the clearing, a buffer between temple and jungle. It was strange to see an area with nothing growing after so long in the Kalparcimex. The sun rose and the first rays of dawn fell upon them.

"XANADROS!" the firemage cried, as loud as he could shout, yet still his voice seemed tiny against the din, before the great scale of this place.

"XANADROS!" All along the wall now, recipitors loomed. They stared down at Sandros, still as gargoyles but for the flicking of their triple tongues.

"This again," Xanadros said, rising from the earth in a thousand twisting threads of darkness, ten paces away from where Sandros and Gregary stood. "They keep calling me."

Before Sandros could get over his surprise to utter a word, the ranger was annihilated, three streams of acid finding their mark simultaneously. Without even a scream, he dissolved, melting into a splash of pitch black nothing hissing against the earth. The spell Sandros had readied was forgotten completely. Could it be that simple?

The pool of darkness rippled and reformed, and the black mage stood before them with her cloak and veil.

Sandros' mouth fell open.

"Alas! The mighty Xanadros is dead! Weep, ye great bugs of the Kalpa, you shall not see his like again," Ink shouted, raising her gloved hands to the sky.

All three bashyskyla were clicking at once, and Ink looked up at the rising sun and winced. From the sheath at her side, she produced the parasol and spread it, striding lazily toward Sandros.

"You lived! And such powerful friends you've made, little scribe. Slayer of the wicked ranger, how they shall cheer for you in Ten."

Sandros could not speak, could not even move in his terror. Ink stood next to him and he was suddenly very aware that if the bashyskyla tried to kill her, he and Gregary would die too. He prayed that Ristarisk really believed his pigshit about mage pacts. Ink turned to them, spinning the parasol between her palms. The three giant beasts tracked her with their ruby eyes.

"Vulgar bashyskyla, forever spitting and drooling. Mind your manners, you three, or I will take your sight away. The Kalpa is no place for the blind." Sandros remembered when she'd done it to him, the sudden darkness, the panic...

"Xanadros killed two of ours. He must die. If you oppose us, I will eat you."

"Xanadros is dead. This one slew him. He was burned too badly, the heat got into his bones and kindled. He died in a fever, a curse everlasting on his lips. This place is mine now, his beasts obey me. You trespass."

"Where is the body?" Ristarisk demanded. "I would look upon the one who killed Yither." At his side Matraiene and Jilque rumbled with uncertainty.

"Would you? I sold him, body and soul. He is in the nether realm now. Do you want to try and get him back? I can take you there."

In their own language, the three bashyskyla sang and chirped back and forth, and finally Ristarisk clicked its mandibles and the other two were silent.

"You lie. We shall shatter this place and dig him out."

"I see. Tell your idiot lackeys that the time-eaters are still hungry. I can sell them three bashyskyla just as easily as I can sell them a ranger. Your pet scribe can't save you, either."

"She can do it. Her power is vast," Sandros said, and there was no need to act. The fear in his voice was real.

"Still uncertain? Here."

Twirling her parasol, Ink walked up to Ristarisk, standing so close the monster could reach out and bite her in half before she could blink. Had she trembled, had it seen even the slightest sign of fear, it would have done just that. But there was no fear in her posture, she all but walked into its jaws and stared into its eyes through her veil. From her cloak, she pulled a scorched garment of dark leather, shining lenses set in its sides.

Xan's mask.

"Tell me if you don't smell a man who burned to death in that. You bashyskyla can smell, can't you?"

"Far better than your kind. I smell the flesh, smell the ranger. It is true then. Xanadros is dead."

"A giant felled by a mouse. Plenty of that going around…" She let the threat linger in the air. "Now, leave this place. I tire of banter," Ink demanded.

The three red eyes blazed, and the great bashyskyla teetered on the edge of attack. The recipitors on the wall began to whirr one by one, until they were all emitting a winding howl. They were enormous, twice as large as recipitors should be, and their eyes glinted with predatory interest. They should be no danger to the bashyskyla, but there were many of them. Behind one of them, a dark form rose, unseen by all, carrying the ranger's bow.

235

"I am through with men. Through with all of this. The Kalparcimex will swallow you all. Your kind is doomed," Ristarisk rumbled, its voice buzzing with disgust.

"What of our deal?" Sandros asked. "The ranger is dead, you have your vengeance. Take us home." Sandros kept a wary eye on Ink as he spoke.

"He was already dead, the deal is no deal at all. No prey, no pact. Find your own way out," Ristarisk thundered, and Matraiene and Jilque turned away.

"So you'll plot to kill Xan with them but not with me? Outrageous," Ink quipped, but they paid her no mind.

"You dragged us out here, Ristarisk! Threatened to kill us if we didn't help! You're going to abandon us in the middle of the fucking inner Kalpa?"

"It should be payment enough that I don't devour you," Ristarisk said, turning its back on them.

"I don't care! I killed the ranger! You can't just leave us!"

"I can." The three bashyskyla were already rumbling away, leaving them to their fates.

"Sandros, no!" Gregary shouted, seeing the wild look in his brother's eyes. All around him, the air was swimming with heat.

"Sandros, yes!" Ink cried from his side. "Burn them all," she urged, a spark of malevolent glee shining in her eyes.

"THE PACT IS BROKEN! DOOM AWAITS YOU ALL!" The words exploded from Sandros' mouth, and the bashyskyla halted in their tracks. Ristarisk wheeled to see Sandros was gone and a twisting column of red flame stood in his place. Gregary was running in the opposite direction as fast as his legs could carry him while Ink looked on, entranced.

For a moment, the bashyskyla seemed uncertain whether to retreat or advance, and then Ristarisk chirped something and the three charged, trying to get into range to hit him with their acid.

Then Sandros called the Red Wind.

For a moment, the din of the Kalparcimex was drowned out as the Red Wind blew with an otherworldly roar. The screaming sear of the flames met the howling whistle of the winds, and all the air around them ripped toward Sandros as he blazed white-hot at the center of the vortex. Exulting in the holocaust, the firemage reached out a hand and a river of living flame roared toward Ristarisk. The torrent of flame took the bashyskyla fully in the face. Sandros cried in ecstasy and the fire burned so hot the nova of light eclipsed everything, drowning the clearing in glare.

At last, the flames relented and Sandros hung in the air, looming on a column of twisting fire. He lifted his hands to the other bashyskyla, ready to incinerate them as well, when Ristarisk began to laugh.

It was the bashyskyla laugh, the rat-tat-tat of the vents on its side, and the other bashyskyla joined in. Sandros wobbled in the air and then fell to the ground, his concentration lost. His most powerful spell, his last measure, and the bashyskyla bathed in the flames as if in an afternoon rain and emerged completely unhurt.

Behind him, he heard the black laughter of the sorceress, rising along with the great insects. Gregary stood apart, his eyes teary from the glare, trying to make sense of it all.

"Fire doesn't hurt them," Sandros breathed, his eyes wide with terror.

"Devour him alive," the bashyskyla at Ristarisk's right barked, and Ristarisk moved forward to do just that. Gregary rushed to Sandros' defense, holding Xan's sword before him. Standing before the great bashyskyla, it was as if he meant to fight an ox with a sewing needle.

"Save them!" A high shout came from the wall, but the brothers did not look for the source with Ristarisk barreling down on them.

"Stop," Ink demanded, appearing before the brothers. "These are mine, I claim them."

"You claim them. You claim the ranger. You claim this place. You order me about. I tire of your pretensions, human. You are just like the fool who stood before Arkiend and dared to barter. Share his fate!"

Ristarisk cocked its head to spit acid. At ten paces away it could not miss. But neither could it see, all three of its ruby eyes grew dark, and at its sides its companions creeched, their eyes as dark as Ristarisk's own. It spat, furious, but there was no sizzle of flesh caught in the stream. The bashyskyla roared forward, slamming the ground with its great armored legs, but there was nothing but earth beneath them.

Ink and the two brothers emerged from a pool of darkness back by the wall, far from the rampaging bashyskyla. At once the two brothers began to scream.

"It's nothing you babies, just a—" Gregary's fist cut her short as he slammed it into her eye, a move of pure animal terror. She was caught completely off-guard and the punch knocked her flat as the two brothers took off running for the jungle, screaming like madmen.

Osolin slid down the sloping wall, landing hard and rolling, then she dashed to Ink's side. "Are you all right?"

Ink rose to her feet, blinking rapidly and swaying. Osolin had to hold her up.

"Come back, you fools!" she shouted after them. "IT'S JUST A JAUNT THROUGH THE SHADOW! DON'T BE CHILDREN!"

The brothers did not heed her. Osolin and Ink could hear Sandros babbling something about the Void and Gregary shouting, "NO NO NO!" as they sprinted away.

She rubbed her eye where Gregary had walloped her. Already it was swelling shut. "Gods, they're more cowardly about it than you were."

"Because it's horrible!"

"Well, get ready for it."

"No, don't!"

Ink reached out and drew her through the shadows, and the pair emerged at the top of the wall behind the row of recipitors. Osolin fought to hold back her screams. It was easier the second time but she was still shivering all over as if she'd been thrust into ice water.

From the wall they watched the bashyskyla smashing around the earth, spitting acid wildly about.

"Three blind bashyskyla," Ink sang out after them. One of them spat in their direction, but it was fifty yards away, and the acid merely hissed against the ground. The three monsters began to move toward her voice, two colliding in their confusion.

"LEAVE THIS PLACE OR DIE!" Osolin shouted and to her surprise, Matraiene and Jilque paused. But Ristarisk rumbled forward, headed right for the temple. Sight or no sight, it would level this place.

"Can you stop it?" Osolin asked, unslinging Xan's bow. "I don't think I can make that shot"

"I'm spent."

Osolin nocked a silvery tink spine arrow, looking for an opportunity. As Ristarisk thundered forward, its head wove back and forth, but it was too high, there was no way to strike the vulnerable spot. She held her breath, waiting for her moment. The monster was nearly halfway to them, and she let the arrow fly, a streak of silver catching the ruby light of dawn. But Ristarisk's head shot up at the last moment and the spine deflected off its armored brow.

"Shiiit…" Osolin hissed, reaching for another arrow. If only she had the crossbow…

As she nocked the arrow, the monster crossed the center of the clearing and a great cry went up along the wall.

The recipitors howled in unison. In a single dark wave, they sprang from their posts and leapt to the earth below. Swift as coursing hares, they bolted to intercept the great bashyskyla, a dozen of them pouncing at once.

The recipitors attacked Ristarisk from every direction. It spat acid and scythed the air with its claws but without sight, it could not connect with the swarming recipitors. They bit at its legs, they dug at the seams of its armor, they nipped at its head, and in a panic, Ristarisk rolled over, hoping to flatten them.

Most leapt clear, though one was caught on the other side. The recipitor curled into a defensive ball as Ristarisk's bulk drove it into the earth. When the behemoth's weight shifted off, the recipitor sprang unhurt from the dirt and nipped again at the leg, tearing through the bashyskyla's thick armor with its rock-crushing mandibles.

Ristarisk screamed in rage, wheeling around and around, seeking the one who dared harm it, and this time the recipitor was not swift enough and the bashyskyla bit it in half. Ristarisk continued wheeling, listening for movement and then biting, but the recipitors adapted, keeping ahead of the murdering maw.

Blinded and beset on all sides, surrounded by the hooting cries of Xan's dogs of war, Ristarisk at last turned to flee, swinging back for the jungle. The recipitors harried the bashyskyla as far as midway across the clearing. The moment it crossed midway, they disengaged. How well they'd been trained! They seemed to strut as they returned to the temple, bounding up the high wall with ease. Two remained behind with the slain recipitor, and Osolin thought that they might be mourning it, until they lashed out with their triple tongues and began to eat their fallen comrade. She narrowed her eyes and turned back to Ink.

At her side, Ink slumped to the ground and sat with her head pointed at the floor, with a hand over her left eye. The punch had left her loopy. Osolin watched her with concern, certain she was concussed. Finally, Ink broke out in a giggle.

"What's so funny?" Osolin asked.

"He gave me a black eye," Ink said, bursting into laughter.

Osolin looked out at the jungle, hoping Sandros and Gregary would come back. But they were long gone.

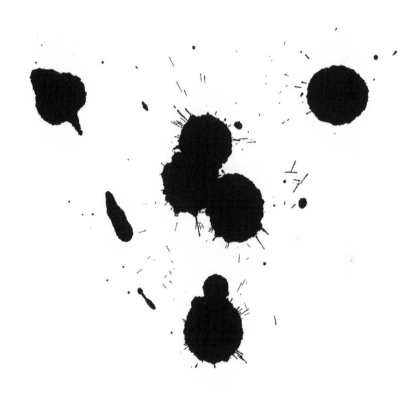

"Where did all these blankets come from? How in the hell did you get a bed here?" Xanadros lay on the mat, sweltering under too many blankets, looking at the huge bed that had been set up to his right. The lights were also different, someone had set lantern shades over his bare firefly globes, with thin silver snuff chains dangling from them. Looking around his home, he barely recognized it.

"Shhh..." Ink pointed at the bed, where Osolin was asleep. She did not stir.

"Most I brought through the demiplane. The bed was too big, though. I had Raspy help with that." Ink brought Xan a cup of water from the spring, and he took it gladly. His mouth was as dry as the Chyskatys.

"Raspy?"

"The big recipitor that leads the dawn pack. He likes me, I've been giving him strawberries. Made good time too, carried the whole thing from Emily's landing in two days. Yamel says hello, by the way, and Ahel grunted at me, which I assume means the same."

"You took my recipitor to... hold on. Give me a moment here." He stood up slowly, his muscles threatening to revolt, but he refused to listen. He walked to where the spring's stream disappeared under the wall for an eyelid-fluttering piss that went on for an eon. A privacy screen had been set up there, a black curtain on a thin wooden frame, and he stared at it dumbly for a minute afterward, feeling out of place in his own home.

Shaking his head, he went to the spring, finding the area around it almost completely blackened. His bar of soap was like a block of pitch. He slipped into the water, trying in vain to get rid of the lingering sense that there were tiny shards of silver digging into every crease in his skin. When he emerged, he almost shouted, thinking his shelves and their priceless jars were gone. But then he realized they were just covered by curtains. She'd put curtains over his collection. He was too stunned to protest, and she was at his side with a towel, rubbing him down. That was another new thing, there were towels now.

"Are you still burned?" she asked, gingerly patting him. "It's impossible to tell."

"Not any more. The silver..." Just saying the words made him wince.

"Do you remember anything? From while you healed?"

"Nothing," he lied. And for a moment, the two looked at each other uncertainly, deciding together to believe it. To speak of the Blackstar was to summon it.

"Good," Ink said, and the concern slowly eased from her face.

"All of this... you know, I have been alone for better than ten years. By choice. I don't know how to live with people. And this slave..."

"She's not a slave, I freed her. Did you wake up swimming in your own piss and shit?"

"No?" she continued when he did not reply. "Then thank her. You've been unconscious for nearly a week. She fed you, cleaned you like a babe, and not because I bid her, either. I trust you can adapt to the situation."

His eyebrows raised for a moment, but if he was ashamed, it was only for that instant. He looked over and saw that they'd replaced his stove, and nodded with approval.

"What do you want out here?"

"You."

"And what about her?"

243

"Her too. I'm greedy."

"So you've just set up a little harem for yourself out here on the fringe, is that it?"

"I didn't know you were so old-fashioned, Xanadros. It didn't seem that way when I had my tongue up your asshole."

"I'm not a concubine. This temple is my home, not some stable of whores for you to fuck."

"I hear..." She drew close to him, and he put up a hand to shove her away but she melted through it, and he felt her heat pass through his arm. Without a body to hold it up, her robe fell to the floor.

"Jealousy," Ink whispered, and she wrapped her arms around him from behind, her breasts pressed against his back. Her hands roamed around to the front of him and found him already beginning to stiffen. She bit at the hard corded muscles at his shoulder, just hard enough to leave the imprint of her teeth behind.

"I waited so long for you to wake. You can have her too. I'm greedy, not selfish." She gripped him tightly now and there was no beginning anymore, he was rigid.

"I'm not going to take someone in thrall," he said, and the anger had slipped out of his voice. His head rolled lightly on his shoulders, he was still shaky on his feet.

"I freed her. She doesn't need convincing from me, either. You beat her in combat, that does all kinds of things to a woman like her. The way her eyes linger on you... I think that's the biggest cock she's ever seen." She ran her hand up and down his shaft for emphasis, felt a tremor run through him.

"And the way she's been caring for you... you know healers are forever falling in love with their patients. Like artists with their models, they see something no one else does, something hidden..." She tightened her hand around the head, then rubbed the very tip with her finger, finding it already slick. "...vulnerable."

He cried out from the white, flaring intensity of it. He nearly came but her other hand mercilessly gripped his balls.

"Not yet. I've waited days for this." She walked toward the bed without letting go, leading him by his cock. Osolin was still asleep, sprawled out beneath the black sheets. He wanted to protest, but her grip was powerful, and he knew what she was capable of.

"Mmmmmm... you'll have to go slow. We don't want to wake her." Ink turned around, about to slide to her knees to suck him when she felt him lifting her up by her waist. She gasped with surprise. She'd meant to tease him, to draw this out, but he had picked her up and held her where he stood. He kissed her with such fervor, such desire, that she couldn't wait either.

She wrapped her legs around him and slowly slid down, feeling the taut muscles of his stomach rubbing against her. She dug into his back with her nails as she slipped lower and lower. Both of them shut their eyes and moaned when they met, and for a moment, they just hung there in space in one long gasp.

Then he was slipping into her, and she took him in a fraction of an inch at a time, with a hundred tiny strokes. Her arms were braced against his shoulders, tight as the strings of a fiddle, quavering as she halted, unable to bear it, and then she relaxed for the smallest instant to accept more. She was trying so hard to be quiet, but when she had all of him inside of her, they both cried out, swaying. On the bed, Osolin was stirring, but they were far beyond the place where anything else mattered. The brush with death had woken a primal urgency in him.

Xan thrust her down against the bed, never slipping out of her, and fucked her so hard the whole frame inched across the floor with every thrust. Osolin woke wide-eyed and rolled away from them. She looked shocked but they were oblivious to her, oblivious to everything but each other. They were both crying out with every thrust, straining at the edges of themselves, melting into the feeling of something vast and important rising over them. When it came it was as if the moon had crashed into the Arc and shattered them both. They exploded into a shuddering oblivion that went on and on.

When the world reformed, he was still on top of her, still pulsing inside of her, waves running through her, vibrations rearranging every part of her. She saw tears glistening in his eyes and felt them trickling down her own cheeks.

She was flooded with it, the whole experience too much for either of them to contain. They stared into each other's eyes, neither daring to speak. He began to pull out of her and she looked so panicked that he stopped, and instead he rolled over, still inside of her, so that he wasn't crushing her with his weight. She was on top of him now, and she craned over to lick at his ear.

"Never stop," she whispered.

She arced her back, rolling her head on her shoulders in a cascade of ebony hair, and he was still hard inside her. She began to slowly roll her hips, carefully at first, not sure she could take more, and he moaned, lifting his hands to cup her breasts, his thumbs brushing over her nipples.

Beside them, Osolin was frozen with uncertainty. She should have gotten up when they began, should have slipped behind the screen to let them screw, but the moment where she could leave seemed to have passed, now Ink would say something...

There were too many feelings striking her at once. She felt ashamed that she meant so little them that they would rut in bed next to her like animals. A hot, jealous anger that this man who'd bested her was inside of her lover. A subservient whisper that it was because she wasn't good enough.

And beneath it all, she was excited. She'd never been so close to two lovers like this. She was captivated by the sounds they made. She felt their motions through the mattress, she could smell their lust... she had only to reach out a hand to become a part of it. Would they reject her, laugh at her, or act as if she wasn't even there?

Ink's gaze fell on Osolin, and her dark eyes seemed to pierce the turmoil inside Osolin. Ink smiled sweetly for a moment. Then her lips parted and her eyes closed tightly as she slid downward.

The smile was permission, and Osolin's hand was on Ink's thigh without her even thinking about moving it. The tightness of Ink's muscle, the way it trembled as she raised herself slowly up and rode back down, made Osolin shiver. Osolin's other hand slid down her stomach and slipped between her legs, she was thrumming with want.

Ink's eyes followed, and she grinned widely, nodding that this was what she wanted. She reached down to stroke Osolin's face, but she couldn't reach, and Osolin squirmed closer, still touching herself, not quite daring to get too close to Xan.

Ink tugged the blanket away from Osolin and ran her hand through her Osolin's short hair, her fingertips brushing against the thief's ear and down her neck. Ink sighed, and Xan's head turned, noticing the other woman in the bed for the first time since they'd begun. For an instant, Osolin was unnerved by his bright green eyes, afraid he would shove her roughly away.

But there was something there, some recognition of the time she'd spent caring for him, nursing him as he lay writhing and helpless. He let go of Ink's breast and his fingers brushed against Osolin's hip, and she felt a flush of excitement. They were including her, accepting her. Xan's hand slid up to cup her breast, and Ink's brushed down her stomach slowly, intently. The difference in touches was bewildering, the rough callused strength of Xan's big hand, the soft expert delicacy of Ink's trailing fingertips… she wanted this, wanted both.

Ink slid off Xan and her fingers made their way between Osolin's legs, discovering how hot she'd gotten. Osolin's cheeks were burning with abashment, and she saw the dark grin again. A moment later Ink's mouth was on her and she cried out, forgetting herself. Ink's tongue pulsed against her, and she saw that Xan had moved behind Ink now. Osolin could feel Ink's mouth press harder with each thrust.

It was so much… she was nearly there but Ink withdrew, and she made a little cry of protest. Smiling, Ink climbed up and straddled Osolin's face, leaving her writhing with need. She kissed Ink, tasting her excitement, tasting Xan, and she was thrusting herself at the air shamelessly, wanting desperately to get there.

"Please…" Osolin said, coming up for a breath.

"Please what?" Ink asked, looking down at her.

"I want…"

"Say it," she ordered.

"I want to be fucked. I want to come."

"Beg."

"Please fuck me. Please."

Ink beckoned over her shoulder, and Osolin felt Xan's hands on her thighs. Ink grabbed Osolin's hair roughly and pulled her face against her slit.

"Look at me," Ink said, and their eyes were locked together. Ink watched every little twitch, each movement of Osolin's face as Xan entered her. The jolt as they touched, the tinge of fear, the slow shuddering pleasure spreading through her. He was very slow, very deliberate, and Ink held Osolin tightly against her, exulting in it, her own excitement mounting as Osolin got closer. Ink meant to come after Osolin, to watch the look on her face, but it was too much, she shut her eyes and threw back her head, drowned in an explosion of wonderful heat. Moments later, Osolin tensed and cried out against her. As she shook, Xan groaned and then Ink slipped onto the bed and panted, totally spent.

For a moment, Xan remained inside Osolin, and their eyes met. Earlier, it had just been Ink and Osolin, his role only mechanical, but now the moment lingered between them and something passed between their stares. Then he leaned down and kissed her.

He's in both of us, Ink realized, and the thought stirred in her, lust and jealousy wheeling around each other. She felt a stab of worry, *what if he likes her better,* and the old familiar loneliness began to seep in, the apartness.

She was thinking about just vanishing, sliding through the nether and going somewhere else, when Xan slid out and Osolin turned on her side, breathing heavily, everything spent. She shut her eyes, and Ink knew she would fall asleep swiftly after.

Xan moved beside Ink and put his arms around her, and she knew she had wanted this, had started it, but she almost pushed him away anyway. Then he held her, those green eyes sought her own, and there was that solidness about him, the part that said *You can trust me. I won't change.*

"You'd better not," she threatened, and he didn't understand, but was wise enough not to argue. She pulled the blanket over all three of them and picked the warmest spot, between the other two. Xan hugged her from behind while she hugged Osolin, and sleep came slowly, caught between two heartbeats.

"Sandros..."

The flute at his side had begun to smolder, its end lit like a brand, burning against his skin. The moment his eyes fell on it, the flame vanished like a disobedient child, yet the proof was there, the end scorched and blackened.

The brothers had come through a rough patch of the jungle, where the cane grew thorns like daggers, and little fist-sized jumping fleas were forever erupting from underfoot, screaming like tea kettles. One had caught Gregary beneath the jaw and nearly knocked him unconscious. When he recovered, they cut a cane stalk into a pole and probed the ground in front of them as they walked, trying to trigger the little monsters before they drew too close.

They reeked of smoke now. They'd thrown away Ink's banes, afraid Ink might track them down by their magic. As Brakkar had before them, they swiftly learned the agony of walking the Kalparcimex without banes. Sandros' solution was to cloak them in a cloud of pungent smoke, and it seemed to keep all but the most determined insects at bay. It seemed worth it if they could elude her.

Yet it was for naught. As the brothers emerged from a long corridor of the mine mites, the sorceress stepped from the shadow of a blaythorn bush, emerging from its spiraling thorns in a million shadowy threads. Sandros flung an arc of flame at her, burning away the shadows, and an instant later Gregary swung Xan's sword through her, but it passed through with no resistance.

"Behind you," Ink said, and this time Sandros' eyes gleamed with prismatic light.

"That's another eidolon. Don't attack it. What do you want?" Sandros had a dangerous glint in his eyes.

"I came to save you. You two are running to your doom. It's all over now, the bashyskyla are gone. Osolin is fine."

"What of Brakkar?"

"Lost. He must have thrown away his bane just like you dolts. I found it far up the Kliyick River. That's the one I found Osolin in as well, moments from a truly gruesome death. I saved her, and I will save you as well if you let me. The river ahead of you is the Borast, it flows into the inner Kalpa. You're lucky I marked you or I would never have found you."

"Curse your touch," Sandros groaned. Even if he'd remembered the stain on his hand, what could he have done? Cut off his hand?

"I'm here to rescue you, fools. I can take you back to Ten." It was the real Ink who spoke now, standing behind them while the eidolon was before. He was nearly sure of it.

"The way you dragged us through hell before? I'd rather die," Gregary said. At his side, Sandros nodded.

"You absolutely will," Ink said, and her words hung in the air. There could be no dispute. They were both surprised they'd lived this long. "I will take you back to Ten, and you can go back to your home."

"We don't have a home anymore. We're banished. We failed in our quest."

"What do you want from me? Do you want me to go back with you and slay all the tinks? End the one who banished you? We can go right now. I'll spirit you all the way to Joymont if you're man enough to bear it."

"No." The word was heavy as a stone. "No more deals with you. No more black magic. Leave us alone."

"You two are leaving the jungle. I don't need your approval. I can just take you. But it will be harder on you." Her voice grew hard, and even from behind her veil they could feel the weight of her stare. But Sandros stared right back, wild-eyed.

"Fuck you. Fuck you for toying with us, for lying to us, for stealing away our friend, for leading us on this fool's errand for a laugh. You're an evil, selfish cunt who poisons everything she touches. Xan was right about you. Leave us, or I'll kill you." The pure flame danced just ahead of Sandros' thoughts. The slightest movement from her and he would give all three of them to the fire once and for all.

The black mage was silent, trying to answer his words. She could not.

"So be it." Her voice was cold, empty of anything human. She faded away and left them.

For a while they stood there, listening to the insects. That was surely their last chance to be free of this place. Finally, Gregary nodded his approval. Better to die than to fall into that one's clutches. They walked forward, their last tie to civilization severed. For nearly an hour, nothing dared to approach them, as if even the insects could smell how close Sandros had come.

Finally, they heard water flowing, and Gregary hacked free of the undergrowth. They found themselves high on the banks of a swift-running river. The Borast was dark and wide, perhaps two hundred yards across. Their hearts sank as they looked upon it, for they had no clue how they would ford it. As they looked at the other side hopelessly, the water bulged, and the huge shell of a shives broke the water.

The beast stood up, perhaps twenty paces away, trailing a web of river vines, and looked at them before it disappeared beneath the surface. Beside Sandros, a spray of orchids shriveled from his heat.

"Are you..." Gregary began, but he didn't know how to finish. He kept a careful distance from Sandros, which the mage did not fail to notice.

"It's the noise. I can't concentrate to keep the fire in check. Can't have an instant without the fucking din in my head, breaking my mind apart. How can you stand it?"

"Ten more steps."

Sandros looked at his brother blankly, his eyebrows furrowed. Whenever Gregary wanted to impart something, he would pause like this and make sure he had your full attention. It was perhaps more irritating because it worked even better when you knew he was doing it.

"I just keep saying that to myself, 'ten more steps,' and then I count them, and when I get to ten, I say it again. After a while, I just keep counting, I was almost to nine hundred when you... when your flute caught fire."

"This is beyond counting. I'm afraid it's only going to get worse. I went too far... let something go… and I don't know how to put it back in. Back there with the black mage I nearly… the Scourer was right."

"Fuck the Scourer. If we can just get out of this place, get you somewhere quiet where you can rest and recover, you'll be fine. I know it."

"I don't know how much longer—I would leave you, just wander off and burn up, but you'll never make it out alone."

"Don't even talk about it."

"I have to talk about it. Just being close to me puts you in danger. Eventually I will lose control. Especially..." Sandros paused for a moment.

"WITH THIS FUCKING RIVER HERE!" Sandros shouted out at the river, and the shives resurfaced to peer at him, and sure enough, a liefly spun off from the trees overhead, happily singing "FUCKING RIVER."

The liefly zipped around and around them and then, mid-cry, it burst into flames, the song becoming a frantic scream. It plummeted into the river like a meteor, hitting the black water with a hiss, and then the surface was broken by the thrashing foam of three formless things trying to eat it at once. The watching shives looked from the spot where the liefly crashed to Sandros and ducked back down under the surface.

"I can't do it. I can't make it out of here. I just want to—"

"Hey Sandros," Gregary cut him off before he could complete the thought. "Remember when we borrowed that boat?"

Sandros had his hand clawed in front of his face in frustration, as if he were crushing an egg, then he blinked, the memory knocking him out of his fury.

"'Borrowed' is a kind word."

"Well... we did bring it back."

"Only because Joymont made us. Gods, my arms ached for weeks after we rowed that awful thing back up the Malsk. And that stupid fisherman still wanted us flensed, though we were just children. What an asshole."

"Still, remember floating down the river in it, just fishing and camping on the banks? Remember how you almost caught that goldscale but fell in the river trying to pull it in? Or when I ate all those berries you told me not to and nearly shit myself inside out?"

Sandros smiled and nodded. "I used to think about that trip all the time when I was in the tower of the Scourer. The whole way down, I knew we had a hiding waiting for us at the end, and I just didn't care. I've never felt so free."

"I thought of it too, when I marched with the army away from home the first time, and the whole time I was at barracks. When we set out to keep the peace and adventure in Joymont, that's what I really wanted. To be a boy again, floating down the Malsk in a stolen boat. With you."

"I'm sorry I got you into this mess, sorry I'm losing it, and can't get you out. It was a stupid idea."

"We couldn't have known." They were both silent for a while.

"Hey Gregary..." Sandros used Gregary's own trick against him, the idea that had seized him burning bright.

"Yeah?"

"Do you want to see the inner Kalparcimex?"

"What do you mean?"

"I mean, I can carve us a boat, burn a trunk into a canoe, the same as I did the flute. Oars too. We can float down this river, follow it deeper than even Xanadros dared. Maybe we'll even make it out, maybe it flows all the way to the lake."

Gregary stood there wide-eyed for a moment before he could even start to think about it. It was surely suicide, and he could see the air around Sandros shimmering with heat—his brother was so excited by the idea he couldn't keep the fire in check. For a long time, he thought of saying no, telling Sandros they would take their chances marching upriver, and he would listen. The whole thing felt like a passing fancy, one they would regret swiftly and greatly.

But as he looked at Sandros, Gregary saw that he would not make it on the march upriver. He thought of the Red Wind his brother had called, the molten tornado. The inhuman, hungry glare in Sandros' eyes as the flames roared, and the utter defeat when the bashyskyla emerged unscathed. Gregary knew how losing a battle could hurt, and Sandros had taken this one hard. He seemed more than half unhinged.

Whatever was in Sandros, clawing to be free, was too wild to withstand the din, the constant danger. However far it was back to Ten was too far, the way too tangled and perilous. They had died the moment they entered this place. All that remained was to choose the way they went.

Gregary thought once more of that old fisherman, how they'd been so terrified of him when he'd bellowed at them and waved his boning knife about, and how they'd mocked him to each other on the long walk home, until he hadn't seemed so frightening anymore.

"Let's find a good tree," Gregary said, grinning. At last, they were free.

A dark pair looked down from the high wall of the temple, reclining and drinking lemon tea. Xan was wearing nothing but a shirt and a ragged pair of work pants. In his pocket he carried one of Ink's banes. It was a novel thing for him to be outside without his jungle suit on. He was enjoying it, pushing back a twinge at the back of his mind that said this was all too easy, too unreliable. He looked out at the trails left in the earth by the conflict, the blackened swath where the fiery tornado had wheeled, the patches of earth deadened by acid. He tried to picture the battle.

The shadows shifted and Ink poured from nothing to sit in the empty chair between them.

"No sign of them?" Osolin asked, looking out at the swaying trees. A storm was coming, and the song of the Kalpa bowed with expectation.

"They have abandoned their banes, just like the priest," Ink said, her voice bitter and cold. Xan and Osolin shared a look, they had both seen this side of her.

"Fools will be fools. Now and forever. I can send the recipitors after them," Xan resolved.

"Can the recipitors bring them back unharmed?"

"Only in pieces."

Osolin shook her head and gave him a sad-eyed look. Not for the first time, he found he could not refuse that look, and at last he nodded.

"It's a chance, leaving them alive. If they survive and make it into the inner, they could make a deal with the Empress or the Weaver or even Arkiend." Xan said the monster's name bitterly. "That mage has already made me regret my mercy. But just the same… they're only fools. Lost in the Kalpa."

"What happened to you in the inner?" Ink asked. There was a long silence afterward. Without his mask on they could see it pained him even to recollect.

"It was after I went to Joymont, to warn them they were building a kingdom in the path of the Kalpa. They didn't listen. They were stubborn, stupid. I determined I would try to save them in spite of themselves. I spent months getting into the inner, no easy feat. That was when I devised the jungle suit. Deep within the inner, sorcery can't be trusted. I spent a long time learning from Yither, sort of the village idiot of the bashyskyla, and I began to make my forays into the inner. I found this place, and many other wonders of the Kalpa. I stopped being just a scholar financed by gathering insects, and became a true ranger of this place."

"It took nearly two years, but finally my name grew large enough that Arkiend grew intrigued. The bashyskyla could not understand how a human had entered the inner and lived, nor why. If you think you have seen monsters in this place, they are nothing before the god of the bashyskyla. To say he was gigantic and terrible falls far short. We have no words grand enough to describe a monster like Arkiend. A living, malevolent mountain, ancient beyond ancient, alien and unknowable. Like a fool, I tried to plead with him, to convince him to spread the jungle south and west instead of east. This is what I got for it." He indicated his ruined face.

"The bashyskyla control how the jungle spreads?" Osolin asked when Xan had recovered.

"Think of how far north and west we are. There shouldn't be a jungle here. It should be a conifer forest. Yet down there, a jungle like nothing else on the Arc. More types of plants and trees than you'll find anywhere else. All wrought by the bashyskyla."

"How?"

"They dig. As they nest, they dig down so deep they cut into the very veins of the Arc itself. They draw its heat upward and build a climate for themselves. The hot springs, the lava vents, all are their doing. I think they plant the selas trees too. Look out at all of those selas poking above the canopy. Every one took root in an abandoned bashyskyla nest. I'm still researching those, I can only guess their purpose at this point. The Kalparcimex spreads as their nests do, and they are breeding faster now than they ever have before."

"I went to Joymont to warn them a decade ago, as Wiyitrup was completing his nest in the east. Now the jungle has grown all around it, and a selas has taken root there. In Joymont, they're already getting the outlier species, the ones that range far to hunt. Tinks, and probably they've already got juggerworms in their rivers, maybe an adolescent hroradrora or two haunting their woods."

"So they're truly doomed."

"What's more, it's not just them. Joymont lies between here and the Wyrth. A three-hundred-league stretch of land with long, bitter winters with hard freezes. On the other side of it is Wyrth…"

"Where it's already warm from all the volcanoes…" Osolin answered. Keenly she remembered the oppressive heat of Wyrth.

Xan smiled as he nodded at her. He'd begun teaching Osolin to read and write, and favored her with the same grin when she did well. That smile never failed to stir her to do better. It was a far cry from working with Ink. The sorceress had tried to teach her letters before Xan, and they'd both gotten so frustrated with each other they nearly came to blows.

"Exactly so. Not only is the temperature right, but that rich, volcanic soil… they'll reach Wyrth and their population will explode. In a thousand years, the Kalparcimex might cover the whole of the north, a great empire of bashyskyla stretching from here to Yarlsbeth."

"Swallow the stars…" Ink breathed. Her eyes glinted with amazement.

258

"The Wyrth legion will fight them," Osolin said, remembering the ranks and ranks of black-armored legionnaires she'd seen tromping through the skull-paved streets of Urth'Wyrth. "They'll lose," she realized as soon as she'd said it. Xan nodded.

"Why are they breeding so fast now?" Ink asked. "Why hasn't this happened already?"

"The war among the four gods has been going on since the dawn of time. About a thousand years ago, the bashyskyla started winning. The spiders say it used to be far drier here, more suitable for them, and their numbers dwindled as the rains grew more frequent. Then selas trees began to appear. The spiders hate them, won't go anywhere near them, and now their range has shrunk to a fraction of what it was. The wasps say the armor of the bashyskyla used to be thinner, their aim less keen, and they lament their own progeny as weak and lazy. Both sides suspect an alliance between Arkiend and the Red Empress, but the wasps suspect the spiders of the same, and the spiders suspect the wasps. Whatever the cause, the bashyskyla wax while the others wane, and so spreads the Kalparcimex."

"Is that... is that why you're breeding the recipitors? Do you think you can stop them?"

"Yes. I thought to turn the tide. I thought I would have longer. In another twenty or thirty years... I could have carved out a sizable piece of the Kalpa with the recipitors. I'm making progress with my other experiments too. But now I no longer have that time."

"Why?"

"When I slew Yither, when you blinded Ristarisk and its mates... the war began there. The bashyskyla will come, they will raze this place. Much will be lost, the hatcheries, the experiments, my materials... Even if I flee with my recipitors, it will set me back five years or more."

"What if we fight them off?" Ink asked.

"An army of bashyskyla?"

"I fought off three," she grinned.

"Can you fight off thirty? If Arkiend itself comes lumbering up from the core to crush us?"

"I just got this place the way I like it. Curtains and everything. I'm not leaving. Do you really think you can beat them, if we buy you enough time?"

"Five years ago I would have laughed. But you've seen the recipitors. That's just six generations of selective breeding. They're getting bigger, smarter, fiercer. They're utterly fearless and loyal unto death."

"Your pack would have taken down Ristarisk, had it remained," Ink said, and Xan's eyes gleamed with excited pride.

"Do you really want this fight? The bashyskyla will be slow, cautious. They'll wait to strike until they are certain. If we hit them first, make them wary of assembling an assault… we could buy months, years even," Xan mused. "Two against the tide…"

"Three," Osolin said beside them. In their excitement, they'd nearly forgotten her. Xan wasn't only teaching her letters. On his workbench he'd begun sewing a new jungle suit and building a new crossbow.

"Three," Xan agreed.

"Three," said Insolade, reaching out to her lovers. Hand in hand in hand, they watched the storm roll in.

260

In the belly of the shives he smoldered. The sweet, throbbing heat was the sunrise and the moonfall, the world was set to the hammering time of his, her, their heart. Strange dreams in the gorewomb, of his body melting gladly, his flesh surrendering to her insistence and becoming fluid, accepting. In the womb he could feel the slightest motion, as if his nerves had grown branches, spreading to every surface, and perhaps they had. He could feel the barrier between the cocoon and the body of the dead shives. It was not like breathing, but it was not so different, drawing something in and pushing something out.

He had felt his hands and feet disintegrate, his arms and legs melting, his manhood gone. When their heart began to thunder with panic, she was there to whisper that they weren't lost, she had transmuted them into raw, fluid possibility. *Augmented.* She meant to trade them for something better, and again she gave him the vision of the red warrior, swift and terrible, of the strength to devour, to conquer, to flood the world with their young. The vision gave him a feeling that would have throbbed and ached, but he no longer had those parts. He was just a collection of floating organs. He knew not what they all did, only that they were not immune to the change, she was modifying them too, some changed and some melted and he knew not why. Only that she had a plan, and it was far too late to reconsider.

She changed, too, and he could feel her growing longer, spreading out, entwining more deeply with him. He had no body left to express the pleasure he felt, the giddy rush of her wanting more of him, the warm sense of envelopment, of exchange, and the pride, feeling her grow, sleek and geometric, like a rose wrapping around his spine. How beautiful she was.

We. We are beautiful. We are strong. We.

We, we, we... he felt the thoughts that were so nearly his own changing, growing more subtle and nuanced. She'd been an infant when they met, and she was maturing rapidly. Again he began to worry that he was not good enough for her, that she would leave him behind. Again she reassured him. Endless was her patience. He radiated joy, that something so wise and patient had chosen him.

In time, a second heart began to beat, in perfect time with his old one, and then slowly it grew stronger, until it drowned out the other, and he realized it was gone, that she had replaced every part of him, except the numb, isolated seat of his thoughts. He could feel the new heart beating, the new organs thrumming, but they were not his.

Is this it? The last stage of being consumed? He could feel that she had grown right up against the base of his brain, and now the deepest fear, the death-cry rippling through the whole cocoon. It was the end of Brakkar, the end of everything. He felt the same expectant terror he'd felt the first time he'd been buggered, the panicked feeling that he could not take this into him, that he would be ripped apart. For the first time, he saw the same fear in her, saw that the next stage terrified her just as much as it did him. But she was stronger.

No life without death. Necessary. We are almost there!

She began to grow into his brain, spreading out with the most delicate care, yet still it was like a maelstrom ripping through him. Great waves of memory and sensation roiled and crashed, emotions flooded through him, raw and unadulterated, and she would stop, giving him time to get used to the feeling of her inside of him, of being two things at once, and he wanted to urge her on and scream for her to get out at the same time.

He wanted to implode and be reborn a star. The part of him that could feel the passage of time was broken, the transformation went on for a billion years and it was over at once. They screamed as one, hearing their own ecstatic agony echoed. Their thoughts were like two ringing bells that slowly drifted into the same tone, and once the waves overlapped, they never diverged again.

All the while, the new body coalesced around them: the hard gleaming armored plates, the long powerful limbs, an armored skull with a headdress of wicked spikes to protect the newly born gestalt brain.

She woke then. Not the red queen and not the blood priest, but a new thing that exceeded either. At once she felt comfortable in the body, while another part of her marveled at the new femaleness of it, the sleekness, the shining potential to produce young, the novel, powerful urges that accompanied it. There was a sharp, insistent hunger already kindling, a sense that this place had quickly grown far too small, too close, and she tore her way out of the cocoon, ripping her way out of the rotting carcass of the shives.

For a long time she stood there, the blood red fluid drying on her armor, and she was simply there, trying to get used to the shock of seeing, the vision unlike what either of them had known. Touch, smell, taste, all of the senses so keen that they cut, the new world so real that she had to stand rigid, to learn what to filter out and what to keep.

When she could move, she looked around and peered into the place where she was born, the carcass nothing else had dared to touch. She gave a regal smile. Of course, nothing had dared provoke her wrath. As she did, her tongue felt the fangs, and again there was the strange combined feeling of "this is right" and "this is new" as the experiences of her parents reconciled. The imperative to eat grew stronger and stronger and she began to listen for prey, but it was only the animal part of her, the least part. Her body moved to seek nourishment while her mind whirled with schemes and ambitions.

The greater part of her was already thinking of dominion, her natural urge to rule, and here she was sharply aware of being more than just a red queen. She was a new thing.

She dreamed of more than a territory in the Kalpa, of more than enslaving a pack of insects to spread her young. She knew of towns, of whole cities full of soft flesh and limitless hosts. The mere thought of them all sent quickening shivers of pleasure through her abdomen. She would spread so far...

In the memory of her father, she saw the great volcano, the streets paved with shattered skulls, the great threat slumbering within the Arc. She envisioned great armies, waves of her servants crashing into the black-armored defenders, saw herself ripping the demon's heart out and devouring it, taking his power for her own. Saw her children spreading throughout the lake, a red tide that would become a great empire.

So much power! So much potential!

Again, she smiled. She could barely wait to begin.

Thank you for reading Xan & Ink!

This book is far better thanks to the
outstanding efforts of these friends.

Thank you all!

Margot Atwell
Spathi Wa
Hubert Chao
Brendan McMullen
Solmyr
Obscenitor
Jessica Sigafoos
Corinne Lenk

Please feel free to send any thoughts to
Zak@Zakzyz.com

About the Author:

Zak Zyz has worked as a welder, electrician, roofer, and cryptologic linguist. He is currently a sinister systems administrator in DUMBO, Brooklyn. He hosts *The Surreal Symphony*, a late-night call in show, and Strategically Correct, a cutthroat boardgaming society. Zak has been published on *Tor.com* and appeared on *Hour of the Wolf*. His first novella, **SURVIVAL MODE**, was published in 2015. *Xan and Ink* is his first novel.

If you enjoyed Xan & Ink, check out:
SURVIVAL MODE
A lone fugitive's struggle to survive on an alien death moon!

Coming in 2017:

Lemon, Maybe, and the Electric Lady

Four super-powered misfits from Hell's Kitchen unite to save New York!

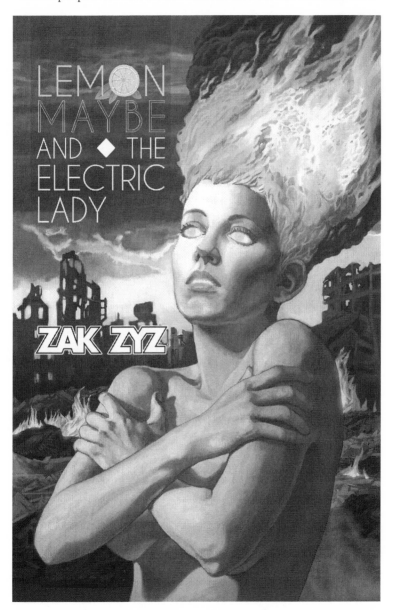

Join the Gutpunch Press Mailing List! Once a month, you'll get all the latest Gutpunch news, cute dog pictures, exclusive beta reader invites, and a chance to win fabulous prizes!

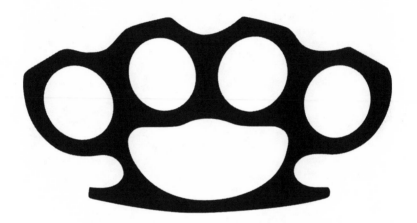

Sign up today for a FREE copy of
SURVIVAL MODE!
www.gutpunchpress.com